KILLER
POTENTIAL

A NOVEL

KILLER POTENTIAL

HANNAH DEITCH

WILLIAM MORROW
An Imprint of HarperCollins*Publishers*

HarperCollins books may be purchased for educational, business, or sales promotional use. For information, please email the Special Markets Department at SPsales@harpercollins.com.

FIRST EDITION

Designed by Elina Cohen

Library of Congress Cataloging-in-Publication Data

Names: Deitch, Hannah, author.
Title: Killer potential: a novel / Hannah Deitch.
Description: First edition. | New York, NY: William Morrow, 2025. | Summary: "Thelma and Louise meets Gillian Flynn in this darkly funny and provocative debut novel, an edge-of-your-seat thrill ride that follows two unlikely female fugitives wanted for murder on their high-octane run from the law"—Provided by publisher.
Identifiers: LCCN 2024011603 (print) | LCCN 2024011604 (ebook) | ISBN 9780063356481 (hardcover) | ISBN 9780063356498 (ebook)
Subjects: LCGFT: Thrillers (Fiction) | Lesbian fiction. | Novels.
Classification: LCC PS3604.E349 K55 2025 (print) | LCC PS3604.E349 (ebook) | DDC 813/.6—dc23/eng/20240510
LC record available at https://lccn.loc.gov/2024011603
LC ebook record available at https://lccn.loc.gov/2024011604

ISBN 978-0-06-335648-1
ISBN 978-0-06-343633-6 (international edition)

25 26 27 28 29 LBC 5 4 3 2 1

For my family

Part I

The Cost of Living

1

I was once a famous murderess. I killed a wealthy family, Manson-style, and then I went on the run. But my thing wasn't about starting a race war to reach the land of milk and honey, or secretly wanting to be a Beatle. According to the news, I was just another fame-hungry killer, desperate to carve my face on the Mount Rushmore of great American psychopaths.

It isn't true, but still: the former-murderess thing is a fun line. I've thought about sticking it in a dating app bio. Two truths and a lie: (1) I'm a PhD dropout, (2) I understand how the stock market works and it's made me millions!!!, (3) I was once a famous murderess.

I was also once an SAT tutor, which is how I came into contact with the family I most certainly didn't kill. One of the bullshit rules of grammar we teach (I'm using the royal "we" of SAT tutors, my kin, my comrades, my fellow con artists peddling horseshit for rent money) is about the difference between passive and active voice. I do things. Things are done by me. The first is active; the second is passive. Passive voice evades. It invites folklore. Crimes committed without criminals. Subjects obscured and disappeared. Active voice is better, but passive voice is useful. If you're a murderer, for example.

Acts were committed by me. It's easier to tell the story like this. The "me" is almost an afterthought; it becomes the least important part of the sentence. Now it's about the act. The Victors were found dead. The Victors' dead bodies were found by me.

Now when I think about the day I arrived to tutor Serena Victor and discovered her father cradled in sea kelp in the koi pond, blue and bloated and unquestionably dead, I can almost imagine it as a film I watched. When I stumble upon the bloody, bashed-in sinkhole of her mother's face, I'm like a ghost encountering a crime scene. I have no material form. I touch nothing, removed from the universe of ripple effects and entropy. I'm just a passenger.

But of course, I did things. Decisions were made: I made them. Violence was done: I did it. Crime scenes were fled: I fled them. People were hurt: I hurt them. Someone was loved: I loved them. Not everything I did was bad. Just most of it.

I think a lot about a story I read as a teenager. Jorge Luis Borges's "The Garden of Forking Paths." In the story, a Chinese professor discovers the work of his ancestor Ts'ui Pen, who wanted to create both a labyrinthian novel and a real-life impenetrable labyrinth. The novel remained unfinished and unintelligible, and it was widely believed that the labyrinth was never located; in fact, the novel and the labyrinth were one and the same. The professor meets a scholar of Ts'ui Pen, who tells him that what Ts'ui Pen envisioned was a labyrinth not of space—a real, physical maze—but of time. Our decisions are not choices that eliminate all other possibilities by their certainty but a multiplication of time in which all other possible choices do exist, carving simultaneous planes of time into existence. In other words, all decisions are being carried out, at all times, all at once.

There's a universe where I don't ever go to the Victors' house. My roommate and I drink too much the night before. I send them a text: "So sorry. I'm violently ill. Can we reschedule?" Later that day, I'll learn about the murders on the news, the same way the rest of the world will. I'll absorb pundits' bloodthirsty speculation and true-crime aficionados' breathless Reddit theories. I'll tell the anecdote at parties: You know the Victors, the wealthy family murdered in LA? I used to tutor their kid. I've pissed in their toilet and drunk their tea and taught their daughter trigonometry. I wouldn't even be a footnote.

Now I'm the story. I wrote it. It wrote me.

2

Serena Victor was my Sunday afternoon. Serena was one of my catchall students. I'd been working with her for almost eight weeks. We met for two hours every week: SAT prep for the first hour, and general homework help for the second. I wasn't Serena's first tutor: Dinah mentioned that I had a predecessor, but they'd had to let her go. The implication was clear. *If Serena doesn't succeed, neither do you.*

Usually, Serena needed assistance with AP Language and Composition, and sometimes with AP Chemistry. Serena had been out of school for the past couple weeks, so I was working on catching her up to speed. Serena's mystery ailment wasn't contagious, her mother assured me, but it was bad enough that Serena stayed home, where her parents could keep an eye on her. SAT prep remained the primary focus. On practice tests, she scored roughly a 1350. Her highest was a 1480, her lowest a 1220. For a kid with expensive liberal-arts-college aspirations, math was surprisingly her best score. I liked teaching math the best. The elegant formulas, the tricks and repetition. It was harder to apply a reliable methodology to coaching reading comprehension. My students' progress was nonlinear and unpredictable, the dips and impasses in scores more difficult to explain to their parents.

These parents typically fell into one of two categories. They were either cloyingly grateful for "all my help" or deeply suspicious of my skill set and pay rate. The Victors, however, genuinely appeared to like me. Peter, Serena's father, worked in finance. Some kind of banker, I think. That's all I knew. Money accrued on other people's debt; zeroes multiplied in bank accounts while he summered in Mallorca and Monaco and Martha's Vineyard. He was short and unnaturally tan, his dark blond hair streaked with silver. He was normally absent during my sessions, but on the rare occasion he greeted me at the door, he had the disarming mildness of a lone man in a house full of women. I knew his type. He was the sort of dad who fancies himself the peacekeeper, the even-tempered voice of reason to balance out all that unhinged estrogen.

I'm not sure when Peter met Dinah, or how, but I know she was a moderately famous actress before they married. She quit the business after she had Serena. At the height of her fame, she featured in an Oscar-nominated drama about an underdog track-and-field star who achieves unexpected victory. My friends and I got high and watched it once. Dinah played the hot girlfriend who refuses to leave the protagonist's side after he gets a knee injury, which, thanks to her unwavering support, he bravely overcomes. I liked the movie more than I'd been willing to admit.

And then there was Serena. Serena Victor was a shy seventeen-year-old, with shiny cornsilk hair and a face like a porcelain doll. She wore dresses and skirts and shaggy thrifted sweaters, and her legs were dusted with peach-blond fuzz. When I first met her, her hair fell nearly to her waist. By week three, it was chopped to Jean Seberg length: this was the reference she told me, which was her way of letting me know that she knew who Jean-Luc Godard was. I suspected that despite her prettiness, she was unpopular at school. She coveted identity through her taste in literature, film, and music, and she was easily embarrassed and judgmental. I was unfairly predisposed to dislike her. Her shyness reminded me of the anti-social rich kids I'd gone to college with, roving across campus, chain-smoking and moody. I could see her future perfectly. An MFA in poetry, or a PhD in Early Modern Literature. Playing at bohemian poverty in a two-bedroom Victorian townhome in the

Mission. I knew enough about her boyfriend, Lukas, to understand the kind of guys she went for. I'd seen photos of Lukas on her lock screen and in the Polaroid she kept taped to the back of her iPhone case. His hair was longish and unkempt, dirty blond, a dishwater version of Serena's shiny goldilocks. He had a very square jaw and very concave cheeks like wax melted over a skull. Lukas was a vegetarian, and rolled his own cigarettes. By her early twenties, Serena would've traded Lukas in for shinier models, variations on the same men, whose cultural tastes signpost their alt credibility. The faded merch for bands no one's heard of, the oily hair, the vintage sneakers, the mustaches, the hand-poked tattoos. They'll be rich, just like Serena, but they'll hide it well. In the end, she'll have a fiancé in tech, maybe Swedish or Norwegian in origin, who develops apps and does a lot of MDMA and considers himself an authority on American hip-hop. Or he's an NYC-bred trust-fund kid who works in real estate and plays in a Dinosaur Jr. cover band on the weekends. Meanwhile, Serena paints, or buys art, or starts an expensive wellness clinic while she finishes her dissertation on melancholia and the female body in English pastoral poetry.

If I sound cruel to you, or petty, I won't try to defend myself. If it's any consolation, I can assure you that Serena's feelings remained protected from my bad mean thoughts. I was very good at pretending that I liked her to her face, and let's be honest: it didn't matter if I liked her or not. She lived in the most beautiful house I would ever set foot inside, a house I would never be able to live in myself, a house so fantastical it didn't look like it belonged to my world at all. But there it was in the Los Feliz hills, nestled among the English Tudors and Spanish Colonials and Swiss chalets.

In the living room, the only light bled sea-foam green through a prism of stained glass, modeled after Klimt's *Tree of Life*. Warrens of hallways appeared without logic, improbable and surreal. Dinah

Victor's furniture was Old Hollywood, long velvet couches and medieval chandeliers. Persian rugs, aquamarine Moroccan tile in the bathroom, opalescent tubs like the belly of a shell, with golden claw feet. For two hours every week, we worked in the dining room, and occasionally the living room or kitchen. During those two hours, half my mind focused on the task at hand: teaching Serena about parabolas and misplaced modifiers and the Pythagorean theorem. The other half traveled those rooms, feasting on every detail. The hundred-dollar cake of soap made of jasmine and saffron. Comma splice. The live-edge table cut from Portuguese wood. Polynomials. De Gournay hand-painted silk wallpaper. Parallelism.

I confess, in moments of weakness and self-loathing, I am susceptible to real estate porn. I like them old. Zillow is where I get my fix. But for the Victor House, I had to put my expensive art history degree to work. The architect was a surrealist artist named Emmanuel Besos, a Spanish aristocrat who came to California to work in the film industry, still in its infancy. He built sets for musicals and historical epics: staircases so vast they disappeared into clouds, fairy-tale ballrooms and gardens and mountain ranges. The Victor House was one of three residential homes he designed in Los Angeles in the 1920s. He wanted to use the house to experiment with a new way of constructing servants' quarters. Besos conceived a maze of secret passageways and hidden doors, designed for staff to remain out of sight. According to the article I found, the passageways were a myth: no one had ever found proof of them, and they didn't exist on the official blueprint of the house. They were just one of Besos's whims, never materialized.

The routine with Serena was always the same. I parked on the street. I drove a black 2003 PT Cruiser that I inherited from a dead great-uncle. It looked threateningly shitty on the Tesla-lined street. From the trunk, I took four books: Princeton Review SAT, College Board SAT, a math workbook, and whichever novel she'd been assigned for AP Lang. That week it was *Frankenstein*. I walked up the drive, over the moat (yes, a real moat), through the lush front garden of succulents and lemon trees, to the huge oak front door, which, on the Sunday this story begins, was already wide open.

This was unusual.

"Serena?" I didn't go in. From the doorway, I could smell the house's familiar scent: that stale must that so many houses in LA possess, all those 1920s estates that decorate the hills. Dinah Victor liked expensive incense and mint tea. I could smell both of these too.

"Serena?" I called again. Still no one answered, except the dog, who came skidding out of the darkness and launched himself at my legs. He bit my ankle.

"Pickle, you bitch."

The dog bit my ankle again. Soft, wet bites that didn't pierce the skin but were incredibly annoying.

"Dinah? Hello?"

I remembered Dinah hadn't been home the past few weeks. It was Peter who'd been answering the door.

"Peter?" I called out.

Nothing. I stepped inside. The main entry hall was low-ceilinged and dark, and there was a dining room to the left of the foyer. This is where Serena and I normally worked. I set down my stack of books. Sounds filled the house. From somewhere in its moody acoustics, I heard a thump. A faucet was running.

I went back to the main hallway. Sunlight begged to enter, dripped beneath a crack of shutters, scattering coins of light on the scarred hardwoods. Next to the dining area was a small bathroom, which I normally used as soon as I arrived. This was part of my routine at every house I tutored: a moment of privacy to piss or shit in a beautiful bathroom, to gather myself for the performance of Evie Gordon, SAT Tutor. The Victors kept paper napkins in a gold dish. Sometimes I wondered if this was so the help wouldn't use their hand towels. "The help" was a supple category, one I was never sure I belonged to. That's the thing about private tutors. We're not teachers. We don't carry authority like that. And yet, between me and the kid, there is at least the illusion that I'm in charge: a silent contract observed between the two of us that we will mutually participate in this performance. Sometimes, to get the spectacle going, the parents want to call me "Miss Gordon." I assure them, benevolently: No, no. Please, call me Evie.

I returned to the dining room, expecting to find Serena. She still wasn't there. I sat down anyway. I thought about turning on a light or throwing open the curtains. My phone was in my pocket. I texted Serena and Dinah separately: "Hello! I'm here."

A phone vibrated, somewhere in the house.

So someone was home. I thought about sending a follow-up smiley face. Serena and Dinah liked touches like this. It made it less awkward that they paid me and allowed them instead to think I was just Serena's older friend who really liked correcting her grammar. For some families I've worked for, this illusion helped: being reminded of the transactional origin of our relationship made them feel gross. The Victors were like that. Dinah always offered me tea. She wanted to know what I thought about Afghanistan, and which Virginia Woolf novel was my favorite, and what my tattoos meant.

No one was coming.

I checked my phone. Neither of them had responded. I listened carefully to the house, for the sighs and murmurs of floorboards. I had been so sure I heard a sink running. Now I couldn't hear anything.

Slowly, I got up from the table. It seemed important to stay quiet, for reasons I didn't yet understand. I crept down the dark hallway, past the bathroom with the expensive soaps and lotions, past Mr. Victor's dark study, until I arrived at the kitchen.

I'd been in here a few times before, for tea, for small talk, and once, for tutoring at the booth-style breakfast table beneath the stained-glass window. The range was French and antique. Copper pots hung farmhouse-style from a thick wooden rafter. The walls and floor were stone: the room felt like it belonged in a castle, like something from another world. An arched pair of doors led outside to the back garden.

One of the doors was open. Nearby was a suitcase, and a dropped handbag. Maybe Dinah had returned from wherever she'd been. Light poured from the open archway into the kitchen, thick and syrupy and swirling with dust motes.

"Dinah?" Tentatively, I pushed the door open even farther and stepped outside, cupping a hand over my eyes to shield them from the sun.

Terra-cotta tiles made a winding path, flanked by iron trellises writhing with ivy. A dark blue pool, like something out of a Roman bathhouse. Mint and basil wafted from the vegetable garden. Ripe tomatoes on the vine. A garden opened to a backyard draped in cypress trees. A Jacuzzi, which I suspected was infrequently used. There were Lovecraftian cacti and succulents, with thick spiked tongues furred with spiderwebs. Smooth plant flesh in alien colors, purples and mints and tangerines. Rows and rows of teeth. There was a footbridge, and beneath it, a koi pond. There was so much to look at, so much color and life and sunlight, that at first I didn't see Dinah or Peter at all.

It was Dinah whose body I registered. I don't remember a lot of details. The brain anesthetizes. I could see her clearly—she was as real and material as you and me—but she immediately took on a kind of unreality. Whatever Dinah was, it wasn't a person. Not anymore. Dinah was meat. Her face was tissue and viscera. Beside her was a blood-splattered rock.

Peter's head was in the koi pond. His face and throat were

bluish purple, his body white. A koi fish was swimming dizzily near his open mouth. As it swam around his head, it left behind a stream of bubbles, so it almost looked like he was breathing. I had never seen a dead body before, let alone two, but I knew enough to tell they were freshly dead. The blood on Dinah's bashed-in face appeared wet and shiny, and neither body smelled yet.

I couldn't scream or make any sound. I just fled. I tripped over something. A rock, maybe. Blood roared in my ears, a jackhammer deep in my skull. My body was moving of its own accord, back down the tiled pathway, through the ivy and the mint, into the cool, dark kitchen, and the even darker hallway, past the study and the bathroom and the dining room to the front doors, which still stood ajar.

As I lurched for the doorknob, I heard a horrible sound. A human sound.

It sounded a lot like "Help."

I'm not a good or virtuous person: I want to make that clear. At this point, I wasn't even going to call the police until I'd put some distance between me and the crime scene. I'd tell them the truth: Hello, Officers, I'm an SAT tutor, wrong place, wrong time, you know the story, you get it. Please get it. Sorry for fleeing but I didn't feel like dying, not now, not today. Not for them.

But there was something about that "help." I followed the noise to the staircase. Beneath the staircase was a little door. It had a round, vaguely sinister cottage shape.

"Please," said the voice. It was low and throaty. It didn't belong to Serena.

There was a wrenching sound, and then a gasp of pain. A plaintive, broken sob. I tried the door. It was locked.

"I can't . . . I can't reach it—" That awful, whispery croak again.

"Fuck." I jiggled the door handle as hard as I could. It wasn't budging. The person was crying harder now.

"Please," the voice gasped, "please—"

"Fuck, fuck, fuck—" I threw my body into the door. The hinges shook. I did this again and again, numbing my shoulder to the pain, until finally, the door crashed open. I looked inside.

Eyes in the darkness. Haunted eyes, staring from a face made of hollows. I couldn't tell if they belonged to a man or a woman or a child. Their head was a choppy mess of bleached and black hair, the dark roots so greasy they looked wet. Features glitched to life like a computer screen rebooting. Ragged lips. Filthy, caved-in cheek-bones. A handprint, raw and prickled with blood at the edges, bruised their throat. The room beneath the stairs had a low, slanted ceiling, and the prisoner—a woman, I was realizing, roughly my age—was cowering near the wall, head wedged against the sloping ceiling. She looked like a boy in a seventies punk band, living off heroin and cigarettes and whatever she could scrummage out of dumpsters. She wore black combat boots, black jeans so thin they clung to her matchstick legs like tissue paper. A yellow T-shirt that I suspected had once been white, and a leather jacket. We stared at each other, stunned. Her chest, which was as flat as a boy's, heaved with effort. She didn't move.

I came inside. It took me a second to realize the woman was tied up. Not with rope, but with frayed electric cord, littered with bite marks. She'd tried to chew herself free. She was tied to the lowest rafter about five feet into the room, which was narrow, crawling on and on, deeper than my vision could perceive in the darkness. The woman shivered as I came nearer. The smell. A terrible smell clung to her, but it wasn't like sweat or filth. It was rot. Expired fruit and roadkill. How long had she been under the stairs?

"I'm going to untie you," I said softly.

For a moment, I was afraid she might try to attack me out of some terrified animal instinct. I thought of cornered stray dogs, baring their frothing teeth. But she didn't fight; she moved back as much as she could to make room for me. The cord looped around a rafter, and there was almost no slack. Her hands curled into fists, then flexed open, struggling for blood circulation.

When I touched her hand, she jumped. I could hear the wheeze of her lungs, as if every exhalation were shuddering out of something punctured. Her lips, a sour breath away from mine, were so chapped they bled. A cold, strange patience entered me and worked at the savage knot until it loosened enough to tug her wrists free. A spasm took over her hands. She stared at her knuckles and fingers like they were something that didn't belong to her. She looked up, her eyes finding mine in the dark.

I was so focused on the woman, and the labored rattle of her breath, that I didn't hear the sound of approaching steps. It was the woman who alerted me: she seized me by the arm and dragged me with her into the main hallway.

It took Serena a moment to register us. She was texting as she entered the house, but her face changed when she saw me and the woman.

The woman immediately darted for the open door, but Serena blocked her with a startled scream.

The woman froze, clutching the stair rail in fear, her eyes darting between Serena and the door.

Serena fumbled for her phone, her voice shrill with panic.

"Nine-one—"

The woman charged for the door. Serena slammed it shut, still clutching her phone.

"Nine-one—" she tried again, screaming, but the woman was able to pry the phone out of her hand and vault it across the room.

It landed right at my feet.

Serena looked at me, and then at the phone.

Unthinking, I snatched it up and held out my hand in warning.

"Serena," I said slowly. "Let me explain what's happening. I don't think you understand."

I didn't understand what was happening either, though I could put together what Serena was imagining. She thought the woman was an intruder, and she intended to call the police on her.

On both of us.

Serena was breathing hard, like a cornered animal, as she slowly backed farther into the hallway. With a sob, she grabbed a lamp off the entryway table; it had a heavy golden base.

"Don't come near me—" she babbled, lifting the lamp like a bat. "I'll—I'll—"

"Serena, please, just let me *explain*—"

She screamed in terror as I moved closer, her hand scrabbled along the wall, as if searching for something.

A landline.

Here's how I saw the following chain of events playing out.

Step One: Serena believed she'd caught me and a dirty stranger trying to burgle her house. If the police arrived, we would be arrested.

Step Two: The police and Serena would discover her parents' freshly murdered bodies in the garden, and we would be swiftly charged with murder.

Step Three: A gory and sensational trial.

Step Four: *Orange Is the New Black: The Evie Gordon Spin-Off.* A life sentence.

And so here was the third of my major mistakes, after rescuing the bound woman and coming to work today, period.

I tried to take the landline.

Serena didn't hesitate. She lifted the lamp and swung it at my head.

It's impossible to describe pain, and it's even harder to remember it. I'd never been hit that hard by something that heavy. It felt like the space between my ears was empty, a cup without a brain, filling sluggishly with blood. I thought my head might shatter like an egg, blood and yolk streaming down my face. I crashed against the stairs, against the woman, scrambling backward. Serena's phone skittered across the floor. Blood was dripping down my face, and I felt the woman take my hand and pull me to my feet, kicking Serena's phone away.

The lamp was coming at me again. I staggered backward and grabbed the first thing I could to shield the blow. It was a vase, much heavier than I thought.

"Serena, stop!"

Serena was screaming without words. Raw, involuntary sound. She reared the lamp back and took a swing. I threw the vase, as hard as I could.

The sound of it striking Serena's head was meaty and dense. She fell, still trying to scramble away, even as her eyes rolled back in her head.

She went limp.

I crawled forward in shock.

She wasn't moving.

I felt her pulse.

Nothing.

I dug my fingers deep into the soft tissue of her throat, searching and searching for it.

I couldn't feel it.

I climbed on top of her, peeling her eyelids open and finding nothing, only blue tendrils, curling around the whites of her eyeballs. I brought the back of my hand across her face. Her head lolled uselessly.

She couldn't be dead. It wasn't possible.

I felt for her pulse again.

Still nothing.

"No . . ." My voice sounded strange. "No. No—"

My mind started to bend.

"An ambulance—we could—we should—"

We couldn't and shouldn't. If we called an ambulance, we would be inviting paramedics to a crime scene. They would have me arrested for murdering the entire Victor family.

But this is what people do. On TV, when this happens—when a death happens, when a person is alive and then they're not, when it's not old age and it's not cancer, it's a gun it's a knife it's Colonel Mustard with the candelabra in the ballroom, it's someone grabbing the heaviest object they can find and swinging it as hard as they can—the police come. On TV, you call the police, and the cast of *Law & Order* shows up, and the bad guys go to jail and justice is restored and you watch the next one and it happens all over again and again and—

I was crying. The woman—who was not crying—took me by the jaw and turned my face toward the mirror above the entryway table. I'd looked into this mirror so many times. Sneaking cheeky mirror selfies for an Instagram story, checking my teeth for stray lettuce from the Taco Bell I'd destroyed in the car on my way over. This mirror probably cost thousands of dollars. A precious, gold-framed antique. I confronted the fact of our reflections. My Target jeans, my secondhand boots. The blood streaking down my hands and face. I'd seen me before, in Netflix true-crime documentaries about serial killers, in mug shots, in B-movie thrillers. I knew exactly what conclusions a cop would draw if they saw me next to Serena's dead body.

In the mirror's reflection the woman's eyes bored into mine. *Look at us,* her eyes said. She looked like she'd just crawled out of the toilet in *Trainspotting*. I looked like Carrie, from the movie *Carrie*.

She wanted to run.

"Please" was the only word she could manage, and it took everything out of her to say it. She closed her eyes, her lips trembling in her effort to produce another word. She was shaking.

Something had happened to her in this house. She had been

hurt here. One of the Victors had hurt her. Peter or Dinah. Maybe even Serena.

Maybe all of them.

"Serena?" a voice gasped behind us.

My nervous system gave a final, deathbed spasm.

I almost laughed. Of course there was one more.

It was a teenage boy. I recognized him immediately, from the photos on Serena's phone.

Lukas. Serena's boyfriend.

He saw me, covered in blood. He saw the woman. He saw Serena, his girlfriend, still as a corpse.

"What the fuck—" He rushed forward. "Oh my God, Serena, *oh my God*—"

We were already running. The choice was made for us. The woman grabbed my hand and hauled me past Lukas, who was starting to scream. My vision spun, kaleidoscopic, taking in plants, moat, grass, blinding sun. The street. My car. The woman took me by the arms and shook me until she came into focus. Her eyes, again. Black and alert.

"Keys," she said.

"Keys," I repeated.

I could barely even see.

She dipped her hand into the front pocket of my jeans and took my keys out herself, pressing them into my shaking palms. Somehow, we got into the car. I turned the key in the ignition, and adrenaline took over. The woman was in the passenger seat, staring in shock at the sun-soaked street ahead of us. In the distance, a police siren wailed.

"Where are we going?" I asked.

We. That's how fast the decision was made.

3

The sun was setting as we fled. The traffic was always bad in Los Angeles, but Sundays were marginally better. Still, I'd never been more grateful for LA's filthy, crowded highways, where it was easy to disappear into the graffiti, the anonymity of cars driving to and from work, Amazon vans and tow trucks, Teslas and Porsches and vintage Camaros, rusted Civics and Corollas, a sleek white limousine. My PT Cruiser entered the stream. My head pounded. It was full of questions, a rush of noise so dense it felt like silence. The hands on the wheel didn't look like mine. They were someone else's. Evie was not here. Evie was at home, nursing her hangover with an indulgent Sunday brunch. Evie and her roommate, Harvey, were slumped across the red couch they'd bought for forty bucks on Craigslist, watching trashy reality TV.

The city blurred past: billboards advertising superhero movies and shady 1-800 lawyers to call if you got in a traffic accident. Apartment complexes, tent cities, chemist-lab coffee shops. A Scientology celebrity center. A tiki bar, Valvoline, McDonald's. A haunted hotel. We made it to the 101. Blood was congealing in my ear, thick as wax. I jumped when the woman touched me.

She'd removed the rag of her shirt, leaving her in a bra and leather jacket. There was a crumpled, half-full water bottle I'd abandoned weeks, maybe months ago, in the passenger-door side compartment. She took a trembling sip, bringing the warm plastic to her lips like a sacrament. Then she poured a few drops onto the shirt and brought it to my ear.

I navigated traffic while she cleaned me. She was gentle with my head. I held my breath against her smell.

"They could've seen my license plate," I said.

This is what I thought about, of all things. My car, the rusted North Carolina license plate I'd never bothered to change. Lukas would've looked for it as we sped away. He would've given the number to the police when they came. Have they arrived by now?

The road unfocused, then sharpened again. Cars. A billboard for a new HBO show about a pill-popping pharmaceutical rep high on her own supply. A truck full of chickens pulled up beside us. Three cars behind me there was a cop SUV.

"My license plate," I repeated.

The woman nodded in my peripheral vision, agreeing.

The license plate was a problem.

Serena, dead, a problem.

One problem at a time.

"Should we—" I started, licking my dry lips, tasting blood. "Should we . . ."

Should we call the police. No, no, no, fuck that for a thousand reasons. Should we pull over and think. No, we can't stop, we have to get out of LA. Should we call our moms and dads and ask for help. Should we tell our moms and dads we accidentally killed someone. Should we ask our moms and dads if they'll still love us even though we're murderers. Should we call our roommate and tell him we won't be home in time to watch *RuPaul*.

A hysterical, dementedly wonderful sort of feeling filled my chest. A balloon of mania, coked-up and seasick, pumping like a heart.

My mind conjured faces I hadn't thought of in years. My third-grade teacher, Mrs. Cuttler, who let me take books home from the classroom collection so I could keep up with my reading habit. My childhood best friend's mom, Ms. Diane, who noticed my fear of escalators during a trip to Build-A-Bear at the mall and rewarded my bravery with an Auntie Anne's soft pretzel. Friends I'd had in elementary and middle school, who I hadn't spoken to in years, now dentists and schoolteachers and stay-at-home moms with small children of their own, who never left Hendersonville, North Carolina. I don't know why it was their faces I thought of on the other side of the television screen, their hands covering their mouths in shock when they learned what Evie Gordon—*Evie Gordon, of all people*—had done to that nice family in Los Angeles. I was a good kid. Top of my class. My parents were kind and well-respected members of our community. *How could this have happened?* they'd say. *How could she have gone so far astray?*

I thought about the friends from high school I was still close with, who I went on annual road trips with: Would I ever see them again? My friends from college, who still lived in New York: When would the news reach their orbit? Would the cops reach out to them, or journalists? My friends in Los Angeles, cops hammering down their doors, searching for me, asking questions? My ex— would they go to her too? How would I explain any of this?

What would I tell my parents?

The thought made my mind go blank. A heart monitor flatlining. It was unthinkable. My mom, who smelled like Pantene hairspray and Orbit Sweet Mint Gum, a drugstore body spray called Juniper Breeze, Virginia Slims cigarettes. My mom, who treated every homecoming, no matter how minor, how banal, as if I were a soldier returning from war. She parked her 1998 Chrysler Sebring in the airport parking lot and waited for me in the lobby, squealing when she saw me emerge from the tunnel. My dad and his reading glasses, his eyes magnified behind them like a little boy's. His chunky waterproof watch, his shelves and shelves of history books. His farmer's tan, his sock tan. His slight limp, from an ACL tear he'd gotten playing in his adult baseball league on

Wednesday nights. They were divorced, my parents, but remained friends. We always celebrated Thanksgiving and Hanukkah together, as a family. My parents, who'd never been any good at disciplining me, who'd never felt the need. My parents, who trusted me implicitly. Would they cooperate when the FBI came to their door? When the headline "Evie Gordon Wanted for Murder" hit the news, would they believe it?

The road pulsed ahead of me. There were so many cars in Los Angeles. So many people. Every stop-start jerk of traffic made my head pound. The woman leaned over to clean more blood off me. The closer she came, the more I smelled her. I wasn't getting used to her smell.

"We need—" I started again, wishing she would finish the sentence. "We need—"

Supplies. A first-aid kit. A knife, maybe. Money. Cash, specifically. We couldn't use my debit card. We couldn't even use my phone. If I called my mom and dad, if I told them what I'd done, that I needed help, a cell tower might find my location. My faded debit card, my pathetic checking account, they all scattered breadcrumbs behind me.

"My phone," I said, "can you grab it from my bag?"

She retrieved it haltingly.

"Give it to me," I said.

She searched my face, as if debating whether this was a good idea.

"I'm not going to do anything stupid," I gritted out. "Give it to me."

The woman handed it over.

I chucked it out the car window.

The woman stared at me.

"Cell towers," I said, like an insane person. "Right? That's a thing. I've heard that. They follow us. Digitally. With their signals. I listened to *Serial*. We all listened to *Serial*. Didn't you?"

The woman was staring at me with the exhaustion of a parent listening to the unhinged ravings of a toddler. I knew the cell tower thing made sense though. It made sense. Sarah Koenig had explained it.

"What. Where—" I started again, searching for the right question. Panic lapped against my skull, to drink, to enter, to worm its way in and paralyze me.

"Where are we going?" is what I settled on.

The woman didn't answer. Plastic crunched in her fist as she took another gulp from the water bottle. She offered it to me, wordlessly. I shook my head. Her lips were chapped and bloody. Her mouth was too dark inside, like she'd swallowed ink or drunk too much red wine. I didn't want my mouth touching something her mouth had touched.

"Finish it," I said. "We'll . . . we'll get more." Somehow.

The woman nodded. She finished the bottle. I could hear the water moving down her throat, entering the starved organs of her body like a coin falling down a well.

The cops were probably questioning Lukas right now. Lukas would be telling them what he saw, and his word would be enough. His school uniform, his Hitler Youth complexion, the Vassar College acceptance letter waiting in his mailbox. Serena had told me he'd already been accepted. She'd told me plenty about him. He rode a bike because it was better for the environment. His favorite writer was Jack Kerouac. He was the only kid in their whole school who had an old flip phone instead of an iPhone. He owned a 1957 Les Paul guitar, which Google informed me cost north of seven thousand dollars.

What would Lukas know about me? What might Serena have told him? "Evie, my tutor, she always smells like weed and hates when I take too long to solve geometry problems, she went to a fancy school and acts like a know-it-all, but look at her now, she's a loser." Probably something like that.

And what would he say to the cops? "Two women covered in blood. That's who I saw. One of them was Evie Something, I don't know her last name, she's my girlfriend's SAT tutor. The other one was skinny and filthy, with short bleached-and-black hair. A stranger. Maybe Asian? Oh, you didn't ask? Well, that would be my guess. Allow me to speculate wildly about her ethnicity in excruciating detail—"

Police would be all over the house by now.

They'd be taping off the koi pond. Taking photos. Blood, ghastly against Serena's translucent skin. Dripping into her shiny, golden hair. Crusted along the blue-veined pearly white of her throat, her forehead. I could see her, pretty and sympathetic in her high school yearbook photo, Laura Palmer–style. A news anchor would tell the world how smart and shy and lovely she was, broadcast live to bored mothers taking quivering sips of coffee, hungry for the killers' wicked names, our troubled histories, our broken homes and vengeful hearts, tasty crumbs to feed their bloodlust.

"She was her *tutor*," the anchor would report, shaking her head. The mothers would gasp. Hands on hearts, mysteriously aroused. "Evie Gordon."

The traffic was thinning, the farther we drove. The sun directly ahead of us, blazing into our faces. I lowered my visor. But the woman just stared into the sunlight, stiff and straight-backed as a vampire confronting the inevitability of death. The road surrendered to desert. We passed what felt like every kind of California landscape: the gentle, Jurassic spines of mountains, the scrub-brush hills, baked earth thirsty for water. We weren't far enough from the city, not yet. The sun had set, but the sky was still an apocalyptic, bloody purple. The color of light pollution.

The woman was shivering violently in the passenger seat.

"The person who killed the Victors," I said carefully, "is that who tied you up?"

Now she looked dumbstruck. Almost confused.

She hadn't known Peter and Dinah were dead.

Her eyes unfocused. Her shivering worsened, and her face became impassive again, as if she was so used to disassociating it had become entirely banal.

If the woman hadn't even known that Peter and Dinah were dead, that meant she never saw the killer: which meant she'd already been tied up in that sinister closet under the stairs by the time the killer arrived.

"Who tied you up?"

The woman stared numbly at the desert.

My stomach sank.

"It was them, wasn't it," I said. "The Victors."

Maybe it was a mercy she hadn't heard them being murdered. Or maybe it was a tragedy. Maybe they'd hurt her badly enough that she would've liked to hear them die.

I glanced at her again. She hadn't spoken a word since we'd fled. Trauma, maybe. The bruise around her neck was a stark, harrowing maroon. She probably needed a hospital. Medical attention. It was risky. I could drop her off and disappear.

But then I'd be alone. And I didn't want to be alone. The woman had helped me. I had helped her. Saved her. That had to mean something. But saved her from what? The "what" skipped across my brain, from nightmare to nightmare. Torture chambers and sex dungeons. Los Angeles houses don't have basements. I had learned that when I moved to this coast. Instead, I pictured a second house, in miniature, tucked away in the closet like a forgotten dollhouse. A horror movie inverse of the Victors' lush mansion. Cobwebbed and pitch-black. The woman huddled in the corner. Laughter echoing through the walls, the music of cutlery, pots, plates. The Victors were philanthropists. Sometimes Dinah offered me the catering leftovers from events she'd hosted the night before. The Victors organized fundraising parties, chaired charities, sponsored the seals and the elephants, every endangered animal except their own miserable kind. Money promised, canapés delicately nibbled, champagne uncorked, small talk of upcoming vacations to Bora Bora, of interesting documentaries viewed over the weekend, of *New Yorker* articles read and summer homes renovated. The hiss of the teapot on Sunday morning. The doorbell on Sunday afternoon. My footsteps, walking right past that door, for so many Sundays. My voice, lecturing on Shakespeare, *Beowulf*, Mark Twain, and Nathaniel Hawthorne, whoever Serena was reading in AP Lang. Looking over her geometry homework, teaching her how to solve for *x*. SAT time tests, eight out of ten, muster some enthusiasm, "good work, Serena!" Packing up my books, exchanging banal pleasantries with Dinah on my way out the door, taking a final piss or shit in their exquisite bathroom. Drying my hands on the plush hand towel, not the help's paper napkins, because minor acts of pettiness are the only recourse I have. My footsteps. The closing of the front door, the squeal of my tires. Leaving her alone, again. The tick-tick-tick of a grandfather clock on the other side of the wall. Footsteps, slow and ominous. Peter Victor's long shadow appearing in an open doorway. The guests were finally gone.

"Is there somewhere I can take you?" I asked. "Home? Someone must be looking for you—your parents, they'll want to know you're okay. I could—shouldn't we—?"

Nothing I suggested seemed to even enter her consciousness.

"What about the cops?" I suggested. "I could drop you off somewhere? The police could—" Arrest the freshly murdered corpses of Peter and Dinah Victor for [insert crime committed against you: Kidnapping? Torture? Sex trafficking?].

The woman said nothing.

The road pounded ahead of me, an endless, unspooling dark ribbon. The sky was darker now, a true dark. Stars, finally, pearled the sky. The red eyes of semi-trucks stared ahead of us.

"I'm sorry," I said.

She looked at me. Her face was carefully blank, like she was concentrating all her energy on its blankness. But her eyes were numb, weary in a way that felt beyond comprehension.

"Not for them," I said. "For . . . for you," I finished lamely. I hoped the apology was vague enough to capture whatever crime had been done to her.

The woman looked away, her face almost sullen, like I was boring her.

"Look," I said. "I can go to the cops. I can say . . . I don't know. I don't know. Something good. Something that absolves you. The truth. It might work. It could work. You shouldn't be here. You don't have to be part of this. I can take you home."

She picked at the dead, bloody skin around her ragged fingernails.

"I did this," I said, lowering my voice. "They're chasing me. They want me. I'm the one who—"

Killed Serena.

And even though I hadn't killed Peter and Dinah, of course everyone would think that I did that too.

"I obviously look guilty," I told the woman. "But you don't. You don't have to be part of this. You shouldn't be. I mean, you were their . . . their—"

I didn't know. I didn't want to say "victim."

The woman jerked, before I even finished the sentence. She was coiled tight, like her entire body was concentrated on containing a detonation. I wanted to hear her voice again.

"How long were you in that closet?"

Red brake lights lanced across her face. A tear drew a path through the filth. Her cracked knuckles swiped it away, as if it were a nuisance. The idea of asking her any more questions made me feel sick. Already I felt sick. Her smell, bloody and rotting. Her silence. How many Sundays had we shared the walls of that house?

How many Sundays had I drunk Dinah's tea and cracked bad jokes and scrolled through Instagram under the table, while this woman suffered only a few feet away?

Bile lifted in my throat, then settled again. Phantoms took shape on the edge of the dark road, lurched, then disappeared. Drivers passed me: they had girls with bags over their heads in the passenger seat. Ropes trailed behind semi-trucks, ropes around broken necks, feet dragging. When I looked again, they were gone.

I don't know what would've happened to the woman if I hadn't found her. She'd said please—I'd heard her voice. She'd asked for help, and I'd given it. I thought I'd given it. But what if instead I'd doomed her to an even worse fate? The police would've searched the house eventually. They would've found her and arrived at wildly different conclusions than the ones they'd be drawing now. The headlines might read: "Horror in the Hills"; "Wealthy Family's Secrets Exposed."

Now she was like me. Her red string tangled with mine.

"Food," I said hoarsely. "You need food. And some water."

She didn't disagree, but she didn't nod either.

"We'll need cash," I continued.

She looked at me in a flat, cynical way.

"I can get some," I told her. "If we find an ATM." They'd be able to track the bank statement, of course, but it was our only option. If we kept driving tonight—if we made it far enough—maybe it wouldn't matter.

We were close to Indio. There was a Walmart. In dark, far-flung corners of the parking lot, families slept under dashboards filled with fast food bags and garbage and stuffed animals.

I parked far from the entrance. The engine cut. The woman licked her mouth with her dark tongue. It was blood, I realized.

"I'm going in," I said.

She looked skeptical. She knew I had no idea what I was doing.

"Stay here and try to clean yourself up," I said.

A sullen indifference took over her face, but her knee was bouncing restlessly. She was scared, I realized. Scared to be left here, alone. Reluctantly I fished the car keys out of my pocket and dropped them into the cup holder. I didn't want to part with them, but it might make her less afraid.

"There," I said, "you can keep the car on, if you want. Stay warm."

The fluorescent lights inside were cold and blinding. I moved quickly through aisles in search of the bathroom, which of course was tucked all the way in the back. There was one employee inside the restroom, a teenage girl with greasy hair, running a mop along the floor in a disinterested way. She made eye contact with me in the mirror, and I caught one horrifying glimpse of my face before I ducked into a stall. I pissed for what felt like hours. Finally, I heard the door shut, and the retreat of the employee's footsteps. I flushed and went to the sinks.

The woman had done a good job of cleaning the blood off me. I still looked wrecked, though, and I stank of blood. I could feel the loss of it, the shaky lightness of my limbs, thinned of iron. My eyes were jaundiced around the iris, my pupils blown. I took a deep breath, arranging my face into a shape I hoped looked casual.

Carefully avoiding the attention of other late-night shoppers—tired moms, gaggles of stoned teenagers—I went back to the front of the store for a cart. I searched the cavernous warehouse aisles, mindlessly grabbing things off shelves. I was not a survivalist. I didn't camp. I had no idea what the fuck I was doing. I filled the cart with water, Tylenol, a first-aid kit, a few dozen cans of soup and nonperishables, jerky and dried fruit and nuts. I grabbed a folding knife. Irish Spring, so we could clean ourselves. An armful of clothes: sweatpants and T-shirts, guessing at sizes. I almost bought her clothes from the kids' section. She was that skinny.

At the self-checkout, I kept my head down, paying in cash. Afterward, I took the shopping bags to the ATM outside. There was a security guard smoking a cigarette near the automatic doors. He watched as I fed my card into the reader and withdrew all the cash from my checking account. I had to do this in multiple rounds, since there was a $500 limit. I took out all the money I had: there was about $650 in my checking account, and $2,300 in my savings. I could feel the security guard watching as I stuffed the bills into my pockets, picked up the shopping bags, and went to the parking lot.

I thought I'd remembered where we parked. There'd been a red Kia Soul nearby and a blue Honda Civic. The Soul was still there. But not my black PT Cruiser.

My heart thumped as I searched the grid of cars, weaving between streetlights flickering with moths, arms aching with heavy shopping bags. I could still feel the security guard watching. His eyes following me as I darted between vehicles, searching desperately for my own.

But it was gone. And so was she.

4

Believe it or not, I wasn't always an idiot. I was smart, once. Talented and Gifted.

The title was bestowed on me when I was eight. I was a straight-A student, and I read fast. My second-grade teacher selected me to be tested for the TAG program. The test was strange: One page was a series of what looked like blank cans. Armed only with our wits, we had to turn the cans into something else. I turned mine into different animals: a fat little sausage dog, a parrot, a whale shark. One kid, Greg Cusimano, just wrote different Campbell's flavors on them. Greg Cusimano wasn't Talented or Gifted. Another page gave us a series of complicated shapes in a matrix, and we had to figure out the pattern. This determined whether we were capable of serial reasoning.

I have incredible serial reasoning. Every Thursday, the chosen ones were scuttled off to a separate room for our TAG classes. Ponytails swinging, smug smiles blazing, we left the half-wits behind. By age eleven, all my classes were TAG: TAG math, TAG language arts, TAG social studies. In eighth grade, TAG became honors. In tenth grade, honors became Advanced Placement. By senior year, my schedule consisted entirely of AP classes.

I was raised in Hendersonville, North Carolina, a small mountain town near Asheville. It was only a half hour's drive from the Biltmore estate: "America's Largest Home." Billboards advertising entry tickets for the Biltmore crowded the highway. They took our fourth-grade TAG class on a field trip, where we oohed and aahed over the swimming pool and bowling alley. My dad was a public-school teacher whose claim to local-paper fame is that a group of conservative parents once charged him with promoting witchcraft. Books of sorcery—in this case, Roald Dahl's *The Witches*—have no place in the classroom. My mom cut hair at a salon. Growing up, my idea of rich people were families who had pools in their backyard, the girls in my middle school who had real Coach purses, and Paris Hilton. My family's idea of balling out for dinner on Friday night was a reservation at Chili's, apps included.

I don't know if it was this trip to the Biltmore, or too many late nights stuffing my face with Chips Ahoy! over episodes of *MTV Cribs*, or the fact that all my teachers repeatedly told me I was brilliant, but somehow, my parents and I got it into our heads that I would be Something. Someone. I won a scholarship to a private school. After school, I swept hair at my mom's salon. I babysat on the weekends. My first business was a mercenary, under-the-table essay-writing scheme. I charged forty dollars an essay. It was a word-of-mouth phenomenon, trafficked by football players and grammatically stunted STEM prodigies. My AP US History teacher was the only one who appeared to catch on: she interrogated me one day before class after I carelessly used the exact same turn of phrase for three different students' essays, including my own. I explained that we were in a study group. She couldn't prove otherwise.

As one of only a handful of scholarship kids, I probably should've been an outcast at the expensive Asheville private school. But this never happened. I had a boyfriend named Nick Faust. Nick was my blond himbo shiksa. He drove a camo-print Jeep Wrangler and burned like a vampire if he wore anything less than SPF 70. He came from the kind of family that bred golden retrievers and watched football together on Sunday nights and privately felt super weird about their kid's bolshy Jewish girlfriend. I was a homecoming princess. I was the captain of the girls' soccer team. In the era of late-stage Myspace and early Facebook, I developed a talent for cyberbullying. I worked and studied and worked and studied until the sun just barely cracked over the soft peaks of the Blue Ridge Mountains, slept for an hour and a half, then went to school. At night after soccer practice, after work, after dinner, after hours and hours of homework and AP essays and problem sets and writing other students' essays, I shaved my legs, whitened my teeth, and subjected my curly hair to the tyranny of a drugstore flatiron until I was knife-sharp and gleaming.

I was salutatorian, in the end. The title of valedictorian went to a kid named Warren Calvin Manning III, whose father was a city councilman and whose mother was a former pageant queen with a diet pill empire. In revenge, my friends and I—friends I'd taken from Warren, friends I'd fought for, friends I never should've had—got high and toilet papered his house, a plantation-style mansion in the most luxurious cul-de-sac in the country club. A country club all my friends lived in except me.

You're just like us, I could feel them thinking as they pet and admired me. It was the highest compliment they could imagine.

No, I thought. I'm better. You were born. I was made.

No, that's not right either. No one made me. I was my own creator.

The irony was that I thought they were rich. I didn't even know what being rich meant, not yet. Not until college. I chose a school, ironically, that didn't consider SAT results in its admissions criteria. Tuition costs had tripled since my parents' generation, and among even those staggering numbers, the school that accepted me was one of the most expensive of all. I was gifted with a scholarship and generous student aid, though we still had to take out loans. But it would be worth it, they told us. This college is special, and you're special for being among the lucky few granted admission. They didn't even grade us—that's how special we were. We transcended those arcane systems of judgment. Here, we could watch black-and-white films and write bad one-act plays and incur abstract piles of student loan debt without fear. A special college full of special students, each of us out-specialing each other in the same special uniform: the combat boots, the coke residue under our noses, the Sylvia Plath in the *New Yorker* tote bag, the rejection of our birth names and our natural hair colors, the queer adaptations of *Fiddler on the Roof* using only puppets, the mental illness, the quoting Foucault during sex, the daddy fetishes. Each of us was just as special as the last.

I became friends with kids whose parents ran entertainment empires, kids who were technically princesses of small African countries, kids rich enough to ship their pet horses overseas. Kids whose Malibu palaces would make Warren Calvin Manning III's five-bedroom McMansion with the pool in the backyard—the biggest, grandest house I could imagine—look like middle-class garbage. And here I was, among them. Rolling joints in fairy light–strung dorm rooms. Barhopping in Manhattan. Being invited to vacation in Saint-Tropez.

I fit in here too. I learned the special college's very special rules. Flung into this new, rarefied landscape, where eighteen-year-olds knew words like "tartare" and "escrow," I seized on their language like a junkie. It's not that I thought I could disappear among them. If anything, they coveted the dirty token of my membership, the perverse social capital my bumfuck status accrued them. It had never occurred to me that I could be made to feel more provincial than I had at the private school. The world was huger and scarier than it had ever looked on MTV, the climb to the top much bleaker and more difficult than I'd imagined. The gap between us embarrassed me, and my embarrassment embarrassed me more than anything else.

You have so much potential, said my parents and my teachers. I'd heard that line my entire life. Surely their confident consensus had to mean something. I was a gravitational field, charged with ions, seeking a power line to electrify.

And then I graduated, and I could not get a job. I looked. I kept looking for two years. There were still possibilities. There are always possibilities. The rags-to-riches fantasy is so deeply engraved into the American consciousness that it's cellular, the invisible strand in the helix of our DNA. A doe-eyed chimney sweep works hard and catches the eye of a Wall Street Prince Charming. Bootstrapping stories have kept capitalists' dicks hard since the Gilded Age.

But the thing about potential is that it's purely speculative: it's the province of stock traders calculating their fantasy math, college athletic scouts playing God with teenage cattle, meteorologists prophesying the fury of oceans. Slowly, the scales began to fall from my eyes. I could see now that I'd been sold a false bill of goods. And yet no matter how much literature I read, how much theory I fought to internalize, I still felt contempt for myself and my country-mouse naivete—for my family and where I came from, our tacky furniture and paper plates and coupon hoarding, our Holiday Inn vacations, and for my parents' idiot faith in my talents and gifts, for my own idiot faith in the romance of social mobility, and for how magnificently I'd fucked up the possibility of fulfilling the promise of either.

As a kid, money seemed so straightforward. Paris Hilton had it because she was an heiress and the Real Housewives had it because they married rich and Leonardo DiCaprio had it because he's a famous actor and the Huxtables were a doctor and a lawyer, and to be honest, I was never sure what the deal was with the kids on *Gossip Girl*, but I knew enough about trust funds to form a reasonable hypothesis.

But in the years after I graduated, wealth took on a different, more elusive form. She was a woman in cat-eyed sunglasses and a headscarf, a femme fatale, a serial killer: she had become, in other words, a great mystery. *The* great mystery. How did the intern afford his beautiful apartment in Chelsea? How do the improv co-medians I popped benzos with at shitty dorm parties already own a house in Westchester, only a couple years out of college? What does a "consultant" do? I searched for clues. I tried to question the suspects carefully at happy hour. I made pitiful attempts to connect the dots: a corkboard, red strings that lead nowhere, a Post-it that just said, "secret porn star???"

I became an SAT tutor. The story of my postcollegiate decline isn't that interesting, so I'll run through it quickly. After graduation, I lived in a large apartment in Bed-Stuy with eight to twelve other special people (some listed on the lease, some squatters, some girl-friends of squatters; I was on the lease). Academics, aspiring rappers, weed delivery service couriers, assistants, nannies, servers, and DJs. The apartment was filthy. The couch covered in weed crumbs and ash. The sink crusted with midnight shrapnel: lentils and late-night pancake batter, eggshells, and fruit peels. Wild mushrooms grew in the shower, which didn't have a curtain. Without the reliable narcotic drip of an education to remind me how special I was or steady employment to occupy me, my self-worth became unstable and indeterminate. For thirteen months I was high from the min-ute I woke up until the second I fell asleep. I got violently ill in the spring and decided to stop smoking, even cigarettes. I fell into a nicotine-withdrawal-related depression, and I badly needed money. I sold some eggs. I was desperate enough to go on a handful of Seeking Arrangement dates: I made a couple hundred bucks for an hour and a half of overpriced dinner and awkward conversation.

Finally, through an old roommate, I landed a temp job at a creative agency in the Flatiron District. Parabola-shaped communal desks, warehouse ceilings, a cold-brew tap, a retro Smeg refrigerator full of kombucha. I was paid fourteen dollars an hour to "input data," but really, I was there to be a piece of hip female furniture. I searched for jobs, usually while at my job. I half-heartedly juggled office romances. I checked my email. I applied for more jobs. I went on my final Seeking Arrangement date with a guy who spent the entire dinner trying to convince me that he was Keanu Reeves's cousin. Impulsively, desperately, I applied for graduate school after seeing an ad for an architectural history program on LinkedIn—if you've ever wondered what kind of schmuck goes for those ads, the answer is me. The deadline was in ten days.

I was accepted. I moved to Los Angeles. Now, when my parents called, or my nosy relatives asked, or my high school nemeses stalked me on Facebook, I could at least say I was a Master of Arts, which sounded more impressive than Minimum-Wage Temp at Job I Don't Understand. I heroically recovered my specialness, then was spit back into the nonexistent job market. Too special to hold down a real job and too broke to pay off my ninety-nine-thousand-dollar student loan debt, I returned to the precarious employment that had steadily funded me during and after college: test prep tutoring. In New York and Los Angeles, this paid sixty dollars an hour. I averaged four or five students a week, and I made them meet me for at least two hours a session. Do the math and calculate whether or not I was living beneath the poverty line: that would make a cheeky SAT question.

Besides the fact that I could barely afford my rent, the job itself wasn't terrible. I got to see so many beautiful houses. Every Tuesday and Thursday I drove almost an hour and a half from East Hollywood to Calabasas to meet with a girl named Spencer. Named after Diana Spencer. She lived in a sprawling country club, and her neighbors were Drake and a Kardashian. My Wednesday, Jagger, was the sweet, disaffected son of a Grammy-winning R&B producer in Bel-Air. His mother was almost a Real Housewife of Beverly Hills. We worked on the ACT next to his infinity pool while sipping LaCroix. Monday was a smart, beautiful, horrible girl who lived in a gorgeous house on the edge of the Silver Lake Reservoir and went to one of the finest private schools in the country. She spent most of our lessons quizzing me on my math skills, trying to catch me in a slipup. She never did, of course. She was sly, I am slyer. Talented and Gifted, don't forget.

5

There weren't any TAG seminars on how to deal with mall cops. I'd been in trouble with the police only a couple of times, all substance-related, all minor. My scariest brush with the law was in high school when I got caught trying to buy weed from a dealer who I didn't know was on parole. They brought in three more cops and a police dog to search my car, as if I were a drug kingpin, and not a high school junior trying to buy an eighth for my friends.

The Walmart security guard was approaching. I braced myself for the worst. He stubbed his cigarette beneath his heel and walked toward me lazily. Taking his time. He had all the time in the world.

"Hey," he said. Even that, the way he barked "hey," seemed to name me as criminal.

"Looking for something?" he said. Up close, he appeared young. I was a fresh twenty-nine, and he was definitely younger than me. Mid-twenties, at most. He wasn't tall, almost my height, roughly five seven. His hair was chopped into a military crew cut, and he had a hangdog sort of face, with big, sober, bloodshot eyes.

"What?" I asked, to buy myself time.

"Are you looking for something?" He repeated the question slowly, like I was an idiot. "You've been walking around this parking lot for like—" He glanced down at his watch. "Ten minutes."

"You were timing me?" I said, my insolence automatic and unthinking.

His face clouded over. He'd punish me for that. Already, I could see the shape this conversation would take—the interrogation, the digging through my bag. It could've gone a different way. I could've smiled or acted scared. That's all he wanted, my trembling deference to the mall-cop badge pinned proudly to his lapel. There was a gun, a very real gun, in his holster.

"You took out a lot of cash," he said. "What for?"

"I don't have to answer that."

He looked me right in the eye. "What's in the bags?"

"Stuff."

"Stuff," he repeated, in the same soft monotone.

I was afraid now. "Can I go?"

"Doesn't seem like you've got anywhere to go," he said. "You've been wandering around."

"I'm not loitering," I said. "I clearly just bought shit from your store."

"Hey," he said. "Hey. It's okay. I didn't say anything about loitering." His mouth twitched, amused by my edginess.

"I'm trying to find my car," I said. "I think my ride left."

"They left you? Man. That sucks," he said, in that same amused way.

"Yeah."

"So," he said, "you need a ride?"

"No."

"You just said you did."

"I didn't," I said. "I said I have one, but I think she left."

"Who's 'she'?" His eyes were steady and pupil-less.

"No one." Fuck. This was a bad answer.

He flicked an eyebrow. "No one?"

"My friend," I corrected, but it was too late. My heart felt like it was being squeezed inside a fist. I couldn't break eye contact first.

"Which is it?" he said. "No one, or your friend?"

"My friend."

"So . . . your friend's no one to you? Damn, that's kinda savage."

"I don't know why I said that."

"You seem nervous," he said, definitely amused now. "Are you nervous?"

"No," I said, trying to keep the tremor from my voice. He was getting what he wanted. I was sure he'd get a fantastic jerk-off session out of this later.

"Can I go?" I said.

"Soon," he said. "One more question. What's with all the cash you took out?"

"I didn't take out that much," I said.

"Sure looked like it to me."

"You were watching me?"

"It's my job."

"Cool job," I said.

A reaction, finally. He knew I was mocking him. I could see him making a decision.

"I get it," he said. "I'm not a real cop, right? So you're like, this guy's an asshole. He can't really mess with me."

"Is that something you think about a lot? Not being a real cop?" I couldn't resist.

He grinned at this and took a challenging step closer.

"Nah," he said. He had small, gummy teeth. Self-conscious, he closed his lips. "I make more money than them."

"Do you?" I said. "That's cool. Can I go?"

"No," he deadpanned. His smile disappeared.

A tremor quivered down my arm. My muscles ached from the weight of the bags, but I was shaking more from fear and exhaustion than anything else. I couldn't believe this was how I'd get caught. Barely three hours out, and nailed by a mall cop.

"I'm just kidding," he said. "You can totally go."

I didn't feel relief. His permission seemed like another power play, another fight I was being set up to lose.

He was too close. I took a step back. He nodded indulgently, playing at generosity. I turned and started to walk. Anger and fear clouded my brain, but there was adrenaline too. Just keep walking toward the street. Just keep going.

"Hey!" he shouted behind me.

Dread snapped through me, and I froze. Half turning.

"Ha-ha," he said. "You actually stopped."

I turned completely now, my brow knitting in confusion and fear. "What . . . ?"

"Hey, it's okay," he said. "I'm only messing with you. Seriously. You're good. You can go."

I didn't move. "Okay," I said slowly.

He crossed his arms, watching me. I turned again and started to walk, resisting the urge to run. If I run, he'll chase me, I thought. He'll join the hunt, with all the others. Just breathe, stay calm, and keep walking. Don't stop. You'll think of something. You have to. You don't have a choice.

It was only when I reached the street that I allowed myself to glance back. He wasn't following me. He hadn't moved at all.

I shivered on the side of the road. It was all palm trees and desert, and the desert at night was cold. I was a few miles away from Coachella Valley. Some wayward wannabe hippies might drive by and take pity on me. Palm Springs wasn't far either. Maybe I could catch a ride with some couple on their way to their Airbnb: to where, though, I had no idea. Hitchhiking felt laughable, but it was the only idea I had, other than walking. Walking nowhere. Walking until the cops drove by and found me, or the security guard when he was done with his shift.

I couldn't believe she'd left me.

A wild laugh curdled in my chest. She'd left me. The longer I repeated it to myself, the more unreal it felt. I guess I couldn't blame her. Without me, she might be okay. She might make it.

I didn't wear a watch and my phone was pancaked somewhere on the 101. It had to have been at least an hour since I'd left the woman in the car. Who knows how far she could've made it by now? A hospital. Nevada. Home. Wherever home was. I didn't know, and I didn't care. Any goodwill I'd felt, any desire to feed or clothe her or nurse her back to health, was gone. She could get fucked.

I kept walking. At least thirty more minutes must have passed. The night mutated around me as I clung to the shoulder of the road, braced against the howling wind. Streetlamps were few and far between. Palm trees were planted with haunting regularity. Somewhere near, a pack of coyotes was howling. My arms, carrying the bags full of soup and water and clothes—things I'd mostly bought for her—quivered.

Police would be combing Los Angeles for us by now. I'm sure they'd gone to my apartment already. My roommate, Harvey, would be slumping out of bed, terrified to answer their knock on our door. Our faces would be on the news. Or mine, at least. Audiences at home would watch and feel confident in our guilt. The story's tentacles reaching far enough that by tomorrow, everyone I know would see my name attached to murder. My friends and ex-teachers and former colleagues and exes would find out through social media, word of mouth. In the morning, my parents would turn on their TV and discover their only child—their little miracle, their baby girl, their Evie—was a killer.

I shut down the thought before it could penetrate deeper. If I dwelled on it too long, I didn't trust myself not to do something stupid.

The desert was unforgiving. There was nowhere to hide, no bushes to duck behind, no leafy trees to climb. It was all sand and prickly things, snakes and scorpions waiting to dart out and attack. The streetlights were so infrequent I could barely see a few feet in front of me. There was nothing to do but walk. Even if I wanted to curl up in the dirt and surrender, I knew every dystopian scenario would march through my brain, single file. My skeleton, threadbare with flesh, a sated coyote gnawing happily on his dinner. A tarantula settling on my sleeping face. A mall cop hunting me for sport.

I could not stop walking, no matter how weak I felt. I thought of blood-soaked Final Girls in slasher movies, staggering away from chain saws and butcher knives, a hockey mask glowing white in the dark.

Frantically, I started digging through the Walmart bags for the switchblade I'd bought. I clutched it. I'd never used one before. In fact, I was terrified of knives. *Grey's Anatomy* makes me queasy.

And they think I'm capable of triple homicide?

I curled my fingers around the knife's handle and tried to imagine actually using it. It was impossible. My grip was sweaty. The yawning hugeness of the desert impressed itself upon me.

Headlights lanced across the darkness behind me, briefly illuminating the lonely road. The motor rumbled, punishingly slow, before drawing to a halt beside me.

It wasn't the security guard.

6

It was her.

She was behind the wheel of a gray Nissan sedan. She pulled onto the shoulder, a few feet ahead of me. Dumbstruck, I went to the passenger window, which she'd already rolled down.

She unlocked the door and made a *get in* gesture. She was chewing gum, tapping idly on the steering wheel. Her elbow reclined almost lazily against the open window, and she had a baseball cap pulled low over her eyes.

"How did you get this?" I said.

A muscle moved rhythmically in her jaw as she chewed.

"Where the fuck is my car?" I raised my voice.

She closed her eyes impatiently and reached across the console to swing open the passenger door.

I was angry. An amorphous, origin-less sort of anger, like I'd had an infuriating dream I could no longer remember. Now the anger had a target, and it was her. I wanted her to talk. I didn't feel like being patient anymore.

"Get out," I said. "I'm driving."

She held eye contact with me, searching and wary.

"Move. Now," I repeated, advancing toward the driver's side, and she did as I asked. I threw the Walmart bags into the back and climbed into the driver's seat, examining the unfamiliar gears. The tank was half-empty. We'd need to fill it soon, especially before we entered the barren stretch of I-10 up ahead. I shifted into drive more aggressively than I needed to. *She left me* thumping in my brain like a chant.

But she'd also come back for me. She'd gotten us a new car. I'd told her the license plate was a problem, and now it wasn't. Unless she'd done something really bad to get it.

I glanced over at her as she rifled through the shopping bags, grabbed a bottle of water, spat her gum out the open window, and downed it. She looked okay. She'd even cleaned off some of the blood. There were no new injuries I could see, no sign of a fight. Just that same giant handprint darkening her skinny throat. I had thought I'd have to be the one to steal the car, not that I had any idea how to pull it off.

But she did.

Beside me, the woman peeled back the tab on a can of soup and drank it cold, in long, wet gulps that turned my stomach. She caught my eye as I streamed onto the highway and offered me a sip. I shook my head.

It occurred to me, suddenly, that we didn't even know each other's name.

I could tell her mine. It would be like a gesture of goodwill. I didn't trust her, but I wanted her to trust me. I thought that would be useful.

"My name's Evie," I said.

She looked up from her can of soup, her lips parting in surprise. The expression made her appear younger, though I guessed she was probably about the same age as me, maybe a little younger. Thirty, at most.

Evie. I could see her mouth move around the shape. She didn't make a sound.

"You don't have to tell me yours," I said, "or maybe you can't with the . . . no-talking thing."

A knot worked in her throat. She looked away.

"I know you can, though," I told her. "Talk. I heard you. In the house. You said 'please.' And 'help.'"

She didn't respond. Of course she didn't. She just stubbornly massaged her bruised wrists.

The adrenaline slowly faded from my bloodstream. I was so tired. Darkness sank into my skull. My vision was muddy. At night, the desert felt like another planet as it moved past us. Mirage-like mountains in the distance, dry wind. I didn't have a map, but I knew the way. I'd driven east before, twice actually. Once on the I-10, and once on the I-40, on a road trip with an ex-boyfriend—Christian, an art student I dated for almost four years after college. We hiked in the Grand Canyon, and he complained nonstop about the heat. We were miserable in Vegas, wandering around slot machines I couldn't afford. When we got back to Los Angeles in the afternoon, I broke up with him at La Cita, in downtown LA, drinking cans of warm beer on the patio. The only other person there was a drag queen with a magnificent curling mustache. When Christian went to the bathroom, probably to cry, the drag queen leaned over, lowered her pink shutter sunglasses, and told me she thought we were the most beautiful couple she'd ever seen.

Gravel kicked violently beneath us as I swerved onto the shoulder. It was two in the morning. I was so tired I could barely think. A car honked at me melodramatically as it drove past.

The woman caught my eye. She jerked her chin at a billboard off the highway. Rodeway Inn, sixty-six dollars a night.

"We can't sleep at a motel," I said. "No place will let us book a room without an ID."

The woman reached into her pocket and fished out a slim piece of plastic. I took it from her, staring at it in disbelief. A woman's face stared back. She looked nothing like me, other than the fact that she was roughly my size and weight. At least she had dark hair. She was ugly, but I couldn't be offended by that now. "Naomi Morgan." She was thirty-one years old, five foot seven, 125 pounds. She was from Fresno, California, and she was an organ donor.

I looked at the woman, who was gazing out the window. I caught the tiniest twitch of self-satisfaction. She had thought of everything. It should've comforted me. Instead, it only heightened my wariness. Her face was impassive, offering me nothing. Under the surface was a motherboard making impossible calculations, plotting chess moves more steps ahead than I could ever fathom. I tried to picture her casual thieveries: the car, the ID. I couldn't. It was impossible for me to imagine. Maybe that's why she was so successful at it.

I needed her. It was shameful, how much I needed her.

The car swerved again. I was exhausted, distracted. The woman reached over to steady the wheel in a cool, self-possessed way that surprised me.

Another car honked as it passed. I looked at the speedometer. I was only going forty-five miles per hour.

With a too-sharp jerk of the wheel, I turned onto an exit ramp. I drove onto the shoulder and put the car in park.

"You know how to drive?" I said. It wasn't meant to be a question and came out bitchier than I intended. Besides, I already knew she could. She'd stolen us this car. She came back for me.

The woman nodded. The corner of her mouth gave a small, scathing twitch.

"Okay," I said, irritated for reasons I didn't completely understand. "Okay." Still, I was reluctant to move. I liked driving. I always had. On every road trip, with every partner and friend group I've ever had, I was always the driver.

Finally, I opened the door. She climbed out of the passenger seat. I threw the keys at her, but she was too startled to catch them. They fell in the grass, and she had to dig through the dirt to pick them up. I felt a little bad about that.

We climbed back inside. The passenger side smelled like her. The empty soup can rolled across the floorboard. I knew it would annoy me, so I chucked it in the back and took a fresh one from the Walmart bag for myself. Campbell's Chicken Noodle.

"I won't fall asleep," I told her as she stepped gingerly into the driver's seat. "So I can help you . . ." I felt helpless already, without the wheel, the gear shift, the keys. "Navigate. And find a motel." I didn't say that I didn't want to fall asleep because I didn't trust her, though that was part of it too. Maybe she knew this. Maybe she'd felt just as uneasy when I was the one behind the wheel, and she was stuck, weaponless, in the passenger seat.

She turned the key in the ignition. Her fingers were long and fine-boned, alive with twisting veins, chapped and raw at the knuckles. She brought us smoothly back to the I-10. I downed the soup, which was thick as egg yolk and salty. Mealy cubes of chicken stuck in my teeth. I washed it down with half a water bottle and offered her the rest.

Now that I was in the passenger seat, I could study her more closely. She didn't seem as small anymore. She might've been only a little shorter than me. Her arms, in her ragged leather jacket, were wiry with muscle. There was something intimidating about her face in repose: the cruel twist of her mouth, the way her features settled into a wintry indifference.

She seemed to sense I was observing her. There was something self-conscious about the stubbornness of her mouth, a certain edginess in the way her eyes remained fixed ahead.

But then, very suddenly, she looked at me. As appraisingly as I was looking at her.

"What," I said.

It wasn't a question. It was just something to say, to respond to. Finally, there was a suggestion of movement between us. Reciprocity, exchange.

Her lips parted, and my pulse skipped.

But then she turned back to the road, and her face clouded over, became impenetrable again. We drove like this in silence until we crossed the Arizona border. Then I fell asleep.

7

By six a.m. the following morning, our faces were all over the news.

Well, my face. The woman's identity remained anonymous. All the reporters had was a rough sketch based on Lukas's description. There we were, side by side on the old-fashioned television screen, a lonely blue glow in a still-dark motel room. The headline beneath the anchors' grim faces read: "Brutal Hollywood Slaying: Female Killers Remain at Large." The tip hotline was 1-800-VICTORS. The photo they used of me was taken from my university admissions website, a candid shot, me reading on the quad beneath a dogwood tree. My friends had given me endless shit about this picture. It looked like a stock photo advertising the virtues of college attendance: the iced coffee sweating in my palm, the rah-rah school pride of my sweatshirt. My group chat had sent me a link to the school admissions website—"look gordon ur famous"; "she's a SCHOLAR she's an INTELLECTUAL"—and I had felt, to my surprise, a tiny, embarrassing swell of pride. Only four other kids from my high school class had even made it out of North Carolina for college. Senior year, my school created a banner they hung outside the building marquee, emblazoned with our names and the universities we were attending. They placed me right at the top, like I was headlining a music festival. I was the poster child for the merits of a liberal arts education.

Now I was the poster child for Women Who Kill.

Pearly blue light was already peeking through our motel room's ugly floral curtains. I blinked numbly, tearing my eyes from the television screen. I'd barely slept the night before. There was only one bed. Without discussing the arrangement, the woman had left it to me, claiming the bathtub for herself and shutting the door behind her. It was still closed.

I shivered. Arctic air shuddered out of the ancient AC unit rattling beneath the window. I glanced at the clock again. It was 6:20 a.m. For hours, I'd watched the clock crawl forward, an endless tick of red numbers. I slept in tiny gasps, waking every fifteen minutes or so to lay stiffly in place, paralyzed with terror. By the time I finally gave up and turned on the TV, I felt like I'd cycled through hundreds of unending nights.

At the commercial break, I tried the bathroom. Carefully, I edged open the door.

The closed shower curtain, limned with mildew, betrayed her shape. A stray elbow, a shoulder.

"I'm coming in," I said pointlessly. Her bony fingers crept around the curtain, tugging it just far enough to reveal her face.

"I have to pee," I said.

Her eyes looked even more bloodshot than mine. Clutching her pillow to her chest, still dressed in the same yellowed, blood-stiff clothes I'd found her in, she slunk out of the shower past me. I closed the door behind her and peed, peering inside the tub. There was a pilled white towel she'd left draped across the bottom. I flushed and returned to the dark bedroom. She was standing in the center of the room.

"There's soap," I said, in a hushed voice. The motel walls were thin. "I bought some, yesterday. And new clothes."

I went to the shopping bags and took out the things I'd purchased: a basic black T-shirt, drawstring sweatpants, a bar of Irish Spring. She accepted the clothes and the soap warily, as if trying to judge if my kindness was a prank. Was I that much of a dick?

"You should shower," I said.

It came out crueler than I intended. Her eyes narrowed. Maybe I was that much of a dick.

Her shower lasted for almost thirty minutes. She emerged finally in her new clothes, flushed from the heat. There was a damp spot in the dip of her spine, like she hadn't dried off before she pulled on the T-shirt. Her black-and-blond hair was spiky with water, slicked back from her face in a way that made her look like a 1930s gangster, a few roguish strands hanging in her eyes. There wasn't an inch of spare flesh on her, anywhere. The sweatpants, a little big, had to be rolled a few times to fit. They hung off the blades of her hip bones, revealing the pale, slight curve of her waist. I caught a glimpse of a tattoo.

She went for the bags and took out a can of SpaghettiOs, gulping straight from the can. She wiped her mouth with the back of her hand and held the can out to me, her expression cool and indifferent.

"Save it," I said. "I'm going to shower."

I went into the bathroom. The mirror was fogged with steam. I tipped my head back against the spray, turned the faucet as hot as it could go. Only half the Irish Spring was left, that's how much she'd used. I lathered the slim cake of it over my body and stood there, head bowed. The water was a little pink as it ran into the drain. Afterward, I studied my soaked head in the mirror, searching my scalp for wounds. I was entertaining visions of Frankenstein, thick black scars. But the cut from the lamp wasn't as deep as it had felt yesterday. A thin laceration and a bump, nothing more. Toweled dry, I changed into my own new T-shirt and sweatpants and returned to the room.

The woman was cross-legged on the bed, which she'd neatly made. The television was on. I finished the can of SpaghettiOs and focused my attention on the tiny electric kettle on the dresser.

There were two pouches of Folgers instant coffee and two Styrofoam cups. I confronted the pair of them, fumbling over the second cup. We were a *we* now. A set. Everything I needed, she needed too.

I regarded her on the bed while the kettle hissed and popped. A stream of commercials—movie trailers, injury lawyers, mudslinging political ads, pharmaceuticals that would heal your psoriasis, though suicidal thoughts may occur. She watched the television in a way that told me she was really watching me. Her neck pulsed with tension; her body was strung tight as a piano. Hundreds of invisible strings vibrating beneath the surface. The density of her silence was so overwhelming it made her almost inhuman. Or more than human. I thought of her like a presence. Not sinister, exactly, not malevolent. But haunted. Hauntable. A void of gravitational energy, tethered to me like a moon, unknowable like a moon. It made it impossible to relax, even for a moment. I couldn't slacken, I couldn't let my thoughts drift. Everything returned to the impossible materiality of her, cross-legged in the middle of the bed, watching me, and pretending not to. The way I watched her and pretended not to.

The coffee was ready. The woman looked surprised as I handed it to her. Her fingers brushed mine, and we both recoiled at the contact. Her breath was audible as she took scalding sips, as dutifully as a child taking their medicine. The organs of her body seemed more alive, more demanding, than other people's.

But then the trailer for the latest *Star Wars* movie ended, and I appeared on-screen, once again demanding the country's urgent attention. Neither of us said a word as the reporters speculated on every inch of my biography that was publicly available, from the classes I took in college to the fact that I was an Aries, the Dirtbag of the Zodiac. They made sure to mention that I had a minor history of drug use: the weed-to–serial killer trajectory is, as we all know, a well-documented slippery slope. The anchor appeared surprised that I had no discernible history of violence, at least at the time of reporting. I guessed they hadn't yet found Scott Delahanty, the kid I punched on the bus in seventh grade after he spilled a Mountain Dew down my shirt and screamed, "Gordon's tits are leaking!" I broke his nose. They gave me three weeks of Saturday school. I'm sure they'd run wild with that one.

Some other troubling news we picked up from the morning news's best and brightest: Cell towers had located us on the 1-10, near Wilmar, before I'd chucked my phone onto the highway. Bank statements showed that I took out almost three thousand dollars in cash at a Walmart ATM in Indio. A Walmart security guard reported that my attitude was "suspicious" and "hostile." The car I fled in, a 2003 PT Cruiser, license plate PAZ6734, was found near Henderson, Nevada. The occupants were a forty-three-year-old man and his nineteen-year-old girlfriend, who said they found the car at a 7-Eleven in Indian Wells. The keys were still in the ignition, the car clearly abandoned.

Less information was known about the woman seen fleeing with me, though the sketch artist was able to produce a drawing.

Once again, they showed the woman's face, in ink. It was a decent likeness, though many of her subtleties had eluded them. The weight of her dark eyes. The sharp precision of her jaw. Her soft mouth. The hostile and beguiling architecture of her face.

The news anchor moved on to the victims. Peter Victor had been drowned, according to the first coroner's report, though details were still developing. Dinah had died of blunt force trauma. Peter's mother appeared on the screen and said kind things about her son in a quavering voice, though her anecdotes stopped at age fourteen. He was originally from San Francisco, which made sense to me. His Tesla, his gadgets, his twenty-eight-thousand-dollar bike. San Francisco rich people like to pretend they're not rich. They wear baseball hats and expensive camping clothing and think their Tevas and their Patagonias and their small, expensive houses make them normal.

But the reporters were more interested in Dinah because she'd been an actress. The broadcast reminded us of her Oscar-nominated film, showed footage of her at the 1999 Academy Awards ceremony.

An ex-boyfriend of hers was interviewed, Anton Vlassic. He was another actor, still working. I recognized him as the villain from a big-budget Netflix science fiction show that my roommate, Harvey, and I once tried to watch but were too high to understand. Anton and Dinah had dated from 1994 until 1999. She broke off their engagement a month before the Oscars, though they'd appeared together at the ceremony. They were still good friends.

"Why would anyone want to kill the Victors?" the reporter asked him.

"I can't think of a single reason," said Anton. "They are the nicest people. Humble, good, normal people. Beautiful people, beautiful family. I can't imagine who would do this. I can't imagine why. Envy. That's all it could be."

My face again. My name. The woman's face. Anonymous Jane Doe.

Was it a random act of violence? the reporter speculated. Or was it calculated? "Manson-like" was a phrase used three times, I counted. Our gaunt faces. The woman's wild, grungy hair in the drawing. Errant, coked-up hippies, inciting a revolution. I would've had plenty of time to study the layout of the house, all those Sundays I sat in the dining room, all those Sundays they'd so kindly let me into their home. All the while, being the duplicitous psychopath that I was, I sat plotting, calculating, stewing. Finally, my plan ripened. I brought along my accomplice, my vicious lap-dog, my Sadie, my Leslie, my Patricia. Death to the One Percent. Justice for the Ninety-Nine. A warning.

The news report shifted to a detective, standing in front of a crowded gathering of reporters outside a police station. I could see Lukas off to the side with his parents.

"Serena Victor is still unconscious," the detective was saying. "I don't know when or if she'll wake up."

Serena Victor is still unconscious.

My coffee slipped out of my hands, scalding me, soaking the carpet.

Unconscious.

Not dead.

I put a hand on my chest, feeling for my pulse.

I wasn't a murderer.

"I'm not a murderer," I said out loud.

A bottle uncorked in my rib cage.

I could go home.

I could go *home.*

Not Los Angeles. Los Angeles wasn't home. No, I'd drive to North Carolina. My family home: the prodigal daughter, returned. I would drive straight there, without stopping. I could leave, right now, and this nightmarish twenty-four hours would be nothing more than a terrible and traumatic memory. A rock bottom I could point to and declare with all the wisdom of hindsight: *If it weren't for that time I was accused of murder and landed on* America's Most Wanted, *I never would've left Los Angeles!* It would be a funny anecdote, a story I'd tell at dinner parties. My fifteen minutes of fame.

I jumped up from the bed, my mind racing to assemble a plan.

First things first, I'd drop the woman at a hospital—she, too, I realized dreamily, would soon be nothing more than a strange memory.

Then I would drive. I would stop only for coffee and food and bathroom breaks. If I really booked it, I could be home by tomorrow night. By midnight I could be in my mom's arms, feasting on a home-cooked meal, watching the search for the Victors' true killer from the comfort of her couch. How many times had my parents begged me to move back to North Carolina? It was so tempting. My hometown was beautiful. I missed the view of the world from our house. Big, dreamy open skies, suffused with potential.

But I'd been too embarrassed. I'd taken such huge swings. Expensive private college, New York City, grad school in LA, and for what? What did I have to show for it? Where had it gotten me? Even if they'd never see it that way, going home felt like throwing in the towel, surrendering all the hopes and dreams they'd harbored. They deserved much better than me.

It wasn't too late. I could teach at my dad's school, or work at my favorite bookshop in Asheville. I'd return to grad school or learn a new trade. I'd date someone new. She'd be outdoorsy. She'd convince me to like camping. She'd be into some real woo-woo shit, like mushroom foraging or brewing her own kombucha. No more Silver Lake Instagram influencers. No more "entrepreneurs." No more PhD students in comparative lit with secret trust funds.

I would start over.

It had taken years of failure, years of delusional self-grandeur, years of credit card debt and microwave popcorn dinners and, finally, a brush with murder to realize what I needed to do. It was, of course, the simplest answer of all. Isn't it always? I had moved so many times, searching for a home. But home had never moved. It was a tiny miracle of a house, yellow siding, red door, cradled in the cup of the Blue Ridge Mountains. Why had I ever looked elsewhere? Why had it taken me so long? I traveled there in my mind. Petrichor, mountain laurel, wild hydrangea. Black gum and hemlock and sassafras. Tobacco and buttermilk and cinnamon.

I met the woman's eyes. Her expression was so unfamiliar, so different from her usual cold contempt or stoicism, that it took a few seconds for me to understand.

Pity. She was looking at me with pity.

"I didn't kill anyone," I repeated.

This time I could hear how feeble it sounded.

My eyes fell on Lukas Taylor-Hogg, on-screen. The chyron at the bottom read: "FBI Joins National Manhunt for the Victors' Killer." My throat tightened.

It didn't matter that Serena wasn't dead. Her parents were. And there was Lukas, a witness. My DNA was everywhere. I've read and watched enough true crime to know it's the most available surface we read closely. The narrative you can stitch together from the pond scum. The shit that floats to the top, the filth in the foam.

We were pond scum.

I dropped the car keys and sank back onto the bed, forcing myself to meet Lukas's eyes. He was wearing his private school uniform. Today was Monday. Would he return to school after this? Would he take his seat in biology while his classmates buzzed around him, firing off theories about why I'd done it, crafting social media posts with just the right amount of sympathy for Serena and her parents? Which of the Victors' family and friends and loved ones would make it their life's mission to hunt down their killers and bring them to justice? Who was crawling into bed every night chanting the name *Evie Gordon* like a promise, an incantation? *I will find you, Evie Gordon. And you will pay.*

I knew nothing about the Victors. I knew the beautiful surfaces of their house, but I didn't know how they afforded their treasures. A former actress, a banker of some kind. I visited them for two hours once a week. I had other students, other families. The Victors had been, in the grand scheme of things, of minimal importance to me and my life. I came, I did my job, I collected my paycheck, and I left. What they did during the other 166 hours of the week was their business. I'm sure they had little curiosity about what I did with mine.

And yet now, unless the real killer was identified, the story of the Victors would be the story of the rest of my life. It didn't matter that Serena wasn't dead. Her parents were, and I looked like the killer. The headline had already been written: "Evie Gordon Kills Peter and Dinah Victor."

I'm sure my parents wanted to believe I was innocent. So would my friends—maybe some teachers, former students, classmates, co-workers, and exes. If I did the sympathy math, that put me at about eight billion minus forty, give or take.

I couldn't accept it. A future of fugitive hotel rooms, cans of cold nonperishables, this silent, watchful stranger I'd found tied up in their house. Whatever had happened to her there had to be linked to the Victors' murder. Was it possible to have wealth at that scale and lead a completely innocent life? Of course not. I'd seen the proof of their guilt under the stairs, with a bruise on her throat.

"You," I said.

The woman's eyes snapped to mine, focused and inscrutable.

"Whatever you know," I said, "you need to tell me."

Something in her eyes moved. A ghost shifting behind a curtain.

I lowered myself to a crouch. This sort of thing—being sympathetic, patient, gentle—none of it came naturally to me. I wasn't the person you went to for caretaking, comfort, or gentleness. I was an awkward hugger. Stiff, sharp-edged. I was the tough-love friend. I was the no-bullshit friend. I always felt woefully inept whenever anyone came to me after a breakup, a layoff, a simple spell of human sadness. I was terrified, and out of my depth, but what I'd suffered the past twenty-four hours was nothing compared to what she'd been through.

"Please," I gritted out. "Listen to me. The only thing—the *only* thing—that might help us right now is if we can identify the real killer. That's it. We fled a crime scene. We hurt Serena—*I* hurt Serena," I corrected myself.

"If you know anything," I begged her. "Anything. You need to tell me. You're the best—maybe the only—chance we have of figuring out who actually killed them. I barely know the Victors. But you . . ." I trailed off.

Her mouth twitched into a bitter shape.

"You don't know them?"

She shook her head.

"Do you have any idea who might've killed them? Any at all?"

The sympathy and patience I'd gathered was fragile. My rage and impatience flooded back, as routine as a wave coming in.

"Do you," I said, "or do you not?"

I was in her face now. My anger formless, impatient for answers, movement, momentum. I wanted to hear her voice. It was there—I knew it was there. If I could just coax it out of her, if I could swing the hypnotist's watch the right way, I might break the spell. Her voice was a casualty of what had been done to her, I knew that. But I needed answers. I needed to feel less alone in this. And most desperately of all, I needed to know that there was an out. I'd spent only one miserable night in a hotel room. I knew I wouldn't survive many more. I wasn't built for something like this. I needed a direction. I needed to know what my efforts were working toward.

She held eye contact with me in a brutal, uncompromising way. I felt the slightest twitch of fear in my chest. She wasn't scared of me at all.

"I know you can talk," I accused her, taking another step closer.

I circled her. I felt like someone starving who'd finally stumbled upon some meat. She was roadkill.

But then she bristled. She wasn't roadkill at all. She was a predator playing dead. She had teeth.

She held my gaze. Something crawled under my skin, unbearable, claustrophobic. I couldn't predict her behavior, which made me feel like I couldn't predict my own. All my senses were unfamiliar to me. The room spun. At the center of it was her, a lodestar, a magnet. All my most sensitive nerve endings were alert, the needle of them tracking her every movement.

I took a step closer.

She lifted her chin, like a boxer.

"I know," I murmured, my voice soft with cruelty, "that you can talk."

I was too close.

She planted her palm against my chest and shoved, hard.

I stumbled back.

Her chest heaved. She looked wary but unapologetic.

I was pleased. A push was something. It was better than silence.

"I'm not going to hurt you," I told her.

She laughed. It wasn't a throaty laugh. There was no sound. It was all in her face. There was something cruel about the way her features twisted, almost mocking. But the look was too raw, too painful.

You can't hurt me, it said.

Seconds stretched between us.

"I'm not going to hurt you," I repeated.

She stood, stiff and edgy, waiting.

Waiting for me to try.

She didn't believe me. I probably wouldn't have believed me either, if I were her. If I'd suffered what she'd suffered.

"You don't know who killed them?" I asked. "You didn't hear anything?"

She shook her head.

"What about the day before? Or the day before that? Did you hear anything new—anything strange?"

I searched her eyes. She shook her head again—this time, there was a shadow of apology, for knowing so little.

"Are you really never going to talk to me?" I asked.

Her fists clenched. She didn't answer. I didn't expect her to.

I picked up most of our Walmart bags. I couldn't be in this hotel room a second longer. She grabbed the last of them and followed me to the car.

8

The Arizona sun was so bright against the sand it looked like snow. I weaved between semi-trucks and RVs on the 1-10 East. I had no plan other than getting us as far away from California as possible and hiding out until some intrepid young Nancy Drew identified the real killer.

Mesas grew from the earth, blistering and mirage-like in the strange winter heat. We entered New Mexico. I bought us Cokes and ham sandwiches at a rest stop in Las Cruces. Within the next hour, we'd made it to El Paso. Miles upon miles of border fence separated us from Mexico. If we could go fourteen hours straight, by nightfall we'd be in San Antonio. We traded off seats, though I let her drive for only an hour at a time. The panic subsided when I drove. When I didn't, it edged up on me, closing my throat. The woman could tell, I'm sure. I was a restless passenger. Behind the wheel, my pulse settled again. The woman seemed content to let me, though without her voice, without language, it was impossible to tell her true feelings. All I had to read were her surfaces. The way she carried herself, her wounds, and her micro-expressions—and those surfaces betrayed almost nothing of her interior life. I had no idea if she knew she was an object of silent obsession for me, though I suspected she did. We were too stiff, too alert, too aware of each other. If my thoughts were not circling the dead bodies of Peter and Dinah Victor, they were circling her. The bruise on her throat, the bruises on her wrists. My mind tunneled through the unknown corners of the Victor House, looking for her.

We developed a rhythm. Cans of cold soup exchanged without question; water bottles retrieved at precisely the moment I needed them. Radio intervened when silence became unbearable; silence returned when music became overstimulating. It wasn't telepathy that explained the ease of our nonverbal rhythms: it was vigilant observation. We were like rival outlaws on opposite sides of a saloon. Above the surface, we pretended to be cool. Under the table, our guns were steady.

I flicked through radio channels. The woman seemed to prefer the older stations, the Stones and the Stooges and the Dead Kennedys, though she didn't seem to mind hip-hop. I caught her mouthing the lyrics to "Ms. Jackson." The only time she ever objected was when "Hey Jude" came on. She slammed her hand on the radio, shrouding us in silence. Of course, she didn't explain why, and I didn't bother asking. I added it to the short list of things I knew about her:

1. *Can talk but won't.*
2. *Successful (experienced?) carjacker.*
3. *Suffered unspeakable trauma in the Victor House.*
4. *Hates the Beatles.*

It was approaching sunset when the engine started to make a strange, wheezing sound.

"*Fuck.* Not now."

I pulled off at the next exit and into an Arby's parking lot and slammed out of the car. I threw open the hood. Nothing looked amiss to me. Then again, I had no way of judging for myself. I'd never fixed a car in my life.

I felt a hand on my shoulder. I jerked in surprise, almost knocking my head against the open hood.

It was the woman. Her hand skimmed intimately along the small of my back, edging me to the side so she could take a look. The gentle authority of her touch made my pulse skitter.

She bent over the hood. Her spine was long, her shirt riding up as she leaned in, giving me another glimpse of her tattoo. Petals, a stem. Sunflowers, or daisies. I could see each vertebra, following the sinuous curve of muscle that dipped near her tailbone, skin disappearing beneath the waistband of her sweatpants.

Heat prickled my neck, for no reason at all. It made me edgy. It made me want to be cruel.

"Do you know what you're doing?" I said.

She turned and held eye contact with me for so long, and with such contempt, that I felt my heart rate leap. Then she bent to a crouch, ran her long, nimble fingers along a belt, working at the machinery beneath. I watched her work in embarrassed awe. I was out of my depth here. My entire life, I'd coasted on confidence, fake-it-till-you-make-it. Out here, that strategy collapsed. I couldn't fake what I couldn't even begin to understand.

The woman fixed the belt with skill so assured it almost came across as lazy.

When she was finished, she stood, wiping her hands on her knees. She gestured at me to return to the driver's seat to test the ignition.

I did. The ignition turned smoothly. The wheezing sound was gone.

She shut the hood and returned to the passenger seat. If she felt any smugness about what she'd done, her face didn't betray it. She just wiped her hands again and took a water bottle from the bag, gulping it down. She offered the rest to me with a mild look.

Out of sheer stubbornness, I muttered, "I'm fine."

She shrugged casually, twisting on the cap.

I was hungry enough to grab a can from the bag, the closest I could find. Green beans.

"Shit." I'd bought one without a pull tab.

Smoothly, the woman took the can, withdrew the switchblade

from the glovebox, and worked it open. The tendons of her forearm fluttered as she punctured the edge with a forceful thrust, sliced along the curve, then pried the top open enough for me to eat.

I took it warily. The gesture made me feel something I couldn't yet name. The unnamed feeling slithered between my ribs, making space for itself. A secret heat rose from my chest, beneath the collar of my shirt.

"Thank you," I murmured, belatedly.

The woman shrugged, unable to meet my eyes.

"Do you want the rest?" I asked.

She shook her head. All the places where her hand had brushed—the small of my back, my shoulder—pulsed. I brought us back to the highway.

There was a Shell station I entered for gas and Coke. Impulsively, I bought a six-pack of Coors, which I planned to drink later while feeling sorry for myself. I filled up the tank. In the corner of the parking lot, we ate a late lunch of Lay's, powdered doughnuts, and sliced honeydew and cantaloupe that tasted vaguely expired. I felt a little better after food. The woman gestured at the keys, offering to drive. I shook my head. Being behind the wheel was the only thing that made me feel like myself.

When we returned to the highway, I lit a cigarette.

"I want to go to a library," I announced.

The woman's eyebrows shot up, stating her objection clearly. I scowled at the bad-boy slouch of her shoulders, the slacker-in-the-back-of-the-class sprawl of her skinny legs.

"Did you have something to say?" I said with mock concern.

The woman just stared at me flatly. I ignored her irritation.

"Here's how I see it. We have basically two options. One, we flee the country and go into hiding, permanently. Or two, we find the real killers, and we go home. The first option is deranged. So that leaves option two. The easiest thing, of course, would be for you to

tell me what you know about the Victors so we can start Sherlocking this thing out ourselves."

The woman's mouth tightened.

"I got to hand it to you, man," I said. "Your commitment to
the bit is impressive. But here's the thing. I need to *go home*. And
in order for me to go home, I have to figure out who actually
did this. The cops aren't going to do any more investigating. They
think they've cracked the case. Now all they have to do is hunt us
down, lock us up, wash their hands of us—done. It's over. And we're
fucked.

"I don't want to be fucked." I exhaled a determined stream of
smoke. "I want to get out of this nightmare. I want to see my family again. I want to return to my life. My life. *Your* life. You should
get to go back to whatever—" I had no way to fill in the blanks
of this woman's life. "Whatever you did before. Freedom. This isn't
freedom. This, none of this—" I waved my cigarette out the window, at the open road, the rain-dark skies. "This is us watching
our backs forever. This is never getting to have a normal life. This
is crazy. It's crazy. What are we going to do, steal cars forever? Rob
banks and . . . and never see our families again, never see people
again, never—?"

Never talk to a human being and hear them talk back again?

"No. No. We can't do that. We have to get out of this. We have
to get out. Someone did this. Someone who isn't us." I took a final draw from my cigarette and ashed it on the windowsill. "*They*
should be in our position now. Not us. Lukas, Serena—someone
who hasn't even occurred to us yet. We need to piece together
what the cops never will. We don't have phones. We don't have any
internet access. That means we need a library."

We reached Fort Stockton. I followed signs to the public library
and parked out front.

"You don't have to go in with me," I said. "But I think you

should. It'll be faster if we're both researching. We need to split up, obviously." I didn't like the idea of leaving her in the car, not after what had happened at the Walmart in Indio. "If you'd rather wait here, I get it."

The woman shook her head, and I was glad. I wanted her close.

"We'll keep it quick," I said. "We just need to find out how far along the investigation is, if they have other leads. We know the detectives are razor-focused on us, but I'll bet journalists are digging around the Victors. I want to know what they're finding."

It felt good, to finally have a direction. An objective. An assignment to complete. I'd always been good at assignments.

I entered the library first. I was purposeful but casual. The rainy day made the library relatively crowded. It was a relief to have bodies to dart between and hide among. The interior was very seventies, with colorless geometric carpet. There were a few computers uncomfortably close to the checkout desk. The old woman behind it didn't spare me a glance.

I opened Google and turned the browser on Incognito mode. In my peripheral vision, I saw the woman enter the automatic doors. I kept my head down. Fifteen minutes, I'd warned her, that's all we could afford. Any longer than that was too dangerous.

I typed "dinah victor murder" into the search bar. Headlines flooded the screen, one after the other—a blur of "Evie Gordon Evie Gordon Evie Gordon"—but it was the headline at the bottom of the page that I clicked on feverishly.

"Sex Worker Goes Public About Her History with Peter Victor."

9

I couldn't click on the article fast enough. I didn't recognize the publication—something online, something clickbaity. It described a Reddit thread from four hours ago. The original post had already been deleted, apparently at the request of the lawyers managing the Victors' estate, but journalists had grabbed screenshots and circulated them.

The post was written by a former sex worker employed by a service called Highest Bidder. She kept her identity anonymous. She claimed that Victor had spent almost eight hundred thousand dollars on the service. He refused to meet anywhere except his own property. She didn't go into detail about the kind of services he requested, though she did mention that his tastes were "extremely strange." She described him as "cold but not violent" and added that she'd been with far more degrading men, but something about Peter made her feel "dehumanized."

I navigated back to the Google search page, clicking on every article about Highest Bidder I could find. A few sites were circulating the screenshot from the original post, but there was frustratingly little detail other than that. I wanted to know if officials were investigating the lead. So far there wasn't a single quote from the detectives or the FBI. A few gossip blogs and D-list "news" sites had picked up the thread. I might've rolled my eyes at the "Evie Gordon and Accomplice: Sex Workers?" headlines if I weren't about to throw my fist into the screen. Otherwise, no legitimate news site seemed willing to connect Victor's paid sex habit to his murder.

It was me and the woman, of course, who were still the primary—in fact, the only—suspects.

There was only one other article that gave me hope: an *LA Times* story reported that in 2008, Peter Victor was a VP at one of the investment banks that packaged weak mortgages into even weaker securities and then peddled them out like a clearance BOGO sale to investors, resulting in the 2008 housing market collapse. Victor received no jail time for his part in the recession, nor did any other banker on Wall Street. He wasn't even publicly named, per the Justice Department's agreement with the Wall Street banks under investigation, though journalists still frequently threw his name around in the aftermath. Victor relocated his family to Los Angeles in 2009 and opened a small but successful hedge fund. The journalist had even unearthed a 2012 police report filed by Peter and Dinah Victor claiming their house had been broken into. No jewelry, art, or money was stolen; a file cabinet was taken from Victor's office that he claimed contained "confidential" files—

A sudden brush against my shoulder made me jump. It was the woman.

Her touch was clearly intentional, to grab my attention. She didn't linger. She was heading for the exit, her hands in her pockets, head down.

I quickly closed the browser window and fled, trying to appear as nonchalant as possible. As I left, I saw a child watching me, maybe eleven years old. He wore an oversized Dallas Cowboys jersey, and his teeth were stained blue. The kid was staring, open-mouthed. He tugged on his mother's shirt.

I was out the door before anyone else could get a good look.

The woman was waiting by the passenger door, a muscle ticking urgently in her jaw.

We climbed into the car. I booked it out of the library parking lot as fast as I could. The child probably recognized me from TV. The woman must've noticed him watching from afar. She noticed everything.

"You saw the kid?"

She shot me a look that plainly said, *yes, asshole.* She ran her fingers through her hair, a nervous habit.

I took us off the I-10. It was too dangerous to remain on main interstates. By nightfall, we reached a town called Fredericksburg. It was in the middle of Texas wine country, which was exactly as eccentric as it sounds. Old Western storefronts and pastel Victorians flanked a light-strung Main Street. French Quarter–style iron balconies and antique shops, gorgeous, giant magnolia trees stretching into breathless open skies. There were a sinister number of German beer halls and several Tudor-style houses waving German flags. I stopped in a general store and picked up a box of black hair dye, scissors, and winter clothing, along with two pairs of blue jeans, guessing the woman's size. She was still wearing her battered combat boots, so I bought her a pair of white sneakers. I got us both baseball caps and beanies: new ones, not stolen, which was where I assumed she'd gotten the cap she had on now. I was tempted to buy myself cowboy boots. I grabbed a pair of sneakers instead, and foundation to cover the bruise on her throat.

We slept outside a church that night. It was German Lutheran, with Tudor windows carved deep into its cobbled face like a jack-o'-lantern. We passed out immediately, reclined in our seats—you can legally sleep in your car in most Walmarts and some church parking lots, and camping grounds and any land operated by the Bureau of Land Management.

The next morning, I woke up alone.

I lurched forward so fast I nearly hit my head on the steering wheel. Something white fluttered to the ground.

A receipt. I picked it up and turned it over.

getting food + money

The handwriting was small and neat.

I turned on the radio, to distract me from the anxiety of waiting. I scanned the channels. No one was talking about us this morning. Not yet.

I took one of the cigarettes out of my pack, lighting it impatiently as I checked the windows. Finally, I saw her approaching from a side mirror. The woman opened the door and slid into the passenger seat, holding a bag of Egg McMuffins, $478 in cash, and a second ID. The name said "Katie Choi." She didn't look much like the woman, though her height and her age were at least somewhat proximate.

"Holy shit," I muttered, counting through the bills. She produced a hash brown from the bag, which I stuffed gratefully into my mouth. "How? Did you take this from someone? Or did you rob a McDonald's?"

She held up a finger. The first one.

"And no one saw you?"

She shook her head.

"You're sure?"

She nodded impatiently.

"How? Show me."

I expected her to ignore me. Instead, she slipped her hand casually into the pocket of her baggy sweatpants, retrieved a bill, then stuck it in a different pocket. She lifted her shoulder, as if to say, *See? Easy*, and took a long drink of water. She had stolen a whole car, I remembered. My curiosity prickled as I watched her cheeks hollow around the mouth of the bottle. When I wasn't looking at her—when she was merely existing beside me in the passenger seat, barely registering in my peripheral vision—she was completely blank to me. Her stubborn silence made her as anonymous and invisible as a bored teenager. It was only when I observed her consciously that she tightened into a coherent silhouette. I found myself inventing biographical details about her. Her personal history took shape, a story I stole liberally from Dickens, featuring cruel orphanages and street urchins and pickpockets. She was a stowaway, a drug mule, a pair of big owl eyes in the back of a van. A runaway sleeping on a cardboard bed under a dumpster, with a mangy dog companion. Enter kind interlude with poor old couple who leaves cat food for her to nibble on like a stray, a malevolent cop who catches her stealing, a stint in juvenile detention.

Then, in her front pocket, I saw the shape of our knife.

"You brought the knife?" I said sharply.

She turned to face me, her brow knit with confusion. She nodded slowly.

"Why?"

A shrewd, defensive look took over her face.

"To use it?" I demanded.

Now she looked angry. Her anger was cold and disdainful, unlike mine, which was explosive and brutish. I didn't know why I was picking a fight with her. Frustration was making me impulsive. Mostly, I think I just wanted her to fight back. A push, a punch: I'd welcome anything. I had no other outlet. She'd pushed me before.

Today she'd brought a knife to a McDonald's. Did she know how to use a knife? If someone caught her, if she got scared, would she have taken it out of her pocket?

"Look," I said. "If you're going to bring the knife somewhere? Hide it. I can see it right there in your pocket. Don't bring more attention to yourself than you need to."

I wanted to hear her defend herself. There was something dangerous about her cool, studied restraint. I wanted to see what would happen if she lost it.

She took the knife out of her pocket and handed it to me with an innocent lift of her eyebrow. As if to say, *You want to hold on to it?*

"I don't want the knife," I said.

Her eyebrow flicked in mock surprise.

"Just be careful with it."

She nodded in an obedient way that somehow condemned me.

"I'm not trying to be an asshole," I said, which only made me feel like more of an asshole.

She nodded again. *Right*, her face said. *That just comes naturally to you.*

"Keep the knife," I said, stabbing the key into the ignition. "We're leaving."

I wouldn't know how to use it anyway.

10

In Louisiana, I saw Peter Victor. He was behind the wheel of a semi-truck, shielding his eyes from the late-afternoon sun. I saw him again on a side street, leaning against an open doorway, tipping his hat. A skinny woman in Daisy Dukes wrapped her arms around him from behind, whispered something in his ear. He slipped a wad of cash into her back pocket and squeezed her ass. She laughed. A car behind me honked at a light. I caught the driver's reflection in the rearview mirror. It was Peter Victor.

Highest Bidder. Eight hundred thousand dollars.

His tastes were "extremely strange" and "cold," said the whistleblower. "But not violent." What the hell did that mean? What did he do? What was he asking for? What did he need badly enough to pay almost a million dollars for it?

I remember the *LA Times* article: he was a VP at one of the banks responsible for the 2008 recession. He got off scot-free and moved to Los Angeles. Someone burgled his house in 2012 and stole confidential files.

Who did you piss off, Peter?

A Bessie Smith song played on the radio, crackling with age, desperate and lean. I wished I was in a smoky bar, or my mom's kitchen. I could picture the white table, the yellow cushions she'd sewn herself. Wooden cabinets, linoleum floors. A bag of Wonder Bread on the counter, a tub of Crisco. The stale cigarette and frying oil smell. Glimpse of cherry-red nails sifting through flour. She only watched Animal Planet and the Golf Channel, and one or the other was always playing in the living room on low volume, a habit she inherited from her mother. My nana had been a waitress: a shiksa, as my grandpa liked to say. My grandpa was a young rabbi passing through Asheville. He was the first Jewish person my nana had ever met. He got her pregnant with my mother when she was nineteen. His family never spoke to him again.

I wondered if SWAT teams had set up camp in my mom's living room or my dad's kitchen. If they were breathing on the other end of the phone line, waiting for me to call.

Along the highway, Spanish moss draped over the arms of trees like ragged laundry on a clothesline. The sky was a muddy gray. Through the crack of open window, the air smelled like sewage, ozone, and fish. Billboards advertised a Cajun shrimp sandwich and the promising religious stewardship of a reverend named Gus Peppers. "Every Knee Shall Bow," one of them said. Exactly a mile later came another: "Avoid SATAN, Come with ME. Guspeppers.com." His face was Peter Victor's.

Bessie Smith was bumming me out, so I changed the station. "Rockin' Around the Christmas Tree" came blaring out the speaker. The next one over was playing "Feliz Navidad."

"What the hell," I said out loud.

The woman, who had been staring dull-eyed at the passing scenery with her head against the window, flinched a little.

"What day is it?"

Realizing she was being addressed for the first time in several hours, the woman glanced at me warily, then shrugged and turned back to the window.

I did the math. December 11 was Sunday, the day of the murders. Since then we'd been on the road for two whole days. That meant we were only twelve days out from Christmas.

The idea shattered me. I had only ever spent one holiday season without my parents, when an ex-girlfriend was sick with the flu, and I offered to take care of her. I'd visited home a week later, and my mom and I had staged our own mini celebration. She cooked a second brisket and kept the decorations up. A few days later, I left to stay with my dad in his little bachelor pad on the Outer Banks, and we went fishing. Croaker fish fried in cornmeal, my aunt's homemade fudge, a belated gift exchange. He bought me a nice bottle of whiskey and his usual stocking stuffers—a carton of cigs, a bar of Cookies 'N' Creme Hershey's, and lottery tickets. My dad was cheap and practical: his favorite presents were things like tackle boxes and cleaning supplies. I'd gotten him a handheld vacuum cleaner. A famously bad texter, he took poorly staged selfies with it every time he used it, and even sent me before and after photos of his car.

It hadn't occurred to me, really, in a serious way, that I might never see my parents again. My dad, who played Phish too loud from his garage when he did yard work, who encouraged every wild swing I'd ever taken, who looked at me and saw only potential, no matter how badly I'd failed. My mom, who worked sixty-hour weeks at the salon and sent me unprompted "I'm so proud of you!" texts punctuated with dozens of emojis. My parents had given me everything I'd ever needed, insisting they pour every last dollar of their savings into my education. They sacrificed so much. I never wanted to bring them pain or sadness—I could deal with those on my own. I wanted to bring them only gifts.

A single sniffle might have betrayed me, though the woman didn't acknowledge it. Maybe my poker face was that good. Either way, I was grateful she let me have my moment of despair in peace. I wasn't much of a crier; I never have been. A in math, A in history, F in crying in front of others. I prefer a stiff upper lip, which probably isn't healthy. I don't like my emotions acknowledged. Crying is something you do in the shower once every three years, or in the anonymity of a dark cinema during a particularly sad gay movie.

"This is crazy," I murmured to the road. It took me a beat to realize that for several seconds I was just repeating the word "crazy" over and over. The woman was staring at me.

"Something to say?"

The woman flicked an eyebrow.

"You seem like you really want to say something."

The woman ignored this.

"Don't be shy. Say what you want. Go on. It's okay."

I was being patronizing to make her snap. I would've, if I were in her shoes. I would have punched me. Whenever anyone picked a fight with me, I could never resist the bait. I was a stranger to the high road.

But not her. She was cool and patient, unfazed.

I tried to imagine what it would be like if I were a different sort of person, the kind who could say, out loud, *I feel lonely. I feel so lonely I am beginning to think I imagined you. I feel so lonely that I am afraid that if I reached out to touch you, no one would be there.* Maybe I would cry when I confessed this. Would the woman behave differently around me, if I were less like myself, and more like a wounded baby bird? Would my vulnerability reach some hidden tenderness inside her?

I couldn't. I wasn't capable. We were two brutes, scaly and unyielding, together, and alone.

"We need to get food for the night," I said. "Before we find a hotel."

I followed the signs to a Winn-Dixie and pulled into the lot.

"Your McDonald's haul might tide us over for a bit, but we'll need more money soon too," I said. "We're getting fucked on gas."

To my surprise, the woman leaned over to take my hand. She drew her finger along my palm. The brush of her finger made my body as tense as a drum. Belatedly, I realized she was tracing letters for me to read.

YOU BUY FOOD

"Okay," I said cautiously. She was still holding my wrist. Her touch was gentle. "What will you do?"

She caught my eye. Her face was so close to mine. Blood rushed up my neck.

Her finger moved again. My pulse quickened as I watched its movements.

I WILL STEAL

We went inside. I bought us shrimp burgers, Zapp's chips, some grapes and bananas, another pack of cigarettes. When I returned to the car, she was already waiting for me. She had a wallet, and a bag at her feet. In the bag was a six-pack of Heineken.

Her mouth offered something I could only describe as a grin. Close-lipped and crooked.

"What are we celebrating?" I said.

For a split second, I thought she might actually speak.

When she didn't, I offered her my palm.

The woman observed my hand for a long moment. Then she traced a word that made me shiver.

ALIVE

11

I took us to a nearby bayou. The water was glass smooth, a perfect mirror of the wild sunset colors above. Across the river were shaggy trees, the last rays of sunlight bleeding golden through the lace. The air smelled tropical and sour. Algae skimmed the surface. We sat on the edge with our feast. When we finished eating, we reclined in the grass. I wedged open the beer tops with our car keys.

The woman looked content. The bruise on her throat was yellowing, the eye of it soured into a lurid green. She was wearing the beanie I'd bought her in Texas, her short hair flipping beneath the edge. She looked like the skater boys who hung out on the stoop at lunch, too rowdy for our high school cafeteria. I watched her bring the mouth of the beer bottle to her own.

I took a long drink from mine, then lit a cigarette. To my surprise, she gestured for the pack. I put the cigarette between her pink, chapped lips myself. She watched me quietly as I lit it, cupping the flame with my hand, bringing my face just inches from hers. Her cheeks hollowed as she inhaled. She held the cigarette in a practiced way that made me wonder, as I had a hundred times, who she had been before she ended up as the Victors' prisoner.

"You're happy," I said softly. "To be free."

She sucked on the cigarette, examining me for a long time with one eye closed, as if I were on the other end of a telescope. Finally, her lips twitched into an amused grin. *Of course, you fucking idiot.*

I kept forgetting. All my agonizing, all my anxiety, all my fears that I would be on the run forever, that the real killer would never be discovered, that I would die with this mystery unanswered. All this time, the woman was experiencing something completely different. Dread, yes, paranoia, yes, but also relief. Gratitude. A bayou, fresh air, some chips, a cold beer, a cigarette. Hundreds of miles away from the Victor House and the horrors she endured there.

"I have an idea," I said.

I fished out a few crumpled receipts, and a pen I'd nicked from the Winn-Dixie register.

She looked at it with apprehension. Maybe she'd been expecting this.

"I know you don't want to talk," I said, "and I get it. I do."

The woman's face remained cool and impassive.

"But maybe I could ask you things. And if you feel like answering . . . you could write it down."

I didn't expect her to agree. After all, what difference would it make, really, to write the answer down, rather than speak it aloud?

"You don't have to answer anything you don't want to," I promised. "You can chuck this in the river for all I care," I added, gesturing to the pen and paper. "But let's try. Okay? Let's just try."

I cringed at my own eagerness. I sounded like SAT Tutor Evie, trying to manipulate a stubborn math-hating teenager into doing their homework.

But to my surprise, she took the paper and pen easily enough, her fingers brushing against mine. She started doodling a flower, a surprisingly good one. I didn't know enough about flowers to identify it, but it wasn't your garden-variety rose. Rows of tiny buds, mitochondrial and regular, almost sinisterly so. Foxglove, maybe. Something poisonous.

"What was Dinah like?" First question.

She was working on the stem now, tiny strokes of ink. Her expression didn't change as she moved to a new part of the page.

oblivious

"She didn't know about you?" I asked.

I don't know
overmedicated

"Overmedicated," I repeated. "Did Peter keep her that way?"

The woman shrugged. I tried to puzzle this information in with the Dinah I knew. She hadn't struck me as particularly sedated, but I saw her for only two hours every Sunday. Maybe she was on her best behavior for me. Some parents were like that: there was something about my job title, my reason for entering their home, that made them self-conscious. They reverted to being students. Others saw me as an inconvenience, a necessary evil, an obligation. Or worse, an uncooperative piece of machinery, a greedy open mouth hoovering up their cash, and to what end? Their child was still stupid after I left.

I remembered a former student, Isaac Goldberg. He lived in Santa Monica in a garish house, Italian Renaissance, all white marble. His family treated it as flippantly as a hotel room. Damp towels hanging everywhere, piles of days-old Starbucks cups and pill bottles crowding expensive furniture. The couch was covered in dog hair, and the table we worked at ringed with coffee stains, packets of takeout soy sauce, stacks of water-stained *People* magazines. Isaac himself wasn't terrible. It was his mother I hated, overmedicated and volatile. I never saw her in anything besides tight yoga pants and sports bras, which revealed her distended stomach, like she'd either recently starved herself or been rescued from starvation. Her addiction to Botox made her expressions unreadable. She didn't know Isaac's classes or even his schedule with me. My appearance at their door always seemed to baffle her.

One day, the mother came to greet me at the door wearing what looked like a swimming cap. It Velcroed beneath her chin and the back of her skull and made her face look like it was being squeezed out of a tube. There were pale yellow-and-green bruises around her eyes and what was visible of her jaw, and the white wrap beneath her ears was dark with blood. She started to scream at me. Apparently, I'd been "canceled," though neither she nor Isaac had informed me that we were stopping their sessions. There was a takeout sushi menu in her hand that she slapped repeatedly against the door frame. The unhinged hysteria of it might've been funny, if I were the sort of person who could be composed and contemptuous in the face of being screamed at, rather than someone who immediately, unthinkingly screams back. It was absurd, really, the whole scene. Teaching children wasn't absurd: that part was banal and monotonous, sometimes surprisingly moving. What was absurd was that it required me to teach in my students' homes. I intruded on what should remain private. I should not have been allowed to see Ms. Goldberg so vulnerable in her plastic surgery compression mask, participating in the daily, delirious rhythms of her pill addiction. Tutoring happens mostly before, after, or sometimes during dinnertimes. I see these families at the climax of their domestic performance, their highest emotional pitch.

If only I'd enforced some other policy. Public meeting places only—libraries, coffee shops. But no. The companies I worked for, the kind that catered to the ultra-wealthy, advertised the "convenience" of in-home private tutoring. We are delivered right to your doorstep. Domesticity swirls around us while we work, dinnertime rituals, familial arguments. Murder.

Dinah, in contrast to Ms. Goldberg, could only be described as "nice." Pleasant, polite, genteel. She was not as grandly hospitable as, for instance, Mrs. Whitehouse, the mother of a boy I used to tutor on Tuesdays. Mrs. Whitehouse had a magnanimous air about her, as if she were playing the part of an aristocrat, one known and beloved for her humane and generous spirit. Her house was among the grandest I'd ever seen, colonial and stately, towering at the end of a circular private driveway. Her son Jack and I worked in a breakfast nook: a medieval table with high-backed chairs and a long, burgundy leather bench. She brought us an elaborate tea tray with snacks, carried it in herself with a slightly sheepish smile, as if embarrassed by her own extravagance. I knew she hadn't prepared the snacks on her own: there was a housekeeper I'd caught several glimpses of. On the tray was a quarter of Camembert cheese, a pot of orange-fig jam with apple slices, toothpicks with cubes of cantaloupe and curls of prosciutto. It was probably meant to be decorative, but I never turned down free food.

Dinah made similar moves, though on a smaller scale. Once she gave me a gift bag from an event she'd hosted that week, full of things she "had no need for." It was mostly expensive skin care and gourmet snacks, chocolate turtles and artisanal olive oil and minty-smelling face creams.

I saw too little of Peter to develop an opinion of his character. He didn't chat much. Dinah liked to linger, indulging in small talk until Serena came down from her room. Peter offered the usual niceties, but as soon as I sat down in the dining room, he retreated to his office.

"What was their relationship like? Dinah and Peter?"

The woman thought for a moment, then wrote:

separate beds

"You mean, literally—they slept in separate beds?"

She nodded, bored.

I was surprised by this, at first, but the more I thought about it, the less shocking it seemed. It's not like I ever saw the Victors interact. If it was Dinah who greeted me at the door, Peter was usually in his office with the door closed. If it was Peter, Dinah wasn't home.

"What was Peter like? How did he treat you?"

Her eyes darted to mine. Something dark flickered in their depths. She paused, then started again. She wrote a single word.

bad

"What did he do?"

The woman put the pen down. She shifted forward, closer to me.

I went still as she gripped my throat.

I held her gaze.

She held mine.

Slowly, I brought my hand to her neck. I drew a finger along the edge of the hand-shaped bruise.

Highest Bidder, I remembered.

"And Serena?"

For some reason, this was the question I was most afraid to ask, the answer I was least prepared to hear. The idea of a teenager, forced to reckon with a father like that. Helpless, maybe, to do anything about it. Or cooperative. A participant.

Or worst of all: a victim too.

The woman wrote her longest sentence yet.

serena is smarter than she lets on

"Did she know about you?" I whispered.

yes
she knew

Serena, answering the door in her little baby-doll dresses. Her sad, dreamy voice. Her nails always ragged. She would peel off little strips around her nail beds, worry at the skin with her teeth. She was often distracted—sometimes infuriatingly so. She would show up at the dining room table with nothing: no notebook, no pencil. Her homework completed on scattered sheets of loose-leaf paper. She did the wrong problem sets, she did only half of what I asked, she did nothing at all and stared at me blankly when I asked why. I told Dinah to buy her a binder. A dedicated SAT notebook, to complete her homework. She never did. It wasn't a priority.

What frustrated me was that I knew, deep down, that it didn't matter if Serena never put in the work. She could still buy her way into a prestigious education, regardless of what score she received.

I remembered the first time I ever met Serena. I commented on her house's beauty. I was dumbstruck by it. I had tutored so many teenagers like her. I had entered so many beautiful houses. But never one like this.

Serena had looked embarrassed, ducked her head sheepishly and said, "It's too much."

I thought of her and Lukas—his bike, his flip phone, their embarrassment. They reminded me of some of the kids I'd gone to college with, tormented by their parents' wealth. I befriended a boy my freshman year who was so embarrassed by his Palo Alto zip code and his trust fund that every time we went into the city, he refused to buy anything more expensive than a street hot dog. Lukas and Serena offered each other models of suffering tailored to their particular circumstances. Serena, especially, wore her suffering on her sleeve. She was not shy about her mental health struggles. Our first few sessions, she took her Lexapro right in front of me. She'd taken time off school for depression. Twice, Dinah rescheduled our sessions, writing that Serena was feeling a "little blue." The last few times I'd tutored her, Serena's eyes were bloodshot and shadowed. She would sometimes stare transfixed at a spot on the wall, the way cats stare spookily at ghosts only they can see.

The "Serena's feeling blue" cancellations made me furious. Partially because I'd had to scramble to find another student to make up for the lost income, but mostly because I couldn't imagine what she could possibly feel so sad about. As hard as I tried to remember that everyone is fighting their own unseen battles and other pillowcase proverbs, when it came to Serena, I simply couldn't look past that house. The stained-glass window, the moat, the pool. That maddening, irresistible house. How could Serena feel anything but rhapsodic, unpolluted joy, living in that house? Every wish catered to, every whim, every taste. It made me sick to see her come moodily to the door, to pop her Lexapro and doodle her tragic little doodles while I tried to explain geometry. What narrative do you write for yourself, I wondered, to justify your sadness? How do you look at the gilded firmament of your life and recast it as miserable and sympathetic?

I've seen these acts of authorship happen, live before my eyes. I used to get cash to ghostwrite them. I'd meet students at the Barnes & Noble in Calabasas and "help" them with their college admission essays. Really, I would just write them myself. I would sip a lukewarm Starbucks chai latte while listening to their sob stories, and then I'd bash out a thousand words while they worked on their homework, occasionally answering my questions when I needed a little more detail or color. Some of these students discussed their alcoholic mothers and brushes with death quite earnestly with me. Others approached their hardships with more cynicism. "Is this sad enough, do you think?"

Maybe they'd earned their cynicism. From a young age, kids today learn that their suffering—no matter how deeply felt, how inexpressible—must be externalized, made coherent and accessible to others. They are taught early that every gatekeeper to their success would demand them to unearth their private miseries and narrate them, over and over, until their value became realized. Once they figured out how to make their suffering legible—even cosmetic, alluring, and profitable—it could become currency. Students rehearse this process before they have the tools or experience to develop any real working theory of self-value. We are all seventeen once. Hopefully. If we get there. Our identities patchworked together by the meager tools in front of us and defended with our lives. Information pouring in from textbooks and teachers and Instagram, refracted through so many lenses it loses all structural integrity. Then, if you're governed by the traditionally accepted logic of upward mobility, you apply for college. You distill your fragile belief system and the raw, unripened biography of your life into an essay and a test score, and you beg for admission into the next stage of your life. Or you pay for it.

I worked with—not with, *for*—the kind of students who pay for it. My services were expensive. Occasionally, I entered an address into my GPS and was surprised to show up at an apartment complex, a sweet, flustered single mom, a promising athlete who needed a little academic boost to win the scholarship. But mostly it was Serenas and Spencers and Jaggers. It was Bel-Air, the Pacific Palisades, Calabasas. I had a mountain of loans to chip away at. I had to pay my rent.

I had lumped Serena in with all those other students. The earnest do-gooders. The shifty-eyed cynics. The ones who think they've gamed the system, desperate to get Mom and Dad off their back. Smart kids, middling kids, helpless kids. I had visited so many houses. I had pissed in so many nice bathrooms. I had taught the same algebra problems to so many confused, bored, hopeful faces.

What if all this time, Serena had been another beast entirely?

"Was she involved?" I whispered.

The woman started to write.

yes and no

I frowned. What did that mean, yes and no? They couldn't both be true. You're either involved in kidnapping a woman and keeping her as a sex slave under the stairs, or you're not. I believe in moral ambiguity as much as the next person, but that seemed pretty black and white to me.

The sun had almost set. The sky was a surreal shade of pink, and the moon looked alien against it.

"It's time to find a hotel," I said, gathering our trash. I felt sick. The beer, the cigarettes, the things I had learned and the things I hadn't. It turned in my stomach. "Let's go."

Something was moving beneath the dark water. An alligator, maybe. Peter Victor. The night played tricks on my mind.

12

By nightfall, we passed the Mississippi border. Around eleven p.m., we reached a town called Pascagoula. There was a Days Inn right off the highway. The lobby looked like it hadn't been updated since the eighties. There was a white Christmas tree strung with blue lights next to a coffee machine. A scruffy-looking terrier sleeping under a plastic folding chair. He opened one eye as the wind chimes signaled our entrance, then closed it again.

Behind the check-in desk was a virginal-looking white man. He could've been any age between twenty-nine and forty-five. His golf shirt and old-fashioned glasses made him look like he belonged in a retirement home, but his skin was as pink and pore-less as a child's.

On his desk was a newspaper. Were we in that newspaper? If I flipped to the front page, would I see my own face?

"Evening," said the clerk, all gentle Mississippi vowels. He had nervous hands. They moved from his coffee mug to his mouse to his ancient desktop keyboard. "Need a room?"

"Yes. Two beds, if you have it."

He nodded, his gaze shifting to the woman.

"Where are y'all coming from?"

"Atlanta," I said casually.

"Atlanta," he repeated, smiling shyly. "How about that. I've never been."

"It's great."

"World of Coca-Cola."

"That's right." A thin smile.

"And where are we headed?" He directed this question to the woman.

"Austin, Texas," I lied easily, diverting his attention.

"For the holidays?"

Affirmative sound. Polite smile.

"You must be the talker of the pair," he said to me, glancing at the woman.

"Oh, she's just tired," I said.

Wan, obedient smile from the woman. I offered the clerk Naomi Morgan. He studied Naomi's face on the ID for several seconds longer than I was comfortable with, then mine. I made some quick calculations: How far had the news of us penetrated? We were probably headlines in California, maybe first- or second-page news in Arizona and Nevada. But what about Texas? What about Ohio or Maine or Mississippi? The radio broadcasts and articles I'd frantically scanned at the library hadn't given much detail about the manhunt, but we had to assume California authorities had told highway patrolmen to join the search. They would be combing the I-15, the I-25, the I-40, and the I-10 by now, and US Marshals would be digging up any useful dirt on us. We could be as far as Salt Lake City or Colorado Springs or Amarillo. Was there an FBI agent who could plug everything he knew about me into an algorithm? Would it spit me out at a Days Inn in Pascagoula, Mississippi? They had no idea which route we'd taken. We were anonymous enough, in the Nissan. So far, no car had been reported stolen as far as we could see, and no one had spotted the woman taking it. But we were just two days out. It was only a matter of time before our faces were everywhere. Four different radio news programs we'd flipped through had at least mentioned the murders. By tomorrow, our faces would be on televisions in

New York, Atlanta, Chicago, Miami, DC. We were never more endangered than we were at this very moment.

The clerk smiled and handed back the ID. I rocked impatiently on my heels as he clicked through buffering web pages to book our room. "White Christmas" played on the radio, and the man whistled genially along. His kindness felt menacing.

Finally, he handed me a pair of rusted keys.

"Let me know if you need anything." He offered an eager smile.

I ushered the woman to our room, shutting the door behind us. I ran to turn on the television, surfing the channels until I found a news program with updates. I stopped when I heard my name.

There were news vans in front of a house. It took me several seconds to realize it was my mom's.

My mom edged out of the front door, shielding her face from the violent flurry of camera flashes with her T.J. Maxx handbag. Glimpse of her zebra-print blouse the sensible flats she wore so her feet wouldn't get sore standing all day at the salon. Reporters swarmed the car. "Why did Evie do it?" "Where is Evie?" "Are you protecting her?" "Where is Evie?" "Why did your daughter kill the Victors?"

The photographers were like something from a zombie movie, throwing their weight against the car. My mom reversed out of the driveway. She looked terrified.

A news anchor replaced her, forbiddingly grim against a cardboard skyline. She had big barrel curls like a Nashville country star and was advocating for the death penalty. For me, specifically, to get the death penalty. When I was caught. Which I inevitably would be. It was only a matter of time. The clock's ticking, Evie Gordon. There are millions of us, a whole legion of concerned citizens, teeth gleaming in the dark. Pitchforks in hand. *We will find you. You will pay for what you did.*

I turned off the TV, resisting the urge to hurl the remote at the wall. I wanted to curb stomp the television until it crackled and popped. I wanted to pluck my mother from the burning pixels and take her to safety. I wanted her to pluck *me* from this motel room and take me home. I wanted to cry.

It was happening. It started in my throat, sudden and burning.

I pocketed a pack of cigarettes and left the hotel room.

Cicadas screamed in the woods beyond the perimeter of the empty Days Inn parking lot. There were no streetlights, not even above the dumpster. The darkness in the South was so much more complete than it was in California. Fewer lights, more stars. The air was so thick with moisture it felt like I could draw my finger through it like sand. I sucked in big lungfuls and stared into the darkness as if I could make meaningful shapes out of it.

My mom was probably a nine-hour drive from here. I could be there by morning, if I drove without stopping. I could slip in through the back, avoid the news vans. I didn't have a key. If I knocked, though, I think she'd know it was me. I think she'd let me in.

Out of the darkness, a door clattered open, making me nearly drop my cigarette.

There was someone standing in the doorway.

"Is that you?" said a voice.

They were backlit, so I couldn't make out their face.

I stumbled back, reaching for the door.

"Don't worry. You're not in any trouble."

The figure took another step, and their features came into view. It was the hotel clerk. He was smiling at me.

"You can't smoke inside, of course," he said, gesturing to my cigarette. "But out here's fine. Can I bum one?"

I couldn't speak. Belatedly, I nodded.

He took a cigarette from the open pack, smiling wider. His teeth looked fake. They were too wide, square, and big, like a horse's.

"I don't even really like smoking much. But every now and then. Can't hurt."

I could feel him looking at me, smiling. I ducked my head, stubbing out the rest of my cigarette, even though I'd barely smoked it.

Right as I reached the door, the clerk said, "So which way are you headed in the morning, Naomi? It's Naomi, right?"

I nodded. Naomi. Yes. That's me. I'm Naomi.

"We'll probably take I-49," I said, opening the door, making it clear I was leaving. The clerk was terrible at reading social cues. "Fastest way to Dallas."

"Huh," said the clerk. "Dallas? I thought you said you were heading to Austin."

Fuck.

"Oh. Yeah. No, I meant Dallas. My parents just moved there, from Austin. Force of habit."

"Does your friend have family there too?"

"My friend?"

"The woman," said the hotel clerk. "The one who's with you. What's her name? I didn't catch it."

"Oh, um. Katie. She's spending the holidays with my family."

"Childhood friend?"

"Yeah. Best friend."

"That's sweet."

"Uh-huh."

"I meant to ask you earlier," he said, with a prim little tap on his cigarette. "What do you do for a living? You look so familiar."

I froze.

"I'm a student," I managed.

He mouthed the word "student" to himself, as though this was of great interest. "College?"

"No," I said, "grad school."

"Oh? Studying what?"

"Law," I said, gripping the door.

"What law school?" he said, advancing.

"Emory," I said.

The clerk followed me. "Sorry, it's just—you look so familiar."

"Huh," I said dumbly. "Well, uh, good night."

"Good night, Naomi," he said brightly.

It took all my energy to walk calmly as I fled back to the room.

The woman blinked groggily when I entered. I started gathering our things and hauling them toward the door.

"We have to go," I whispered.

The woman climbed cautiously to her feet.

"We have to go. *Now*. Right now. That chatty clerk downstairs thinks I look 'familiar.'" I grabbed the car keys. "We can't afford to wait until he figures it out."

The woman followed me to the hallway. We left the room keys inside, moving as quietly as we could. The light was on by the dumpster when we stepped outside, illuminating the lot.

The hotel clerk was standing beside our car, peering into the windows.

He was holding a phone to his ear.

"—yes, sir, just like that, couldn't quite get the story straight. And the woman with her, she—"

The woman moved faster than me. She shoved past me and tackled the clerk to the ground, knocking the phone out of his hand.

I sprinted after her, kicking the phone as far away from the clerk as I could. I stomped it under my heel until it cracked.

When I turned around, the woman and the clerk were wrestling on the ground. He was screaming.

"Them," he gasped, "you're them, you're really, you—"

The woman was trying to cover his mouth. He bit her hand. She let out a savage grunt of pain and rolled off him, cradling her bleeding hand to her chest like a wounded bird.

He scrambled to his feet. The woman lurched out, blood streaming down her arm, and grabbed his ankle. He crashed to the ground, and she crawled on top of him.

The woman withdrew the switchblade. She flicked it open in a cold, effortless gesture.

She brought it to his throat. She made low, hushing sounds until he quieted.

It was only when the clerk was finally still and quiet that I dropped to a crouch on the other side of his head. The woman had one of his skinny arms pinned beneath her knee. The other flailed wildly. I captured it in my fist and held it against the asphalt. The knife gleamed at his throat, patient and hungry. The clerk's eyes were red-rimmed, rolling petrified around his skull.

"You saw nothing here," I hissed. "Do you understand?"

The clerk made a choked, gurgling sound. The knifepoint was trained right on his Adam's apple. If the woman moved the blade a centimeter, she'd slice his throat.

I bent lower to his terrified face, blood thumping in my skull like a heavy bass.

"Do you," I whispered to him, "understand?"

The woman caught my eye, urgent and panic-stricken.

It was an empty threat. I knew it, the woman knew it, the clerk knew it. The minute we let him go and fled the scene, he'd run inside the lobby, pick up the phone, and call 911. And we'd be fucked.

"Shit!" I felt like kicking in his skull as I climbed to my feet.

The woman was still sitting on his chest, pinning him down. I knew, staring into her eyes, that she would kill him if I told her to. There wasn't a question about it in my mind. She could do it. Stealer of cars. Wielder of knives. Killer of clerks.

I shook my head. Understanding dawned on her face.

We could not kill him. That decision wasn't ours to make. He was no one. A Days Inn motel clerk in Pascagoula, Mississippi.

And maybe that meant nothing—maybe there were bodies in his closet, heads in his freezer.

Maybe he had a family. A newborn at home. A high school sweetheart, a nurse, who worked nights just like him so their hours were in sync. A sick mom, a hungry teenager. People who depended on him. He was doing what he thought was the right thing. He had no reason to believe I was innocent. No one—maybe not even my own family—believed I was innocent.

No one except the woman.

She met my eyes. I counted.

A charged telepathy vibrated between us.

One, two—

Run.

She sprang off him, racing toward the passenger door. I unlocked the car and dove into the driver's seat. I turned the key in the ignition and sped out of the lot. In the rearview mirror, the clerk staggered to his feet and screamed for help.

13

We abandoned the map, and the road. I treated the pitiful sanctuary of
the Nissan as if it were the lowliest prey in the world. We must
take a bird's-eye view of ourselves. Only a small percentage of our
minds belongs to us; the rest is their consciousness, their thoughts,
their predictions of our behavior. We must treat our path with the
abandon of anarchists. Dirt roads, back roads, residential streets.
Anything resembling a highway must be avoided. I didn't know
where we drove or how long it had been. The night sanded over
topographical milestones and time stamps, leveling the earth into
an endless, hallucinatory tunnel of sky and street. A gas station here,
a side street for a discreet piss or vomit there. The woman vomited
twice—discreetly, without expression, as if it were routine. Neither
of us slept. When we passed a twenty-four-hour CVS, the woman
abruptly gestured for me to pull over. She directed me to park a few
spots away from a dark, battered-looking GMC SUV. She retrieved
a screwdriver from one of our bags. I was not invited to watch.
A few minutes later, she rapped her knuckles on the window, her
chilly breath visible against the glass. I sank into the cracked leather
passenger seat of our new car. It was her turn to drive.

I awoke in the mountains. Frosted peaks against a pink sky. It
was almost sunrise. We found a Victorian-looking Quality Inn
with an almost empty lot. It wasn't ideal, but we needed sleep, and
we were too vulnerable to risk another church parking lot. The
woman checked us in with the Katie Choi ID. I wore a beanie

and heavy scarf, covering as much of my face as I could without looking suspicious. Every inch of the lobby was decked out in Christmas garland, fairy lights, and tinsel. "Little Saint Nick" played loudly from the speakers. A bright-eyed elderly woman, chipper for her morning shift, booked our room. There were no doubles available, only single queen beds. Since it was already morning, we booked the room for both the day and night.

Our room was flowery carpet, flowery bedspread, flowery curtains. Big, garish jewel-tone prints with eyelet trim. The tub hadn't been updated since the nineties, but at least the water was hot.

The woman immediately went to the windows to yank the curtains shut.

That's when I noticed the blood. A dark pool of it on the back of her T-shirt, near her tailbone.

"Come here," I murmured.

She turned around, confused.

"Your back. You're bleeding."

She felt the small of her back, realization dawning on her face.

"Can I . . . ?" I approached her slowly, reaching for her shirt.

She nodded in a resigned way. Her shirt was gluey with both dry and fresh blood, and I had to peel it carefully like a Band-Aid. She gritted her teeth against the pain.

The laceration was thick and jagged. Blood trickled sluggishly from the wound. Something sharp must have gouged her when she was wrestling the clerk on the ground.

"Go to the bathroom," I said. "I need to clean this."

Her fists clenched, though she didn't disobey. I shucked off my down jacket. Black, synthetic material, Walmart brand. The heat was turned up too high in the room, and I was already sweating. I fiddled with the thermostat. Sweat prickled under my arms. I heard the faucet running as I sorted through the first-aid kit on the bed, selecting bandages and ointment.

The woman stood in front of the sink, facing away from me. Her blood-stiff shirt bunched in her fist. She was braced over the counter, her neck bent. Waiting.

Her back was bare. Twin dimples grooved either side of her tailbone, like someone had taken her by the hips from behind and pressed their thumbs into the soft material like clay. Dimples of Venus, they're called.

Her rib cage sank and vaulted, over and over, as I stepped forward. I washed my hands. The sink was a retro salmon pink. The woman hovered at my periphery. The wings of her shoulders angular, the dip of her spine somehow obscene. She shifted, the long muscles of her back undulating and settling like a collapsing tent. Her tattoo beckoned me closer. Dark petals stretched over the ribs, wilting at the tips. The surface looked velvety.

I wet a washcloth and dabbed gently at the dried blood. She didn't flinch. She just stood at the sink breathing while I cleaned the wound, anointed it with salve, and applied a bandage.

I brought her a new shirt. She pulled it on slowly and accepted the water I offered. The room was still oppressively hot. We moved as if shifting through heavy curtains, slow, almost drugged. The woman's elbow touched mine, and her knee. Her eyes were trained dazedly on my mouth, as if she didn't know she was looking.

Sweat beaded her upper lip. A little pearl. I wanted to put my thumb there and swipe it away.

"Better?" I croaked, and then immediately regretted it. The room had been so hushed for so long, no sounds except the susurrus of our own movements. The shock of my voice was like a slammed door.

"You should finish that," I advised, jerking my chin at the water bottle.

The woman nodded and looked away. Whatever spell was cast was broken now.

I took a shower. When I was finished, I found a vending machine in the empty hallway. Chex Mix, Famous Amos cookies, Welch's fruit snacks. We still had some powdered doughnuts from the car, and the rest of our beer. The woman drank hers fast, and I kept pace with her. She drank a second in quick succession and finished the doughnuts. By the time I was sated enough to climb into the queen bed and attempt sleep, I could hear the shower running again.

Thirty minutes later, she emerged damp and red-eyed from the bathroom. Her T-shirt clung to her torso, still damp. She stood at the foot of the queen bed like she wasn't sure how to enter it. I sat up and peeled back the covers on the other side. An invitation. I didn't want her to sleep in a bathtub again. And I didn't want to sleep alone.

She stared at the pillow with a kind of vacant uncertainty. Slowly, she stepped forward.

I didn't breathe a word as she slipped under the covers and turned on her side, presenting her back to me. I was suddenly, cruelly awake. Morning light came through the crack in the curtains, prisming across the ceiling like we were underwater. The woman's breath was loud and uneven beside me, her body shifting. In my peripheral vision I saw her turn onto her back. Mirroring me. The radiator was silent, the room as hushed and windless as an anechoic chamber. Every breath and rustle like a gunshot.

We slept in jerks during the day. I heard her get up now and then for water, or the bathroom. The longest stretch I managed to sleep was about an hour and a half, between three and four thirty p.m. By five, the sun had already set.

I looked out the window. The pool was covered for winter, but there was a trio of kids sitting on vinyl lounge chairs, playing handheld video game consoles. Slowly, across the hotel lawn, multicolored Christmas lights were coming to life.

The woman was awake too. I turned on the lamp and picked up the remote to find a news channel.

She grabbed my wrist abruptly.

"Don't you think we should—?"

She shook her head so pleadingly that it left me no choice but to give in.

"Okay," I said.

Relief flooded her face.

"No news. But find something, okay?" I tossed her the remote. I couldn't sit here in silence all night.

I left her flipping through channels while I returned to the vending machine, checking to make sure the coast was clear. Peanut butter crackers, Ruffles, single-serving Frosted Flakes. Two Cokes, two water bottles. When I got back, she was sipping a beer and watching *Home Alone.*

I dumped the snacks on the bed and opened a beer for myself. After *Home Alone*, we watched *The Holiday.* Then *The Muppet Christmas Carol.* We finished off the last of the beer and the snacks. I took a shower around nine.

When I was finished, I found the woman at the sink wearing only her underwear, the cheap, boyish kind I'd bought us at Walmart. Fruit of the Loom. She was mopping up a pool of water on the floor. All over the motel room, wet things were hanging— T-shirts and sweatpants and socks that she must've washed in the sink while I showered.

"Oh," I said dumbly. The woman stood cautiously. "Thanks. For doing that."

I felt stiff and awkward in a way I didn't like. Politeness made me feel estranged from her. I missed the nonverbal, almost primitive rhythm we'd shared in the car.

She shrugged, in a self-conscious sort of way.

I left her alone in the bathroom, my towel still tied under my armpits. She slipped off her underwear and started to wash them in the sink. She was roped with spare, whipcord muscle and sharp angles. I looked away and let my own towel drop, climbing beneath the covers.

I turned off the light and heard her climb into bed. Moonlight shivered beneath the curtain. She was closer to me than she had been during the day: not touching exactly, but close enough that when she breathed, her exhale tickled the back of my neck.

When I felt a finger brush my knuckles, I thought I'd imagined it. When it happened again, I turned to face her.

"What?"

The woman's eyes stared into mine, searching for something intently.

She was shaking.

"What?" I repeated. "Are you cold? Should I turn up the heat?"

She shook her head. Her eyes closed. She drew a deep breath and opened them again. Her face was so close I could see the fringe of her eyelashes.

"Jae," she said into the silence. "That's my name."

Part II

Bootstraps

14

Gas station coffee steamed the windshield. On the dashboard were two bruised bananas, covered in pocket lint, and a plastic-wrapped apple, swiped from the Quality Inn breakfast buffet. The car was a stolen GMC SUV, circa 2005. In the back seat was a duffel bag full of stinky football gear, a fossilized Clif Bar, and an empty can of Mike's Hard Lemonade, black cherry flavor. The floorboards were mud-stained, and there was a dirty camping tent and men's hiking boots in the trunk, size 11. Snow was falling. Today would be our fifth day on the road.

We were in the Ozarks, at a gas station off the highway. Jae had grabbed a map from the Quality Inn before we left. I was pretty good with maps. For now all that mattered was putting distance between us and the hotel clerk. Buying time until the Victors' true killer was found, or until we were forced to make a more grandiose plan. I traced a route that would take us farther south. I was afraid of what might find us if we went north. The cold. The congested cities of the Northeast, all those bodies. All those eyes.

"What do you think?" I asked Jae.

She hadn't spoken yet today. Not since last night. Not since "Jae." I was starting to worry that I'd imagined it.

Jae made an agreeable noise. Not a "yes," not a "no."

I drove. The car was quiet besides our sips of coffee, my restless drumming on the wheel, the scrape of the windshield wipers battling snow. I lasted only a few minutes before the hotel clerk's screams disturbed the silence. I saw him staggering from the side of the road, like a horror movie lead who'd finally escaped the cabin in the woods, the madman with the chain saw. The mute girl with the knife.

I scrolled through radio stations. A country song came blasting out of the speakers: something about saving a horse, riding a cowboy.

Jae turned off the radio.

"I can't do silence," I warned her.

"I know," said Jae. "You're terrible at it."

I laughed, embarrassingly loud. I was so relieved to hear her speak again. To confirm that I hadn't conjured it, some new stage of insanity I'd entered. Her voice wasn't anything like I'd thought it would be. It was a voice like a scowl, or a hiss. Its quality somehow rusted, as if the place it emerged from in her body was wounded.

I risked a glance at her in the passenger seat. Thin sunlight struggled against the clouds. A beam of it sliced through the windshield, across her face. Her eyes simmered with amber light. She held my gaze a beat too long, then looked away.

You are Jae, I thought, studying her sharp elfin face. Her long, fine-boned hands and bitten nails. *Jae is who you are.*

"Tell me a story, then," I said. "If you won't let me have the radio."

I hadn't planned to ask her this. Privacy and patience were some of the few gifts I could offer her. Her biography, no matter how tragic or mundane, was hers alone if she wanted to keep it that way. I wouldn't force her to turn her life into some kind of currency, a token I charged in exchange for my loyalty.

But it's easy to be brave in the car, when you're not forced to look the other person in the eye. To say things you wouldn't normally say. To ask things you wouldn't normally ask.

"What kind of story?" Jae asked quietly.

I felt another tiny thrill.

"Any kind."

I heard the click of Jae's throat as she looked to the mountains. "I don't know any good stories."

The bravery was fading fast. Learning her name hadn't sated me: it only made me hungrier. After so many days of silent, lonely company, I would've accepted anything.

"Tell me a bad one."

"I'm rusty."

"It's fine, forget it." I fished a cigarette out of the pack, fumbling to light it. I was embarrassed to be rejected—I'd pushed too hard, too fast. "It was a stupid idea."

Jae reached over to help me. She cupped the flame, steadying my hand with her own. I counted the measure of my own breath, felt its clumsy steps. I was glad to have things to busy myself with— mirrors to address, cars to consult, turn signals to manage. I wanted to want it less. I wanted to know her less. Since that was impossible, I filled in the gaps myself. Her parents were Olympic athletes, or traveling musicians, or wartime journalists fleeing persecution. She was shuttled between cruel governesses in Paris, or neglectful relatives in Malaysia. She fled their oppressive custody and raised herself. She scaled fruit trees for food or plucked farmers' wares from busy market stalls without payment. She hid herself in crates and traveled the high seas as a stowaway. She was an underground boxer in Spain, a car thief in Busan. She was a painter's muse in Morocco, and a street busker in Cartagena. She was Jae. Besides that, I knew nothing about her at all.

"I have been practicing, you know," said Jae.

Her voice was soft. I was so focused on ignoring her, I almost missed that she'd spoken again.

"I'd whisper things," Jae continued. "In secret. When you'd leave to buy us food. In the bathtub, that first night."

"You would practice . . . talking?"

"Yes. I had to make sure I still could. My voice seemed . . . strange." She spoke slowly. I could hear her choosing each word carefully, to make sure she'd be understood. "I hadn't heard it in so long. I didn't like how it sounded."

"I like your voice," I said impulsively.

Jae looked at me sharply, as if she thought I might be mocking her.

"I do."

I did. It was low and rough, deep the way a voice is right when you wake up, in bed with a lover. An audience of one.

"I've never been a big talker," said Jae, once she'd accepted that I was being sincere. "I was always quiet. When I was a kid. My parents thought I'd grow out of it. But I didn't. And then, in the house—"

A knot worked in her throat.

"It's not like I forgot how. You can't forget how to talk. But I was so used to being alone that when you busted the door open it was like . . . a piece of machinery shut down, and I couldn't figure out how to turn it back on. I knew I could still speak. It was just a matter of finding the lever. But . . . finding the lever was hard."

"I'm not gonna make you," I said.

I felt Jae studying the side of my face.

After a long moment, she said, "I know I've made it hard for you."

I didn't know what to say to this, so I said nothing.

"But you still kept me around," said Jae. "You kept us safe."

"*You* did that," I corrected. "I don't know what I'm doing. Everything we've gotten, the cars, the IDs—it's all been you."

"I can get things," Jae admitted. "But you make them happen. You're a talker. People listen to you."

"Because you don't talk."

"Because people don't listen to me," said Jae. "They listen to you."

I couldn't help but laugh in disbelief.

"*I* listen to you," murmured Jae.

It sounded like a confession.

"Tell me a story," I said.

"What's the point?" said Jae.

"The point?" I didn't understand.

"What do you get out of it?"

"What do you mean 'get out of it'? I get to know you. That's the reward. I get to know."

"Knowing me isn't a reward."

I saw a glimpse inside the Victor House, where everything was transactional, understood only in terms of what it cost. This costs more than that. I cost more than you.

"I just want a story," I said. "To make the drive easier. You don't have to tell me anything about you. Just give me something to listen to."

This was it. I felt like a grizzled sea captain, stranded on a desert island. Just me and my volleyball. Was that a rescue plane overhead, or a cruel trick of my imagination? I didn't know how much longer I'd last if it was the latter.

Please, I thought. Just talk to me.

"All right," said Jae. "I have a story."

There was once an artist named Mila. She was from Ukraine, and she was beautiful. The kind of beautiful that made men stupid. She was married to a rich man in Germany, but he did not make her happy. After they moved to America, the rich man did not allow Mila to work, so she spent her days going to a flower shop, purchasing the most expensive and complicated bouquets, and bringing them home to paint.

At the flower shop was a handsome florist named Jordan Park. He told Mila that when he moved to the United States from South Korea, he chose the name "Jordan" because of a basketball player he admired. Mila didn't know anything about Michael Jordan, or flowers, or the music of the Beatles, or any of the other things Jordan liked to talk about and show her, but she went to the shop almost every day to see him. Her English was not very good, but she always attempted to speak it with Jordan, to impress him. His was excellent. She liked to go through every single flower and ask Jordan what each meant. A lotus, for rebirth. Rhododendron for danger. Snapdragon for deception. Sweet William was Jordan's favorite, for gallantry. Mila preferred black-eyed Susans, for justice.

They began an affair. Jordan lived in a small studio apartment, which charmed Mila. She left First Husband and moved in with Jordan. It took a long time for Jordan to feel comfortable revealing the details of his childhood, a life he spoke about so impersonally it was as if it had happened to someone else. His given name was Sung-ho, and he was born in Seoul. His mother had been a singer, though she ended her career when he was born. She was only eighteen years old. His father was a businessman who died in a car crash when Jordan was four. His mother suffered regular nervous breakdowns when Jordan was a baby, so it was mostly his grandmother who raised him. She grew watermelons on Jeju Island. Jordan said it was the most beautiful place in the world.

More beautiful than California? said Mila, surprised, and in response, Jordan laughed. *Yes. More beautiful than California.*

Mila couldn't imagine a place more beautiful than California. Certainly not Ukraine, which was cold and gray, or Berlin, which was cold and gray and everyone was on ketamine. She often wondered why, if Jordan loved home so much, he never spoke of it. He said that beauty was not a substitute for freedom. It became clear to Mila that in Jordan's mind, freedom was another word for

money. He told her about an epiphany he once had, after an inter-
action with an American tourist who bought a watermelon from
him. There were a lot of tourists who came to Jeju Island, to ad-
mire the sea and nibble suspiciously at their food, always stunned
to discover it was delicious. But this American tourist wasn't like
that. He walked and made purchases with confidence: he even
spoke a little broken Korean. He was with a beautiful woman, in a
long blue dress. He wore all white, with leather shoes, and a gold
watch that winked in the sunlight. They bought a watermelon
from the stall Jordan's grandmother managed at the farmers' market. He paid for it with two hundred thousand won—about one
hundred and fifty dollars, give or take. The tourist gave this money
away with such casual indifference. The beautiful woman on his
arm smiled at her partner, and at Jordan, who thought to himself,
One day. One day. At home, Jordan worked and worked but his
situation never changed, and never would, even if he had a different job. He knew his father had not been killed in a hit-and-run,
as his grandmother pretended: he had driven off the freeway on
purpose, to escape the punishing workload and his debts. But in
America, there were many rich people. Hundreds of thousands of
them, it was said, maybe millions—and they did not descend from
kings, but from farmers, like him. There were more rich people in
America than in any other place in the world.

Jordan moved to America when he was twenty-one. Five years
passed. He wasn't rich yet, but he would be. He listened to a lot of
business programs on the radio, hosted by men with loud voices
that grated on Mila's nerves. He bought a book called *Rich Dad,
Poor Dad* and read Mila passages from it. Mila thought it was a
stupid book, but she kept those thoughts to herself. What was the
danger in her husband thinking stupid thoughts? A woman could
go mad trying to rid her husband of all his stupid thoughts. And
this one, at least, gave Jordan happiness and purpose. There were
worse things.

Though Mila never expressed any longing for the luxuries she once enjoyed, Jordan became obsessed with buying Mila a house. She offered to get a job, but he, too, would not let her work. He said it was because her English wasn't very good, but Mila always speculated the true reason was that the idea of being unable to support his wife on his own was too much humiliation to bear.

Jordan took on a second job as a butcher. He listened to American business programs on the radio that preached the importance of property ownership and investment. He saved as much of his paycheck as he could, in the hopes of amassing enough for a down payment. There were lots of new developments going up, in Irvine and Anaheim. Two- and three-bedroom starter homes, advertised with shiny color photos of smiling middle-class families.

Mila became pregnant. The baby was unplanned and expensive. By the time the baby was an elementary school student, Mila had fallen into a deep depression. Jordan believed his wife's depression was his fault. He had not made enough money to buy a house yet, even though many of his friends had. This puzzled Jordan. His friends couldn't have been making that much more money than him.

We took out loans, they explained to him, as though this were obvious. Jordan, humbled, followed suit. He was worried because he didn't have good credit. But to his surprise, the bank granted him a loan.

That was how he moved the family into a three-bedroom house in Irvine. The listing price was $245,000, and the loan, according to Jordan, required him to pay virtually nothing. The interest would simply be rolled into a higher principal balance. The house was located on Carmel Avenue so they called it the Carmel House.

We stopped at another gas station in Arkansas, right outside of Little Rock. Snow ceded to icy rain. It was Jae who secured our next haul of food—things easy to slip into pockets: sleeves of nuts, jerky sticks—while I filled the tank. Jae ripped open a package of nuts with her teeth and poured a handful into my palm. I steered us back onto the highway, keeping my expression as neutral as I could. I didn't want my eagerness to scare her back into silence.

"Mila and Jordan," I ventured slowly. "They're your parents."

Jae acknowledged this with a shrug.

I couldn't picture Jae as a child. She was so competent in every situation. It was hard to imagine her ever being small or depending on anyone or anything except her own cunning.

"What were you like as a kid?"

"I was a kleptomaniac," she said, through a mouthful of beef jerky. "I'm not joking," she added, when I laughed. "Pokémon cards—that's what started it. Everyone at school had them but me. My dad said they were an 'unnecessary luxury.' I told him what the kids told me at recess: one day, the cards would be worth lots of money. But he only trusted that kind of speculation from the stock market pundits he listened to on the radio. Not me."

"So you stole."

"It was easy. I didn't understand why my dad didn't steal too. He wanted to buy my mom these little pearl earrings. I remember thinking, why didn't he just slip them into his pocket? That's what I did. I wasn't even that sneaky about it. As a kid, I really thought I might have superpowers. I could walk around in plain sight and take things off the shelves. No one ever saw me."

"What about your parents? They never caught you?"

Jae shook her head. "I hid my loot in my mom's desk—that's where she kept her art supplies. I knew it was safe there. She never used it anymore—she just slept all day."

"Did her depression get better? Once you moved?"

"To the Carmel House?" Jae was quiet. "For a little bit, maybe. I think she liked the new house. She had energy again. She spent a lot of time making it beautiful. She tore down the wallpaper in the living room and repainted the walls, covered them with her own artwork. Watercolor birds. Once, she even hung one of mine. They weren't as good as hers, but she still hung one. A crane. It didn't last long though, her happiness. She had a secret."

Ovarian cancer. Mila had known for a while. She hid it from Jordan and Jae as long as she could. Jae could understand why: her father believed in working hard, the fruits of labor. His faith in this, and his faith in God, they were the same to him. If he knew about Mila's diagnosis, he would take another job to pay for treatment. Work himself to death. They barely saw him as it was. If Jae were her mother, she would've lied to him too.

Mila moved back to Ukraine to be with her parents. She barely spoke to Jordan. Jae barely spoke to her father either. All he did was work. When he did speak, he only wanted to talk about college. He was obsessed with getting Jae into UCLA. Jae was worried about the cost, but Jordan assured her that loans would help, just like they'd helped with the house. Not going was never presented to Jae as an option. If Jae went to college, she would get a high-income job. Jae's father didn't go to college, which was why he didn't have a high-income job. That's how the world worked. Every Sunday morning, he woke Jae at six a.m. to take a full-length practice SAT. If she did well enough, she could get a big scholarship. It was 2009. Jae was a junior. They scheduled her first real exam for October.

"How did you do?"

"I missed it," said Jae, in a strange voice.

I looked at her. She was holding an unlit cigarette. A muscle rolled in her jaw.

"A month before that," said Jae, "we got evicted."

Jae hadn't begun to process the word "eviction" before the police started moving things into the yard. They told them the bank was claiming three hundred thousand dollars in past-due balances. Jae's dad was stunned.

He was too embarrassed to call one of his friends at church, so he forced Jae to call her friend Kevin Ahn, who he knew came from a rich family. It was humiliating, but she wasn't given a choice. Mr. Ahn found an apartment building the city of Irvine designated "affordable housing." Jordan qualified for a low-income-housing tax credit, Mr. Ahn explained, which Jae's dad took as a personal offense.

The new apartment was in a building called the Inn at Woodbury, which implied it was meant to be temporary. Every night, Jordan pored over bank statements, trying to identify where he had gone wrong. He concluded that his understanding of mortgage loans was fundamentally flawed. Jae shared her own theory, which was that they had been scammed. She thought this explanation might, in some perverse way, give her dad comfort. But it had the opposite effect. A personal mistake for which he—a humble butcher, florist, and Target custodial staff member—was exclusively to blame, left his belief system intact. But the idea that an American bank had knowingly screwed him—and thousands of other people—over? It was heresy.

He didn't hit Jae when she told him he'd been scammed. It was the second thing she suggested—that they were now homeless—that made him hit her. It wasn't a hard slap, though it did leave a bruise. Overcome with guilt, her dad made her stay home from school for the next few days. This wasn't a consolation to Jae. She wasn't popular, but she had Kevin Ahn and Minho, who she skateboarded with after school. And at least there she inspired fear: her baggy clothes, her smears of dark makeup, her deadpan stare. Her grades were good, though her teachers disliked her, interpreting her surly muteness as a provocation. Still, she'd choose school over home every time. At home, it was just her and her dad in their weird hotel-apartment with the white walls and the TV on the carpet, the piles of SAT practice books waiting for her.

She was able to reschedule the test for March. She got a perfect score.

15

"A *perfect score?*"

The gambit had worked. Listening to Jae had successfully sustained my attention for the entire morning drive. Noon came and went. Sunlight triumphed over the rain clouds, glittering innocently on the windshield. It was hard to believe that thirty-six hours ago, we held a knife to someone's throat.

Jae looked embarrassed. "I took a timed SAT practice test every weekend for like four years. What'd you expect?"

"There's only a thousand people in the country that get a perfect score every year."

"What—are you saying your score was bad? You were an SAT tutor."

"It wasn't perfect."

"Did your dad make you practice every weekend?"

"No. I took it once."

"Ah. You were one of those assholes."

I couldn't resist a grin.

"I'm a good test-taker," I said, defending myself. "Which, by the way, is one of the most useless skills on earth. No shelf life. Dud superpower."

"I'm sure it helped you in college."

"Nope. My college was too special for tests."

"How'd they grade you?"

"No grades," I admitted.

Jae shook her head in disbelief. "That's not how it went down at UCLA."

"So you did end up going to UCLA? What was that like?"

Jae shook her head. "It's your turn."

"My turn to what?"

"To tell a story."

"Oh, is that what we're doing? Is this a game? Eye for an eye?"

"They're not free," said Jae, as if I were crazy for suggesting otherwise. "I want one back. My reward."

Knowing you is a reward.

I looked at Jae, still not quite able to believe she was speaking to me. She seemed exhausted. But there was also a relieved, almost bewildered quality to her speech. She spoke in a measured way, sometimes speeding up, rushing through certain parts, as if she expected me to change my mind at any moment and decide that listening to her wasn't worth my time at all.

"Isn't that what people do on road trips?" said Jae.

"What? You've never been on one?"

"I've never left California until now."

I frowned. That didn't seem possible, though the slightly self-conscious look on her face confirmed it was true. All this time, all these states we'd crossed—Jae had never seen any of it before.

"I've been on a few," I said. "My last one was pretty terrible."

"Worse than this?" said Jae.

"It was with an ex."

Now Jae looked interested. "Tell me."

"His name was Christian St. Clare. We dated for four years. We went to college together. It was in the Northeast, a liberal arts school, stupidly expensive. There weren't a lot of other students from the South."

"You're from the South?"

"Yeah. North Carolina. A little town outside of Asheville. It seemed like every other student in my graduating class was from Manhattan or Boston or LA. There was no one else from North Carolina. There were two Louisianans—Christian was one of them. We started dating at the end of senior year. He was rich. It took him a long time to admit this to me. He had a trust fund—he acted so embarrassed about it."

"Why?" said Jae, genuinely curious.

I laughed awkwardly. "Well, because, I wasn't. And . . . I don't know, he didn't want me to see him as some sort of silver-spoon asshole, I guess."

"Did you?"

"No. Honestly, by that point, I was used to people like him." I was fluent in Inherited Wealth. I'd made the right friends. I'm a quick study. I could hang, even if I didn't have the money to back it up. That's what a good liberal arts education will do for you. That was the real return-on-investment for an expensive bachelor's degree: the ability to hang. So long story short, no, it wasn't obvious to me that we were such a mismatch. I had become so adept at moving in Christian's world that I forgot my parents hadn't moved with me. They were the same beautiful, Walmart-loving coupon-hoarders I'd left behind.

I told Jae that it was a meet-the-parents Christmas that made things weird. After three years of dating, Christian's mom joined my family in North Carolina. She was rude, even if she was polite about it. Southern women are talented in the art of the subtle insult. "Wow, I never drink Barefoot wine—what region is it from? Is it Californian? Italian?" I did a bad job imitating Ms. St. Clare's accent. She left a day early even though my parents had booked a reservation at the fanciest steakhouse in town. They'd put down a nonrefundable deposit. My parents felt terrible. They thought they'd done something wrong.

What happened next was my fault. Months prior, Christian and

I had booked a road trip for the first week of January. I should've canceled. We spent days avoiding talking about how terribly the holidays had gone.

"When I finally brought it up—you know what he said? 'You're right. My mom should've hosted herself. It would've gone much better.' I broke up with him as soon as we were back in LA."

We were closing in on Birmingham, Alabama, and starving, but we were too afraid of being noticed to risk a drive-thru or another gas station pickpocketing. I parked at the edge of a Walmart lot and studied the map, ignoring my empty stomach. We were about four hours from the Florida border. The question was how deep into Florida we wanted to go. We'd need to find a place in the panhandle to sleep tonight. Someplace that wasn't a hotel.

And then I remembered.

"What if I knew a house we could stay in?" I said. "An empty one. I know exactly where it is and I'm positive it'll be empty. I've been there, like, four times—they never spend the holidays there, ever."

"Whose is it?" said Jae, with a note of distrust.

I opened my mouth, then closed it. Jae's eyes narrowed in suspicion.

"The St. Clares'," I admitted.

Jae barked out a laugh.

"What?" I demanded.

"So this is about revenge."

"What? No. Jesus. What do you think of me? I'm not insane."

Jae looked deeply skeptical.

"I'm *not*—okay, fuck off." The more I insisted, the less sane I sounded. "Look, it's a beautiful, huge, empty house. We can hide out there for a few days, while we plot our next move. It's safer than being on the road. Especially now that someone's identified us."

Plus, I knew where Ms. St. Clare kept her expensive jewelry.

So maybe it was a little bit about revenge. The house was once described in *Southern Living* as the "West Indies–style jewel of the South." It sat on a street called, no joke, Olde Plantation Road. It was overdue for a home invasion.

Jae still didn't look completely convinced.

"It's a four-hour drive, if we don't stop again," I said. "And we're heading that way anyway. If it seems cool, we'll stay for a night or two. If it doesn't, we'll go somewhere else."

Jae couldn't really argue with that.

By nightfall, we crossed the border into Florida. The clouds overhead were swollen with rain, dark against the night sky. I sped through Pensacola. Tiger Point. Navarre. Wynnehaven.

Mary Esther, Florida. Live oaks dripped with lichen, flickering in the dry lightning like antebellum ghosts. It had been years since I'd visited, but I recognized some familiar sights: a Target I'd slipped into a couple times for a spare swimsuit, a six-pack, last-minute ingredients for a recipe Christian and I wanted to try. Everything except the Target looked like it hadn't been updated since the eighties. A graffitied gas station, a discount food store, a tattoo parlor, and a scuba shop shared a strip mall. The one-street subdivisions with names like Sleepy Hollow and Plantation Oaks. There were three different churches within a half mile: Baptist, Greek Orthodox, Methodist. This was deep Florida Panhandle: not the kind of town that attracts hordes of spring breakers.

Right next to the cemetery—haunted, undoubtedly—was the St. Clares' house. They had no neighbors; the other side was empty marshland. The property had a gate, but it was open, like always. I zipped down the familiar drive until we were shrouded in darkness, moonlight slivering through the canopy of trees.

At the end of the drive was a house. Cream clapboard exterior, Nantucket meets Charleston. Sea-foam trim, tastefully muted.

Twin brick chimneys on the roof, like the eyestalks of a crab. A wraparound porch crowded with rocking chairs, trellises of bougainvillea. Shaggy ferns in hanging baskets, swinging in the storm-thick air. An unfamiliar speedboat sat in the driveway, hitched to an unfamiliar pickup truck. Everything else was the same.

We stepped out of the car. I could hear the crash of the ocean, the creak of the St. Clares' dock.

The doors were locked, as I expected. The windows were not. It took us a while to hunt down an open one—I had to let Jae climb onto my shoulders, the soles of her shoes digging painfully into my neck—but we found one, in an upstairs bedroom. Jae shimmied her way inside, sleek as a cat burglar. From outside, I watched her shadow dart through the house.

I was admitted through the front door like an invited guest.

I blinked. The St. Clares resisted modernism. They favored open windows over air-conditioning, tropical afternoons and torporific heat, strong cocktails at noon. The nostalgic leisure of extraordinary wealth, dreaming of simpler times, strict caste systems, the landed gentry. They had been rich for a long, long time. Black-and-white-checkered marble floor, serene leafy palms, a touch of British colonial in their decor. Gauzy curtains, dark-beamed ceilings, rattan furniture with creamy cushions. A leather trunk in the center of their grand living room, piled with heavy coffee table books and vintage magazines. Timber paneling, dark, distressed shutters. Expensive cane chairs, canopy beds with a bamboo finish. Greenery, everywhere.

This was wrong. This was different.

A huge television had taken over the living room. All the furniture had been replaced with generic, neutral colors: a tan suede couch, a Pottery Barn coffee table, a media console crowded with video games and DVDs. *Step Brothers*, *Rambo*, and *Platoon*. On the walls a framed University of Alabama football jersey, a generic Ikea beach print, and a sign that said "Thankful Grateful Blessed." The fundamental architecture was the same—the pine floors, the blue-tiled fireplace, the French doors. The appliances hummed, a hive mind sensing an intruder.

Jae noticed my expression. "What's wrong?"

"This isn't the St. Clares' house."

16

"You got the wrong house?" Jae's whisper was fierce.

"No, it's the right house," I said. "But they must've sold it. I don't know who lives here now. It's been three years since I broke up with Christian."

I had barely finished speaking before Jae darted for the door.

"What are you doing?" I said.

"We have to *go*," Jae hissed.

I was exhausted. I'd spent the entire day driving. Nonstop, eagle-eyed surveillance. I couldn't imagine stepping back into the car, back into the night, a world of cops and US Marshals, FBI agents and hotel clerks. It was a miracle we hadn't been arrested yet. The clerk at the Days Inn had been screaming for help. How long had it taken for help to come? For a guest to run to the parking lot? To fumble for their phone and call 911? Phantom sirens pinballed around my skull.

"Let's just look around," I pleaded.

Jae seemed wary but exhausted. Reluctantly, she nodded.

We checked every room. Two bedrooms looked like they belonged to teenage boys: plaid bedspreads, lacrosse sticks and footballs left forgotten. Two were guest rooms. The master bedroom was lavishly carpeted, a California king bed, a half-assed nautical theme.

I picked up a piece of mail on the dresser. A catalog—*Simple Surroundings*—sent to a Mrs. Abigail Carlisle. On the bedside table was a Bible and a military thriller, the kind you buy at the airport.

The only distinguishing piece of decor in the room was a moose head above the bed. Its antlers looked like the jaw of some ancient sea creature, a megalodon or a great whale, the vastness shocking in the otherwise bland space. I reached up to touch them, expecting hollowness, the shell-smooth surface of a fake.

They were heavy. The fur, too, was coarse. The eyes had been replaced with gleaming marbles. This was once a real moose, taxidermied and mounted above their bed.

Catching my reflection in the pitiless orbs of the moose head made me shiver. There was a flit of movement in the window.

It was Jae.

"There's a bunch of packages against the front door," she said. "They look like they've been there awhile. And there's an empty dog kennel. I think they've been gone for a few days, at least. Christmas is in what—a week and a half? Less than that? They've probably gone somewhere for the holiday."

"So you want to stay?"

Jae exhaled with resignation. "We have nowhere better to go."

We got to work closing all the curtains. It took a while; the house was huge. I caught up with Jae in what looked like a study. Glossy judges paneling, a big oak desk. Her back was to me, and she was holding a photograph. I peered over her shoulder.

It was a framed magazine article. In the center was a picture of the family, a caption underneath with their names, from left to right. A father, a mother, two teenage sons. Michael and Abigail, the parents. Garret and Devin, the boys. They wore polo shirts in bright, Easter-candy colors, yellow and mint and pink, embroidered with cute animals: the tiny Lacoste alligator, Abercrombie's moose, the whale of Vineyard Vines. Blue skies over their heads, a candelabra tree. Garret—he looked like the eldest son—was holding a rifle. At their feet was the great, muscled corpse of a dead lion.

"And look," whispered Jae, setting down the photo. We turned around.

Behind us was a library of weapons. Rifles and automatics and tiny handguns. There were knives too. Bowie knives, hunting knives. A machete.

"Come on," I said, suppressing a shudder. I was eager to leave. "Let's find something to eat."

We went to the kitchen and tore apart the fridge and pantry. There wasn't much—the Carlisles had done a good job of cleaning out their perishables—but we devoured what was available. Stale-ish kids' cereal from the pantry, Froot Loops and Cocoa Krispies, milk a day out from expiring, gulped straight from the jug. A few slices of Kraft Singles, some out-of-season peaches. A single orange that Jae hastily peeled and divided, juice and pulp dribbling down our chins. We ate kneeling in the blue light of the open fridge, attacking the food with the efficiency of wolves discovering roadkill, silently, without looking at each other.

There was more food in the freezer. Totino's Pizza Rolls. A Meat Lovers DiGiorno pizza. A Stouffer's frozen mac and cheese. We threw all of it into the oven, half dozing on the kitchen floor as we waited for our feast. It had started to rain. We watched the storm pelt the skylight in the kitchen, the solitary beam of moonlight we admitted inside. I'd lived in California for so long that it felt like years since I'd experienced a real thunderstorm. Occasionally, lightning flashed, and there was a strange pleasure in that too, observing it from inside the house.

We were safe.

In the morning, we played house.

Though there were many beds available, we'd agreed it was best to share the king-sized master. If either of us heard a noise, it was safest for us to be together on the first floor, closest to an escape route.

We slept in, savoring the indulgence. We took showers in the master bathroom. White marble floors, veined with pale pink and gold. Vanity trays, crowded with pearly bottles. Jae naked behind the glass, veiled chastely in steam. Me at the sink, brushing my teeth, mind wandering. What kind of people would we be, I wondered, if we lived here? Was I a doctor? A retired athlete? An heiress? Was Jae a tech mogul? A lawyer? How did we meet? What were we to each other? My mind traveled too far.

Jae emerged from the shower. I handed her a towel, careful not to look at her. Or was that worse: Not to look? Was that less casual than looking?

In the kitchen, Jae unearthed some frozen Costco bagels. A pantomime of marital bliss: Jae fixed breakfast; I made coffee and read us the paper. It was a week old. The world was different then. I was an SAT tutor. Jae was a hostage. Different, not better.

Food and a full night's rest gave us the stamina we needed to face the desperation of our circumstances. It had been a relief to get a vacation from the news—the real news, today's news—but we couldn't afford to put it off any longer.

There we were, on ABC. The photo of me from the college admissions website: my smiling face somehow sinister. Jae's sketch scowled beside me. A middle-aged woman was holding a press conference. The chyron at the bottom of the screen said "Rebecca Fitzgerald." She was petite, with a chic French bob and very blue eyes. There was something about her, an uncanniness, that made me feel afraid. I'd seen her before—but where?

I turned up the volume.

"—deep disappointment in the FBI and the US Marshals' failure to track down Evie Gordon and her accomplice. This is why I'm prepared to offer a reward of a hundred and twenty-five thousand dollars for information leading to their arrest."

Jae cursed. Our eyes met in panic.

"As reported Wednesday morning, we have a new lead," Rebecca continued. "Tom Craddock, a Days Inn hotel manager from

Pascagoula, Mississippi, reported to the local police that he had a near-fatal altercation with Gordon and her accomplice on Tuesday night, December thirteenth."

They showed a clip from a different press conference in front of a Mississippi police precinct. Tom Craddock stood behind one of the officers. They had released the audio recording of our altercation.

Of course. He'd been on the phone with the police when he caught us. I'd smashed his phone under my foot, but maybe they were still able to capture the sound.

The din of voices and thuds was as unintelligible as if we were underwater. We might as well have been listening to a dogfight. Animals hissing in a zoo exhibit. Then, from the screaming, smacking, crunching—

"—them, you're them, you're really, you—"

Jae had covered his mouth, and he'd bitten her. I could hear her furious grunt in the footage.

Neither of us looked at each other as we listened. We just stared at Tom's and the police officers' faces, who stared back at us.

A thud, when he'd tried to run, and Jae had knocked him down. A hiss. The knife, maybe. I remembered the cool, practiced flick of it as Jae held it over his throat. Seconds ticked by, so many of them. Had there really been that many of them? And then—

"You saw nothing here. Do you understand?"

The shock of my voice emerging in the low-fi crackle, like a snake in the grass. A B-movie villain. Tom responded with a pitiful gurgle. An entire minute passed. Beside me, her thigh pressed against mine, Jae was so still she must've been holding her breath.

I heard myself swear, a pathetic, tinny sound, crackling in the 911 operator's mic.

And then we ran.

We didn't speak when the footage ended. There was nothing to say. As soon as we tried to assign words to it, to explain what we had done to survive, the engine of our logic would sputter and collapse. Not because it wasn't true. But because it wouldn't sound true. The event, and the sound of the event, those were two different things.

Tom took the mic again.

"As terrifying as that night was," said Tom shakily, his hands folded on the podium, his eyes down, "God must've been looking down on me. I don't know why Evie Gordon and her accomplice spared my life. I've been asking God that question over and over, ever since. Why didn't they kill me? I don't know. I don't know."

The police officer took the mic again.

"Fortunately, Mr. Craddock was able to provide more physical description of Gordon's accomplice, which we've passed on to the sketch artist. They've released the following—"

A new sketch appeared on-screen. This one was much more accurate than the original.

"Mr. Craddock reported that Gordon and her accomplice checked in under the name 'Naomi Morgan,' though it appears that this was a stolen ID. The FBI followed the lead and confirmed that Ms. Morgan is a medical student at UCLA. She believes her ID was stolen Sunday night during a weekend trip with her partner to Palm Springs."

The ABC News clip ended with a final remark from Rebecca.

"If you have any leads at all," she said, "please continue to report those to our tip line, 1-800-VICTORS. Dinah's funeral is in two days.

"I won't be able to rest," said Rebecca, "until my sister's murderers are put to justice."

That's why Rebecca looked so familiar.

We flipped through the other news channels. Our faces were featured on every single one, right above the words: "$125,000 Reward Offered for Gordon and Accomplice."

17

"We need a plan," said Jae.

We were poolside, desperate for fresh air after the news footage. It was chilly, in a pleasant way. Jae was wearing an oversized hoodie she'd found in one of the teenagers' rooms: "United Christian Academy Lacrosse." The baggy sweatpants she wore belonged to one of the boys too, along with the University of Florida baseball hat. She skimmed her fingers across the pool's surface and plucked a dead wasp by its wing, placing it tenderly on the limestone edge. An unlit cigarette hung from her mouth.

"A plan," I repeated dully, flicking the lighter's flint wheel.

It was easier to say the words "we need a plan" than to make one. Truthfully, I was still holding out hope that we could avoid the project altogether. I couldn't let go of the fantasy that the country's finest amateur sleuths were banding together to puzzle out the truth. Was it a wayward sex worker, seeking revenge on Peter Victor? Someone he fucked over on Wall Street—or who'd lost everything in the recession? Or Serena, at her wit's end, a desperate act of vigilantism? Or Lukas, protecting his girlfriend from her father's cruelty?

If only Serena would wake up and tell us. Her eyelashes had fluttered: they mentioned that on the news.

Without a conscious Serena and regular internet access—we'd tried the kitchen desktop and the laptop in the study, but they were password protected—it was impossible to do any Sherlocking on our own. Our best hope was an imaginary Poirot or Nancy Drew, sniffing out the injustice of our wrongful accusation. A blue-haired teen hacker combing through Peter's bank accounts in a dark bedroom. A bored housewife hunting down cell records. Maybe my family and friends were in on it. They'd march to the police precinct and drop a cardboard box of evidence like a microphone. Cue hip-hop sirens.

The head of the FBI would go on television and make a public apology. Jae and I return to civilized society. My parents embrace me on live TV. Cue giant lawsuit. An apology check, for millions of dollars. A Hollywood biopic. Some hot young ingenue would play me in the movie. A talented literary star with a prestigious MFA would ghostwrite my memoir. *(Wo)manhunt: The Evie Gordon Story. Making a Murderer (Evie's Version).*

I felt close enough with Jae to share my fantasies. It was possible she'd been secretly harboring the same hopes.

But to my disappointment, Jae only responded with a pitying smile.

"It *is* possible," I defended. "Why wouldn't it be? I'm innocent, you were their *victim*, and if you knew anything more, you—" I cut myself off with a frown. "You *would* tell me, wouldn't you? If there was anything that would help us—you would say it. Now that you . . . now that we're talking."

Jae's expression was steady. "Of course I would."

A quiet fell over us. Though Jae was trying hard not to look wounded by the implication of what I'd asked, I still felt a little guilty.

"I'm not saying exoneration's out of the picture," said Jae gently. "The police could find out who really did it. But—"

I didn't want to hear a "but."

"But we should probably start thinking about a plan B."

"A plan B," I repeated. "What's plan B?"

"Canada?" Jae suggested.

My fantasy balloon was punctured.

"You want to escape to *Canada*?"

Jae shrugged. "I don't know. It's big. Most of it's wilderness. It seems like an easy place to disappear. And the border isn't policed like Mexico's."

I scrubbed my hands over my face and closed my eyes, trying to picture it. *Canada*.

"The point is," Jae continued, "it's crazy we've managed to evade the cops this long. We'll have a much easier time once we've fled the country."

"*Fled the country*," I repeated, incredulous.

I remembered the news anchor with the eighties Nashville hair, her furious pink mouth demanding my head on a spike. Her followers, delirious with schadenfreude and the promise of a $125,000 reward.

Jae had a point. In Canada, invisibility felt plausible. I had no idea how to cross the border. But capable, world-weary Jae, stealer of cars, wielder of knives? She might.

"If they catch us," I said, "they'll just extradite us back to America."

"So we don't get caught. We haven't yet, have we?"

"So what—if no murderer comes forward, what happens? We just disappear? Forever?"

The enormity of what Jae was suggesting was barely comprehensible.

I couldn't envision the rest of my life as a fugitive. What would that mean? What would that look like? How do you imagine a thing like that? The rhythms of a day, the passing of a season, the highs and lows of a life. I would move through time on no official census of existence. I would be like a time traveler, booted out of the historical record.

And yet.

We couldn't keep going like this. Driving aimlessly, sleeping in motels. This couldn't be our lives. Either we turned ourselves in and hoped they'd understand we didn't do anything, which they wouldn't, or they'd find the real murderer, which they wouldn't, or we'd carve new identities for ourselves from whole cloth. We'd start over. New names, new histories, new futures.

I fantasized about finding some kind old woman who'd have a room she'd rent to us under the table. We'd live in a run-down apartment complex, wash dishes and fix cars. We'd make a little money. And if anyone ever became suspicious, we'd travel somewhere new. Smoky mountain towns in British Columbia. Riverbeds in Ontario. Eventually, the world might forget about us. The trail would cool, the cops grow impatient. A new, shinier crime would take over the news cycle. If enough years passed, we might creep quietly back into our old lives. I could talk to my mom on the phone, now and then. I would still make an impression in the dirt when I stepped. I would exchange oxygen and carbon dioxide. I would leave a chemical footprint. I could still touch and be touched. Kiss and be kissed.

How does someone disappear? What new dimensions of existence could I reach, as a ghost? Beholden to nothing and no one. Free to do anything I liked.

Anything but see my family again. My friends. The people I knew and loved. I would no longer exist as a social creature. I could never go to a restaurant or a movie theater or a bar and observe life swirling around me, participate in it. I could never live among other people. All my potential, squandered.

"Never mind," Jae muttered. "It's a shitty idea."

"But you've thought about it, haven't you?" I said, examining her. "You've already come up with a plan."

I was catching on to how Jae worked. How fast her mind

moved. A computer playing chess with itself, finding the single path to victory among a million fatal contingencies. If there was a way to do it, she'd already thought of it. She wouldn't have raised the idea of something so impossible if she hadn't.

"I have," she admitted. "I was looking at the maps—I think I've found a way, through Washington. I'm not saying it'll be easy. But if we're careful, if we do it right . . ."

"Washington? But that's so far. We'd have to drive through the entire country again."

"I know it's not ideal. But it's the safest way. We can't go east: most ways to cross will be frozen or too densely populated. The Midwest is dangerous too—too much wilderness. Too much snow. Washington will be warmer. We won't go as far west as Seattle, but there are lots of little border towns nearby that won't be frozen."

I tried to wrangle the logic of it, haul it close enough to see. We'd have to cross right through the heart of the country. It would take days. There would be so many moments when we might be recognized. Our faces were on every television channel, every website and newspaper.

"We'd need to change our appearance," I said.

"We still have the hair dye and the scissors," Jae reminded me, "from Texas."

It was insane, what she was proposing. It felt like a long-running bit we were participating in, a joke that grew more absurd the longer we told it.

"It doesn't have to be forever," said Jae. "But for now . . . I don't think there's any other way."

"When would we leave?" I couldn't believe I was even asking this.

"Tomorrow morning," said Jae. "Tonight, we'll change our hair. We'll pack, we'll get ready. We can leave for Washington first thing in the morning."

I studied her. Was I really trusting her with this? Was she really trusting me with this?

Was it even a choice?

I stood up from the pool chair. Jae stood too, cautiously, waiting for the verdict.

"Come on," I said, gathering our things. "I'll cut our hair."

18

Spirals of hair covered the sink counter. I cut my own first. My heavy seventies shag, shorn to right below my ears. I wanted to shave my head entirely—curly hair like mine required diligent maintenance, the kind I couldn't afford on the road—but Jae said I'd look too conspicuous.

"The back of my head," I said, turning to Jae. "Can you help me?"

The scissors made Jae edgy. Gone was the apathetic, almost lazy cunning with which she usually carried out tasks. I was different from an uncooperative car or a soup can. Now her expression was as focused as a surgeon's. To reach the hair at my crown, she had to adjust my head. Jae's fingers were shockingly cool against the back of my neck, but it was she who flinched from the touch.

"You're doing good," I told Jae, which seemed to mortify her more than anything else. The sullen teenager expression had returned, and her ears were red.

She finished. Locks of hair covered the floor. She knelt, gathering them into a pile with a towel.

"I can get those," I said.

Jae's eyes flicked to me, and something shifted in her face. I had taken a step closer to her, by accident. My hips were right at her eye line, inches from her face. She darted back, her eyes lifting nervously to my throat, not quite reaching my eyes.

She stood stiffly.

"I'll dye your hair first, then cut it, after it's washed. We'll clean everything up at the end."

Jae shrugged, affecting casualness.

I'd colored plenty of friends' hair over the years, and I'd watched my mom do it a thousand times. I prepared the mixture from the cheap box of dye and put on the latex gloves. I was good at this.

I brushed the tangles from Jae's hair gently, using a comb I found in one of the Carlisles' drawers.

"You don't have to do that," Jae muttered. "I can do that myself."

"It's fine," I said, gathering her hair in my hand, lifting it from her neck. Her throat moved uneasily.

"Lower your head," I said.

I started with the part of Jae's hair, drawing a thick line of dye along the roots. Her scalp looked white and vulnerable under the parting of my fingers. I used my pinkie to slide through her hair, working section by section. Jae's fingers, on the edge of the sink, were white-knuckled. I felt like a hunter, hushed, and attuned to her movements. Every breath and twitch a whisper of information, an instruction, a reply, a request carried out. My fingers on her neck, my thumb on her pulse, my breath on her ear. Her uneasy surveillance, the bob of her throat, rhythmic and unsettled as a marble rolling in a bowl. It wasn't quite trust, what she was giving to me—we had to transform ourselves; we had little choice—but I could feel her yielding with every minute that passed. By the time my fingers were running through the ends of her hair, she was almost pliant.

"You're done," I said, removing the gloves. "Hold still."

I ran the corner of a washcloth under the faucet and stood in front of her, taking her jaw to guide her where I needed. Gently, I cleaned the dye off her forehead and ears. I took her hip and turned her toward the mirror again to clean her nape. I felt a shiver run through her.

Jae watched me in the mirror, her expression troubled, almost brooding.

"I didn't hurt you, did I?"

She shook her head.

"Okay," I said, stepping away. "Then you're done. We have to wait thirty minutes, and then you can shower."

While we waited, we cleaned up the fallen hair and flushed it. We wiped down the sink. With twenty minutes to spare before her shower, we went downstairs to the kitchen and untwisted the cap off one of Mrs. Carlisle's many, many bottles of Chardonnay.

The wine made Jae less guarded. She smiled easily. Her limbs loosened. I stared. I knew I was staring, but I couldn't stop.

Jae was beautiful.

I hadn't quite given myself permission to give the thought shape before. I'd felt it creep through some dark, shameful part of my brain enough times over the last few days that I'd learned to ignore it. Quiet, dangerous beauty.

Tonight, it was harder to ignore.

"Oh—" I saw the clock. "We've gone seven minutes over."

Jae ducked into the shower. I waited in the bedroom until I heard the water turn off, giving her privacy to change. The bathroom was steamy when I reentered.

"Come here," I said.

Jae stepped in front of me, facing away toward the mirror.

"No, no," I said, speaking in a low voice. I took her by the hip again, turning her. She didn't resist, letting me guide her so she faced me. We were close again, as close as we'd been when I untied her wrists from the rafter in that dark hallway. I remembered how afraid I'd been. How repulsed. The sourness of her breath, her dark teeth and tongue. Her lips were pink now, and a little swollen. She avoided my eyes, staring somewhere near my earlobe.

"I'm going to cut it shorter," I said, "maybe here." I made a scissors motion around a lock of her wet hair, right at her cheekbone. "And here." Her nape.

Jae's eyes lifted to mine in a sharp, guarded way. The tougher she acted, the gentler I wanted to treat her.

"It'll look good," I assured her. "Don't worry."

I combed through her hair a little with my fingers and lifted a lock to Jae's eye line. Then I snipped off the end. It fell back to her cheek, and I peeled it away. Her cheek was shockingly soft.

Jae allowed me the tiniest nod. I started with the hair that framed her face. Then I took her by the shoulder, turned her toward the mirror, and cut the back of her hair all the way to her nape. It began to dry as I cut it. Her hair wasn't that long to begin with, barely chin length. I wondered how short it was before the Victors took her. Based on the state she was in, I couldn't imagine they ever cut it themselves. They didn't even let her bathe.

I shifted Jae to face me again so I could finish, playing with different angles. She was stoic as I handled her, allowing me to move her this way and that.

I pulled away, examining her carefully. I'd done well.

When Jae faced the mirror, surprise flashed across her face. A few strands fell stubbornly over her eyes. She looked like a greaser from the fifties, moody and disreputable.

She liked the haircut. I could tell. Standing next to each other in the mirror, we looked like a pair of low-rent bandits from another era. Highway robbers in an old Western. Actors rehearsing a play for which we were humiliatingly unprepared. Like I was trying to play a trick on my own psyche. As if without my hair, the costume of my old life, I could convincingly step into a new skin.

A new name, a new history. I'd reinvented myself before, in high school and college. It felt like tempting fate to think I could pull it off again.

"You look good, Jae," I said, passing her a new bottle of Chardonnay.

Jae brought the mouth to her own, her neck flushed.

"You too, Evie," she murmured, and drank.

19

We loaded the car so we'd be ready to leave first thing in the morning. Jae gathered all the useful food—granola bars, nuts, cans of nonperishables—and packed them neatly with the folded teen-boy clothes. I found winter accessories in the master closet: down coats, gloves, scarves, hats. For dinner, we cooked the last of the frozen food, a chicken pot pie. Afterward, we took the wine bottle and ventured down to the beach.

We'd avoided the beach all day. It felt too dangerous. The Carlisles' property spanned many, many solitary acres of woods and marshland. The nearest house was almost a mile away, so there was no risk of getting spotted by a neighbor. But the beach? There we risked being seen by a passing boat or anyone walking from the public beach a few miles down the road. Families playing with dogs, evening joggers.

But tonight we wanted to enjoy the last of our vacation before we were forced to return to the hunt. We doubted we'd see anyone else—and if we did, we'd sprint inside. If we got truly spooked, we could jump in the car and leave. The car was packed. We could leave right now, if we wanted.

We crept across the crabgrass. It was windy, but the live oaks were unmoved, their branches vascular and witchy against the night sky. Grass surrendered to sand dunes. The strip of beach was narrow: it was an inlet, technically. Christian and I had once taken some inflatables out, and he nearly capsized when he spotted a baby stingray shimmying along the sand. In the daytime, the water was a clear, calm aquamarine.

At night, it was a black mirror. The moon swam some distance away. We dropped to the sand, sinking our fingers into the dampness. Sea foam crawled up the bank, brushing our feet. It wasn't as cold as I thought it would be. We could swim, if we felt brave enough.

I lit our cigarettes, passing one to Jae. She took a swig from the wine and passed it to me. A crab scuttled near my fingers.

"Can I ask you something?" she murmured.

I frowned. "Okay."

"Have you ever—" She chose her words carefully. "Have you ever done something bad? Something you can't take back?"

"Of course." I shrugged carelessly. "Everyone's done something bad."

"What's the worst thing you've ever done?"

"The worst thing I've ever done?" I repeated, incredulous.

Jae looked amused. "You don't have to answer."

"I was expecting you to ask—I don't know—'What's your favorite animal?' 'What's your favorite color?' 'If you could have a superpower, what would it be?'" I said. "To be fair. I did actually ask someone that once. The worst thing they've ever done."

"Who?"

"I was, uh—" I avoided her eyes. "On a date. I was so bored. I thought, let me ask her literally the most fucked-up thing I can come up with. To her credit, she did answer. She said she hit a guy biking down Laurel Canyon with her car and didn't check to see if he was okay. It was an accident. But still."

"Did you date her?"

"Yeah." I shrugged. Jae lifted her eyebrow in surprise. "I mean, she was really hot. We only went on a few dates."

"What did you tell her was the worst thing you've done?"

"I didn't. She didn't ask me. She wasn't very interested in me, I think."

"I'm asking."

I met Jae's eyes. Jae had already borne witness to so much of my rage. Serena, the clerk. It's not like she was under any impression that I was some pious little angel.

"When I was a teenager, I was a pretty terrible bully," I admitted.

"What does that mean? You threw kids into lockers? Stole their lunch money?"

"Where's your imagination?"

"What?" Jae's grin was sheepish. "I've never bullied anyone."

"What a saint."

"You say that like it's a bad thing."

Maybe I did mean it as a bad thing. People who were too nice made me feel like shit. Christian used to be like that. Whenever we argued, he had this patronizing way of either reverting to his nice-guy shtick or playing the victim.

"Is it a bad thing?" said Jae.

"No," I said. "I just thought maybe you weren't so saintly either."

"I wasn't," said Jae. "I'm not. I steal. Since I was a little kid, I've been—I've been bad."

"You steal from box stores. Big chains," I countered. "It's not like it's just shits and giggles for you. You're not the Bling Ring. You're not stealing Lindsay Lohan's Birkin bag to post duck-face selfies on Instagram—which, whatever, go off. Do your thing. But you? Jae, you're stealing food. Cash. You're just trying to survive."

"You think what you've done is worse than what I've done? The worst thing you've done is bully someone. You were a kid."

"That's your measurement?"

"There are worse things," said Jae.

"Sure," I said, tapping the ash from my cigarette, "but just because I'm not a serial killer doesn't mean I'm not a piece of shit."

"You're very committed to this idea that you're a piece of shit."

I didn't know how to respond to this. Maybe I was.

"Okay, new question," said Jae. "What's the worst thing that's been done to you?"

"These questions."

"You still don't have to answer," said Jae, taking another swig of wine.

"Worst as in what?" I questioned her. "Unjust? Fucked-up? Mean? What are we talking about here? Date rape? A bit of school-bus groping? Or like more large-scale? The crimes of, I don't know, Sallie Mae? What scale of measurement are we using? Jesus, I sound like an asshole." I cut myself off, embarrassed, noticing the look on Jae's face.

"Those are all good questions," said Jae.

"You sound like a teacher."

"I wanted to be," Jae admitted, surprising me. "At one point."

"Really?"

"Yeah," said Jae. "I mean, I'm a college dropout. So I don't know what that would look like. But it's what I wanted, at one point."

"Why'd you drop out?"

"Long story," said Jae.

"Would you go back to school? If you could?"

Jae shrugged. "Maybe."

"I wanted to go back," I admitted. "I thought about it a lot. Doing a PhD or something. I was thinking of applying the next application cycle."

"In what?"

"Dunno. Art history, probably. Architecture focus. I've already got the master's, so why not."

"Wow."

"Are you going to give me the 'what's the goal of getting a degree in liberal arts' speech?"

"No. I think it's cool."

"No, you don't," I chided her, without any heat. "You think it's bullshit. It's fine. It is bullshit. But it's what interested me. It still interests me. And I like teaching. I didn't like teaching the SAT, but I like teaching, generally."

I hadn't actually articulated this plan to anyone before. It felt good to tell Jae. To plot a future. Of course that future was laughable now, but it was nice, even for a few minutes, to forget.

"How many students did you have?" Jae asked me. "When you were a tutor."

"About five a week."

"Did you have favorites?"

"Of course." All teachers have favorites. I liked the well-meaning slackers and the sporty kids. Honors students and sycophants gave me secondhand embarrassment: they showed their desire too plainly. They gave me too much ammunition, too much power over them, and I didn't trust myself not to abuse it. I liked the ones who were too busy with sports or video games or their YouTube channel to covet my attention. I liked the clueless skater boys, who were baffled by everything and delighted by every minor success. They were so different from me.

"So that's the main reason you want to go back to school? To teach?"

"I don't know." It felt lame to admit now, but I've always liked school. It was a performance I understood, a comfortable skin to slip into. "I guess. Yeah. I mean, I'm good at it. I like it. The pay is shit, but you know. It's too late for me. I'm not hirable in anything else. I'm already on this path—there's nothing else on my résumé."

"I can see you as a teacher," said Jae. "You like bossing people around."

"I don't."

"It's okay, Evie." Jae reclined on her elbows. It was dangerous, the way she was looking at me. Some liquid need inside of me solidified, atoms vibrating together like cargo in the hull of a ship. "It's okay to like bossing people around."

"I'll boss you around," I warned her.

The corner of Jae's mouth lifted. "Whatever you want."

I gripped the sand, just to give my hands something to do. The wine was a bad idea. I could feel it moving through the dark sinews of my body like an eel. Making me brave.

But I didn't need bravery. I needed restraint. What I wanted was not possible. Not with Jae.

I forced myself to look away. The ocean was a single highway of rippling blue where the moon struck. Everything else was darkness and noise. Waves, wind.

"Should we swim?" Jae whispered.

She was already standing, knocking over the empty wine bottle. Her sweatshirt went first, abandoned in the sand. I felt, rather than saw, the thud of her sweatpants hit the ground. When I couldn't bear not looking anymore, I allowed myself to stare.

It was cruel, her nakedness. The way only beauty can be cruel.

"What are you doing?" I said.

"I've been inside for a long time." She was drunker than I realized. I could hear it in her voice. "I want to swim."

Water lapped around her ankles. She waded deeper, goose bumps prickling her arms. She ran her fingers through her hair, tousling the roguish, bad-boy swoop of it.

Jae looked at me over her shoulder, beckoning me to follow, but I was already following. I'd taken off my clothes. The water was cold, but I didn't care. I didn't care about anything.

She walked ahead of me, until the water reached waist level, then dived below. She swam out a few feet, then breached the surface, shaking the ocean from her hair with a laugh. The laugh echoed, and I swallowed it down, ducking beneath the surface to meet her. I chased her, and she chased me, and the current conspired against us, or for us, depending on how you look at it. Her knee brushed mine, her elbow, tangling like seaweed, inescapable. Maybe it was always inescapable. Maybe I was wrong to resist it.

Maybe I wasn't alone.

Above us was a sickle moon. A spray of stars, so close against the velvety darkness I could've plucked one with my fingers like a jewel and gifted it to Jae.

Our mouths floated inches from each other. Under the water, I felt Jae's hand cup my hip. Her lashes were spiky, her eyes so dark and wet they reflected everything. Even me. I felt a sharp tug, some final ribbon of self-control unspooling.

"Evie," Jae ordered softly, "don't move."

I didn't move. She came forward. Her hand, when it gripped the back of my neck, was cold. My eyes fluttered shut. I felt her breath ghost against my lips, then my neck. I shivered, gravitating closer to her body heat.

She put her lips to my ear.

"Behind you," she whispered, and it was only then that I heard the terror. "There's a boat."

20

The engine purred gently. It was large, a cross between a speedboat and a houseboat. Its bow a long knife, carving ripples of glass.

There is no elegant way to get out of the ocean fast. No matter what, you'll look like an ass, lumbering, like you're losing a fight against the wind. We scrambled out of the water, tugging our clothes on over our soaked and shivering bodies, yanking our shoes on as fast as we could.

The boat was heading right for the Carlisles' dock. We crawled up the dunes on all fours then broke into a sprint.

"Hey!" a voice shouted behind us. "HEY!"

My muscles felt slippery, like raw meat.

"WHO THE *FUCK* IS—"

"GARRET, GO GET YOUR BIKE, GO AROUND—"

"WERE THEY IN OUR *HOUSE*—"

"YOU STUPID FUCK, IS YOUR PHONE STILL DEAD—"

"SIRI, CALL THE COPS—"

"WHAT THE FUCK—"

"CALL DAD CALL DAD CALL DAD—"

"WHAT THE FUCK—"

"SIRI, CALL DAD—"

"DON'T CALL DAD, CALL THE—"

A terrified glance backward confirmed these boys were the teenagers from the photo. The Abercrombie pastels, the Vineyard Vines. Ruddy faces, shocks of blond and red hair. Two teen boys, holding automatic rifles. Two teen boys, a dead lion at their feet.

Tonight, there was a third teenager with them. He leaped off the boat onto the dock, the others at his heels.

We were outnumbered.

"The car," I gasped, sprinting past the pool, nearly tripping on a plastic lawn chair, "we have to, we have to—"

We vaulted up the steps to the house. My hand was sweaty on the door handle. It took me two, three times before I busted it open and sprinted inside. Pain cracked through my knee as I slammed into a coffee table.

I couldn't hear the boys behind us anymore, though that only heightened my fear. Where had they gone? There was no time to look. I raced for the front door.

The GMC was still in the driveway. We dove inside. I stabbed the screwdriver into the ignition and slammed my foot on the accelerator. Woods streamed past us.

"We're okay," Jae was chanting like a prayer, an incantation, as if saying the words would make it so, "we're fine, we're okay, we're—"

"Okay" was a word that crunched in Jae's teeth. The teenagers' car came so fast that all I saw was a blur of headlights in the rearview mirror, lunar-bright, before we went hurtling into the windshield.

The smell of my blood was rich and soupy. It ran down my face into my ears and nose. Dark spools of it dribbled from my mouth.

I crawled blindly forward on my shredded elbows, spitting out a mouthful of blood.

A boot stepped on the back of my neck.

My vision, for almost ten full seconds, went dark. My eyes were open, I think. I just couldn't see. Who's to say? I'd just gone through a fucking windshield.

"Holy shit, is that—"

"Whatshername—"

"WHATSHERNAME!"

"EVIE!"

"—don't kill her—"

"—reward—"

"—where's the other one—"

"—accomplice—"

"—I said *don't kill her*—"

"—*hundred twenty-five thousand dollars*—"

"—*WHERE'S THE OTHER GIRL*—"

"—*WHERE'S! MY! FUCKING! PHONE!*—"

They were drunk. Their voices slurred together. Useless petals of sound, penetrating nothing. I blinked. My face was in the dirt. I saw shoes. Five Sperry Top-Siders. Hairy, skinny-boy ankles. Feet stumbling, shuffling in the dirt. Where was the sixth Sperry?

Oh yes. On my neck.

"Toby, go look for her," one of them hissed.

"I'm not your fucking butler, Garret," said Toby. He sounded more sober than the others.

"TOBY," Garret exploded. "GO! FIND! HER!"

What I knew: there was a sober teen called Toby—*not* a butler—and an absolutely unhinged teen called Garret. Plus, a third teen whose foot was on my neck.

"Get—" I gritted out, scrabbling forward, my hands clawing the dirt, "the *fuck—off me*—"

A Sperry Top-Sider went walloping into my rib cage so hard I couldn't even scream. I felt the sound travel up from the deepest cavern of my body and get lost in my throat.

Suddenly, the foot left my neck. I scrambled to my knees, gasping, clutching my ribs.

"Grab her, Devin," Garret directed the boy behind me. "Let's get them both to the pool house. Then we can use the landline to call the cops."

I was hauled up by the back of my shirt, my arms wrenched behind me. The scaffolding of my body no longer had any structural integrity.

A boy swam in my vision. He was so freckled he was almost tan. His hair was reddish blond. Dad sunglasses hung around his neck. He was wearing salmon-colored boat shorts and a striped shirt that hung open, unbuttoned. There was nothing underneath, only his sunburnt, underdeveloped belly. He had a long, skinny neck, and a small head, like a turtle. His eyes, when they finally came into focus, were like blue daubs of paint. Unseeing buttons.

He was very, very drunk.

"You," he said, "are *dead*."

"No, Garret," said Devin, teeth gritted with irritation, "the cops want her *alive*."

"SAYS," Garret exploded, spraying us with tequila spittle, "WHO—!"

"Let," I rasped, "*go*—"

Suddenly, the boy holding me slapped his hand over my mouth, hard enough I felt my skull rattle.

"*Shut up*," he hissed in a sour cloud of beer breath.

I closed my eyes, trying to calm my breathing. If I could stay calm, I could think. *Jae.* That was the first thing. Where was Jae?

When I opened my eyes, there was a knife gleaming an inch from my throat.

The tip pressed into my flesh. If I took too deep a breath, it would break skin. *My* skin.

Terror flooded me like a drug. My heart was jackhammering so fast it seemed as if it had disappeared, drilled into the soft earth of my body and buried.

"I didn't do it." My voice sounded faraway, disconnected from my body. "I didn't do it, I didn't do it—"

The boy behind me—Devin—slapped his hand over my mouth

again. My mind and body cleaved apart. When they returned to each other, imperfectly jigsawed, the boys were arguing about what to do with me.

Garret lunged at his brother, his eyes bulging with hate.

I grabbed my chance and ducked. Devin's knife slipped as I escaped. I could feel fresh blood gurgling up, trickling down my neck, but I was running too fast to care. I heard a faraway scream. Feet trampling the dirt behind me. A cry. Maybe a fall.

A savage joy roared up in my chest.

Sprinting out of the woods, her hands slick with blood, was Jae. She was running so fast she almost barreled into me. I caught her just in time, grabbing her arm, which was slippery with gore.

We ran. A weight tumbled into my back. An axis tipped. Moonlight streamed overhead. A midnight sky. A red face I didn't recognize, crowned in Kraft-yellow hair. His eyes so pale blue they were almost translucent.

Devin was much bigger than his brother.

He picked me up and then threw me down so hard I felt something break. Shattered china, floating in the dark channels of my insides. I closed my eyes. I opened them again. Jae's fist flew in my periphery, landing in Devin's face. I closed them. Every breath took effort, like drawing a bucket from a well.

I forced my eyes open. I knew a struggle was happening a few feet away from me—Jae versus Devin—and I turned my neck, gritting my teeth against the pain. Jae and Devin were fighting with their fists and knees and teeth. The choreography of it was slow and primal, like they were fighting in extreme weather conditions. Slow-motion punches. Jae looked sinewy and feral, a wolfishness in the way she lunged. I didn't know where Garret was—inside, probably. Calling the police. I was sure they'd come at any moment. I forced myself to my elbows. The pain dulled to a faint pulse.

Jae had Devin pinned underneath her. He was bucking wildly, but she'd managed to get his knife, and she held it at his throat. He went slack, panting like a bull.

"Evie," she rasped, "Evie, in my pocket, there's a—there's—"

I saw it.

A gun.

I took it from her back pocket, keeping my eyes trained on Devin. It was small, a tiny Glock. I wondered when Jae had taken it from the study.

The woods rustled behind me.

I wheeled around, raising the gun.

Garret froze. Vomit was dribbling down his chin—he must've fallen. His eyes were dazed. He stared at the gun, open-mouthed in shock.

"Get on your knees," I said.

Garret fell. He made a pitiful retching sound.

I pressed the gun to his temple. My arm shook.

Something was loose inside me. A big, slippery something, gnashing its teeth. I was so furious it was hard to keep the reins on it. The rage had been brooding ever since I fled the Victors'. My hands were already fists, my throat raw, blood pressure at 100, 200, higher. The injustice of it all. Why was I here? Why was I picked for this? I hadn't been a saint, it's true. But was this really all my life was going to amount to? Was this always the destination? I wished I'd known earlier. I would've studied less. Worked less. Spent less time away from the people I loved.

Garret's lip trembled. I'm not sure what he saw on my face, but it was enough.

"Don't, please . . . please, *please* . . ."

It felt good to make him beg.

Behind me, I could hear Devin pleading for his life too. Jae had him on his front now, hands behind his back. Garret's head was bowed, his hands folded behind his neck. He was weeping.

They were pitiful, weren't they. They were kids.

I looked over my shoulder at Jae. She looked back at me and nodded.

We ran. Jae led us around the house, toward the pool. We stepped over a third body, moaning softly, dragging himself out of the pool. This must've been Toby. He started screaming when he saw Jae, heaving himself from the water in a panic.

"Where are we going—?" I shouted. "How are we—the car—"

That's when it came into view.

The boat.

21

The journey was quiet. The purr of the engine, the lap of the ocean. I'd driven boats before. A friend in high school had a lake house, and a big group of us would go almost every weekend in the summer to drink and smoke weed, do doughnuts on the speedboat, cling to an inflatable tube.

The Carlisles' house was out of sight, miles and miles of ocean between us now. A laugh spilled out of me, accidental—a release of tension. Once I started, I couldn't stop. It was a terrible, rib-crunching belly laugh.

"Why are you laughing?" said Jae. But she was grinning too.

She reached over and thumbed blood from the corner of my mouth. I could taste it. She looked awful. Her knuckles were a ruin of scrapes and cuts, and her lip and eyebrow were gushing fresh blood. I'm sure I looked just as bad. I glanced at my reflection in the black navigation screen. Blood painted my neck. My eyes were two hollows, like the holes of a Halloween mask.

But I was alive. Jae was alive.

We were free.

I could feel whatever had taken over me in the woods still prowling inside me, its parasite heart beating a step out of rhythm with my own.

"How's your head?" I asked, eyeing the dark ooze at her hairline. Jae shrugged, ever stoic, and began cleaning the blood off me with a towel she'd found in a compartment under a seat cushion. It smelled faintly of mildew.

The boat was clearly expensive. The seats were a creamy white leather, the navigation system state-of-the-art. It was a sports cruiser, with a sleeping cabin underneath. Judging by the state of it, the boys had been at sea for days. The boat was trashed. Crushed beer cans, coolers full of melted ice, soggy potato chips, a hamburger bun floating in a pool of water. Damp swim trunks, sticky puddles of spilled soda and rum, Solo cups filmed with days-old tequila.

We couldn't stay on the boat. The police would probably be arriving at the Carlisles' any moment. They'd call their parents. The US Marshals would know we left by boat, the make and the model. They'd contact the coast guard. It would be over.

I watched the nav system. We sailed down the Santa Rosa Sound, past Navarre. Jae found some clothes in the cabin: they stank of Axe body spray and beer. She looked funny in a cream-colored J.Crew pullover and chinos. I wore a baggy blue polo and kept my own pants—there wasn't much blood on them anyway. Stinky baseball caps, pulled low over our eyes. United Christian Academy. University of Alabama. From afar, we'd look like teenage boys.

Ahead of us was a bridge. A harbor. Restaurants crowded along a marina, strung with lights, dense with bodies, country music blasting. A water tower loomed like a hot air balloon, painted pink and orange. "Pensacola Beach."

I navigated into an open slip at the marina. Restaurants were packed closely together, crab shacks, decks swollen with rain. Picnic tables crowded with beer pitchers, platters of oyster shells and the husks of squeezed lemons, crab legs cracked open by bare hands. I could hear the faint sounds of someone badly singing "Santa Baby." Karaoke night.

We approached the dock. There were so many boats parked in the marina. A few were strung with Christmas lights: we avoided those. Too conspicuous.

At least one of these drunks had to have left their keys.

Jae crept up to a Formula Bowrider while I kept watch, hands slung casually in my pockets, the little Glock cradled in my palm. Jae climbed up the boat's narrow stairs to the captain's seat.

She signaled for me to approach, and I stepped aboard. This boat was much older than the Carlisles', the leather seats cracked, some of the lettering faded. But the surfaces were well-oiled, and the deck smelled like lemon cleaner.

Under the captain's seat was a key.

We followed a long, solitary beam of moonlight into the choppy open bay. We discussed the possibilities of going south, fleeing the country in a different direction. Cancún was a gulf away. If we made it to the southernmost tip of Florida, Nassau or Havana were an hour's ride at most. But the idea of crossing an ocean by boat—not just a strait or an inlet, like in Washington, but a proper ocean—terrified us both. We pictured waves as tall as mountains, swallowing us whole. Sharks eating the meat from our ribs, our skeletons floating miles and miles down through the darkness to the ocean floor. Plus, we would be far more conspicuous in tiny Caribbean islands or Central American cities, especially the ones teeming with American tourists.

It would have to be Canada. That meant wading back into the heart of the country, its insides marching with pitchforks, a hungry guillotine waiting—hungrier now that we'd almost killed a pair of rich teenage boys.

But tonight, just this one night, we would allow ourselves the boat.

I waited until we reached Mobile Bay to drop anchor. A few miles off the coast of Fairhope, Alabama, glittering houses in the distance. We cut all the lights. Unless a lighthouse swung directly at us—and there were no lighthouses within sight—we should disappear easily into the dark.

Jae pressed into my side in the captain's seat. I was pressed into hers. Hip to hip, knees knocking, shivering together. Jae had found a bottle of Malibu, and we passed it back and forth, letting the shoreline become hazier and hazier, rocking in the distance. It was stupid to drink, but oblivion was too tempting. My skull still felt like a bruised fruit, felled from an impossible height. But it wasn't the pain that made me feel so out of control. It was the humiliation, the fundamental wrongness. It was what I had screamed, senselessly, like a child, when the knife point was at my throat: *It wasn't me. I didn't do anything. Why is this happening to me?* My entire life, I had imagined there were choices, a map with a thousand paths to chart. I could choose the right one or the wrong one— mostly I chose wrong—but it was my choice to make.

Tonight, there was no map. There was one lonely road with one lonely end: the door of a cage, with nowhere to step except into its mouth.

And yet I was still here.

Jae's fingers ghosted over the cut on my neck, the tender flesh on my wrist bone. The bruise on my nape in the shape of Devin's shoe. She was so gentle. I felt raw, without armor.

Jae's finger was under my chin. I let her lift my face.

"Evie—" Jae breathed out.

I closed the gap between our mouths and kissed her.

She made a hurt, fierce little sound. I pulled away, heat blazing in my face and neck.

I leaped over the captain's chair and down the stairs and un- latched the door to the cabin, ignoring the sounds of Jae calling my name. She followed me down.

Moonlight bathed the cabin in blue. Jae shut the door behind her, faltering on the stairs. My careful barometer of her thoughts and moods had collapsed. She was a new creature. I was a new creature, stranded without any of my usual defenses. We watched each other with the alertness of predators, encountering the other across some distance. Tentative, terrified, anticipating who would make the first move.

It was Jae.

She crossed the room, pushed me against the wall, and pressed her lips to mine. My mouth was slack beneath hers. Jae didn't try to touch me. It was only that, our lips. I could feel her holding her breath. I held mine too, until I couldn't any longer. A warm spill of an exhale, my lips parting beneath hers. Finally, the touch of our mouths became a kiss. The second I granted permission, Jae descended on me in an urgent, almost despairing way. I was grateful for it. This was all I felt capable of doing, kissing her and being kissed, holding her and being held.

22

The ocean rocked us to sleep. A seagull woke us, tapping its beak against the cabin window. The sky was gray—I spotted some far-away storm clouds. We'd have to keep our eye on those.

Sheets were pooled around our hips. The night returned in pieces. Blood. A gun. A boat. Coconut rum. Jae's lips. My lips. A pirate's life for us.

Sleep had come more easily than expected, nestled into the hollow of Jae's neck.

But then the dream came. Even now it circled my brain, searching for a way back in. In the dream, I'm following a dark green Range Rover. It pulls into a driveway. A family spills out. I follow them inside. They don't see me. There's a mirror in the hallway, and I catch my reflection. I have a knife. I'm wearing a Venetian mask, the long-beaked omen of a plague doctor.

"Are you awake?" I murmured, reaching over to run my fingers through Jae's hair.

She nodded, cracking an eye open—the unbruised one. The other was swollen and sticky, a sick purplish color. I bent to kiss her temple, and Jae tugged me closer. She was still too skinny, but her arms felt strong around me, pure muscle, pure competence, vibrating with violent potential. If someone climbed aboard and kicked the cabin door in, I was confident she could capably get rid of them.

"I think we should hang here until dark. Wait out all of—" I waved my hand vaguely out the window. An army on horseback waiting for us on land. Tanks. Cannons, battering rams. Pitchforks. "That."

Jae nodded in agreement. "There's food?"

"A little. Eggs, bacon. Some snacks in the cupboard."

"What happens if someone comes on board?"

"Comes on board? Jae, we're in open water."

"What if the coast guard is searching boats and they pull up? What do we do?"

"I have the gun."

"Evie."

"What?"

"Someone comes on board and you'll—what?"

"I'll shoot them in the face."

Jae laughed.

"Okay, *you'll* shoot them in the face."

"I saw you last night. I think you're better with a gun."

It was fun to play pretend, to talk to each other like outlaws in some movie. Violence broods in all of us. Summoning it was just a matter of opening a door.

"I thought of something I've done that's worse than bullying," I said, getting up to make coffee.

"Evie, don't."

"Don't what?"

"Don't beat yourself up."

I turned around to face Jae. "You think I'm talking about the Carlisles?"

"Aren't you?"

"I don't feel guilty about what we did. Do you?"

Jae shook her head.

"I'm thinking of—remember? You asked me on the beach. What's the worst thing I've ever done."

"I remember," said Jae cautiously.

"It's a thing I used to do with my friends, in high school."

"Okay."

"The first time we did it, we were all drunk," I said. "There wasn't a lot to do growing up, so mostly we just drank and drove around. We were dumb teenagers in a small town. One time we were on the road, and we spotted this green Range Rover. I don't know who got the idea, but we decided to follow it."

"The Range Rover?"

"Yeah. We followed them all the way to their house. Well, it wasn't their house, actually—they pulled into someone's drive-way, but they didn't get out. We waited in the cul-de-sac. We even turned the car lights off, to make it creepier."

"Who was behind the wheel?"

"I was," I admitted, handing Jae a cup of coffee.

"What did the Range Rover do?"

"Nothing. They just sat there, waiting. Eventually we got bored and left. We felt bad. We were kids—all we wanted to do was scare them."

"Did you ever do it again?"

"With my friends, yeah, a few times. And once when I was alone," I said, "though I don't think I was trying to scare anyone that time. There was this gated community full of big houses I really wanted to see. Me and my dad, when I was a kid, we used to go to open houses all the time. Like really, really big ones, ones we could never afford. It was our Sunday-afternoon ritual. But this neighborhood, the only way to get in was to wait until someone entered the gate code and follow them in. So that's what I did. I wanted to see the neighborhood. It made me feel . . ." I couldn't describe it. It was like poking a wound. Not for masochistic reasons, but to find its origins, like a scientist conducting an experiment.

"I know how it made you feel," Jae whispered.

I sat beside her on the bed, holding my coffee. "You do?"

"I used to work for this catering company. Sometimes we did events: hotels, board rooms, stuff like that. But mostly we catered at people's houses. Big, ridiculous houses. Working there . . . it was like being handed a loaded gun. I could steal one bracelet, one antique, one handbag, and be set for months. Sometimes I'd wander into rooms I wasn't supposed to. I never got caught. But there was a part of me that almost wanted to."

"Why?"

Jae shrugged. "I don't know. To see the look on their faces."

Fear. That's what it was. It didn't matter, in the end. Someone would call the police, kick me out of the neighborhood. Someone would fire Jae, order her to leave. But that flicker of fear, right before the 911 call. That was real.

"When were you a caterer?" I asked Jae.

"After I dropped out of UCLA."

"What happened?"

Jae stared into her mug. "I got a call one day, from my friend Kevin. We hadn't spoken since high school. He said my dad had shown up at his father's car dealership and asked if there was a job opening. He was blackout drunk. He'd been fired from both his jobs for intoxication, and he hadn't told me."

"Shit."

"Yeah. I transferred to UC Irvine, to keep a closer eye on him. I helped him apply for food stamps and unemployment and Medi-Cal. I got a tax refund just in time—that helped us for a bit. He was able to get a job at a Coca-Cola syrup plant in Ontario, on the night shift. I drove him every day, since we only had one car. I started working for DoorDash and Lyft—it just made the most sense. I dropped out of Irvine too. It was hard to care about school. All I cared about was making money. I wanted my own place. My dad was drunk all the time. I worked a lot—it was better than being at home."

Jae's expression made it clear that she didn't want to talk about her dad any more than she had to.

"What was UCLA like?" I asked her.

"I don't remember that much, to be honest. It's kind of a blur."

"Let me guess—you had a super butch haircut," I said. "One of those undercuts. And you wore a lot of short-sleeved button-down shirts with dumb prints on them, since that's what all lesbians wear to be, like, legible as lesbians."

Jae shook her head with an embarrassed grin, which meant I was right.

I was enjoying myself. "How many straight girls did you sleep with?"

"A few." Jae looked away. "But it's not like anyone wanted to date me."

"They just wanted to sleep with you."

"Yeah."

"I would've dated the ever-living shit out of you."

Jae's eyes met mine. Her mouth did a funny thing, and then her grin disappeared.

"No," she said. "I don't think you would've."

"Why not?"

"You just—" She was resisting a frown. The smile she landed on was tight and unconvincing. "You wouldn't. Our paths never would've crossed. Out there."

"What do you mean?" I didn't like what she was implying.

"Just—you know. Different worlds."

"Different worlds. That's some Aladdin-ass nonsense. Am I Jasmine?"

"You're the monkey who steals the hat."

"Abu. Show some respect."

Jae's look was exasperated and amused. She was wrong. I could picture us crossing paths so easily. A dating app, a wedding, a bar.

A dim room dense with bodies, deep bass notes pulsing in the walls. Her eyes in a booth, finding me. Choosing me. Low simmer of eye contact. The cool way she ran her hands through her hair, the stubborn strand that hung in her face.

I would've brought her back to my place in East Hollywood. It was a yellow Spanish colonial from the 1930s. I'd lived in the duplex for almost four years with my roommate, Harvey, a construction worker from Boyle Heights, and, more recently, his boyfriend Van. I thought about the lemon trees, the peach-pink roses and blue tulips threaded through the chain-link fence. The bright orange kitchen and stone floors, the way sunlight spilled so thickly it took on its own dreamy, fog-like dimension of space. I thought of the old Colombian restaurant I passed on the way to my local bar, the red-and-blue Christmas lights that hung year-round, the elderly couples dancing cumbia after ten every night. The Ukrainian cultural center, the pupuseria, the tacos sold on card tables on the street corner.

Next to our duplex was an abandoned house. It used to be occupied by an Armenian family. Harvey and I often heard them hosting parties. One day, out of nowhere, they left. The windows stayed dark for months. Then one night, I saw a light come on in the neighbor's kitchen. In the morning, broken glass littered the yard, and a yellowed mattress had been dragged onto the stoop. One squatter became two. Two became dozens. Sometimes Harvey and I saw them holding a bucket beneath our water tap. They didn't bother us, except for the time I found a man moaning beneath my window, masturbating. We heard the wails of trips gone bad, arguments that turned violent, police raids. A week before the Victors' murder, the city had kicked them out and erected a fence around the yard. A cop car patrolled the street.

I wondered if anyone had climbed the fence by now. I wondered if Harvey was looking for a new renter already. I wondered what he'd done with my furniture. The Ikea bed I bought for thirty dollars on Facebook Marketplace, the blue dresser I thrifted from the Rose Bowl Flea Market. Would Jae fit into this apartment? I tried to picture her in my kitchen, brewing coffee, brushing her teeth in my bathroom. Jae at Trader Joe's, choosing an unbruised banana. The curve of Jae's spine under my sheets. I went further back. Jae in North Carolina, in my private school, wearing the plaid schoolgirl uniform I'd worn for four long years, staring down my teachers with bored, lazy judgment. Jae, with her short bedhead hair like a teenage boy and her long, hollowed body, as crudely elegant as a muscle car stripped to its most essential parts. Her bruised knees, protruding above knee-high socks and oxfords. There was something so filthy and wrong about the image, and terribly erotic in its wrongness. I wanted to kiss her again.

So I did. Jae's hands roamed the length of my back. From the small cabin window, I could see the sky darkening. We needed to get closer to shore.

A thunderclap made the boat lurch.

I climbed out of her lap. "Come on. I'm going to find us an empty slip. We don't have to go ashore yet—but it's too dangerous to be in open water during a storm."

I offered her my hand, helping her out of bed. I unearthed one of the baseball caps and tugged it over her head. Then I kissed her. When I pulled away, I saw the faded bruise on her neck, and felt guilty. Did she want this, the way I wanted this? Was it right to want this from her, after what she went through—after the Victors—after *he*—

Jae knotted her fingers in the back of my hair and kissed me, hard.

"Don't," she murmured. "I can feel you thinking. Don't."

Still, my next kiss was more tentative. Jae had no patience for that. She deepened the kiss instructively, making her desire plain.

I palmed the small of her back, snuck a hand down her chinos, and she made a rough noise of approval, leaning into my touch. I kissed the hollow of her throat and felt her pulse jump.

"I'm going to fuck you later," I said.

Jae's eyes closed, and she smiled—real, unguarded, a smile I'd never seen.

23

The beach house we docked at was pitch-black. Jae tried her best not to be sick as the boat dipped wildly from the force of the waves. It grew calmer the closer we got to shore, but not by much.

"Should we try breaking into the house?" Jae shouted over the wind. "Won't it be dangerous on the boat?"

"We'll be fine—we'll just park here and stay in the cabin," I yelled back. "I don't want to risk breaking in—if we fail, then we'll be stranded in the storm."

Rain spat hatefully in our faces as we ducked back into the cabin. Wind rattled the windows. Jae was shivering. So was I. Our clothes were wet, but we didn't have any others to change into. She ran a towel over her hair, tousling it. Lightning struck a halo of light around her head, disappearing as quickly as it came.

"Did you mean it," said Jae quietly. "What you said. Before."

"What did I say?" I knew what I said.

Jae arranged herself against the wall opposite me, her hands tucked behind her back, as if she didn't trust them.

Thunder cracked. We both ducked instinctively.

"We need an escape plan," said Jae, avoiding the question.

"I told you," I said. "I have the gun."

"A gun won't protect us from the storm."

"If it gets bad, we'll get off the boat. We'll find a car. You'll work your GTA magic. We're golden."

"Right," said Jae, playing along. "It's that easy."

"Tell me what I said before."

"You said—" Jae straightened, like a cadet at attention. "You said you wanted to fuck me."

A throb of need pulsed between my legs. Jae against the wall, her hands still folded behind her back, stiffly waiting to be told what would happen next.

"Did you mean it?" she asked.

The thrill of Jae asking was almost too much to withstand. I wanted to drag out the suspense for as long as I could. To commit the sight of her to memory. The fall of her damp hair, the shallow rhythm of her breath.

"Do you want me to mean it?" I said.

Jae nodded quickly, as if afraid the offer would be rescinded if she waited too long to answer. Or maybe she had read me well enough to know that when it came to her, my bravery was determined by the perimeter she drew. That I could be bold with her only if she initiated the conditions for me to do so.

I closed the distance between us. My fingers curled in the wet hair at her nape. Her breath spilled hot against mine. I didn't kiss her yet. That was the sweetest part, the anticipation, her willingness to wait for what I'd give her. My lips ghosted along the knife edge of her jaw and the dip of her throat. My fingers moved under her wet shirt, feeling her rib cage expand and compress. I slipped my hand beneath her waistband, between her legs. Her skin was cold. I found the place where she was hot. Almost feverishly so.

"Jae," I said.

Her eyes met mine.

I kissed her. Her body arched into mine. I thumbed at the seam of her lips. She accepted it into her mouth, holding eye contact with me.

My eyes traveled Jae's face. I felt the softness of her tongue, the sharpness of her teeth. A drum kicked inside me. Seconds later, I felt it reverberate in her like a tuning fork.

Jae peeled the wet clothes from my body. Her lips moved to my neck. Every nerve prickled to life on the surface of my skin, hypersensitive.

When I was naked, she knelt on the cabin floor and put her lips to my stomach, pressing the sweetest, lightest kiss above my navel. My stomach dipped fiercely. I threaded my fingers in her hair, and Jae made a wounded, hungry sound. She gave another, even lighter kiss, right beside the first, sinking lower, and lower still, and my stomach jumped again, and the heat between my legs pulsed and deepened. A fault line breaking open. It was so good it was unbearable. Good things can be like that. A touch tender enough to hurt.

I was weak when she finally stood, pressing me into the wall to kiss me. I could taste myself. She was still dressed in her damp clothes. I removed them impatiently.

We moved to the cabin bed. I was between her legs, gripping her knees, opening her. She rose on her elbows, her hair falling into her face. She watched me as I lowered my mouth to her breast, took her nipple between my teeth, soothed it with my tongue. She lifted her hips, rocking them against mine. Asking. I reached between her legs, felt the wetness and heat between them. Her eyelashes fluttered, her gaze still locked with mine. I ran my finger over her clit, and her whole body shuddered.

"Good?"

In answer, she grabbed my wrist, pulling. I slipped a finger inside her and lowered my mouth to hers. A wet, open-mouthed kiss, more a shared breath than anything. Her mouth was on my jaw, greedy. My throat. I sank another finger inside, and her body knotted like rope. I twisted my fingers in her hair and tilted her head back.

"Look at me," I said.

There was an audible click in her throat as her gaze met mine.

I fucked her like this, holding eye contact, coaxing an orgasm from her in slow, deep strokes. Her eyes were as dark and luminous as an oil spill. It was too much, to look at someone like this, to be looked at like this. To be trusted to see this much of someone.

Her body jerked, rocking thoughtlessly against me until she sank boneless into the sheets. Her mouth brushed lazily against mine, little sips of kisses while we caught our breath. I buried my head in her shoulder. She cupped the back of my neck, as if afraid I might run.

24

Returning to land was like waking up after several months in a coma and discovering the world had been visited by an apocalypse in your absence. There were no people. There were no cars. There was only rain. The thunder and the lightning dulled around five a.m., though the rain persisted.

We sprinted to the road. Multicolored Christmas lights glittered in the gray morning light. Our breath puffed as we trudged uphill through the woods. A quarter mile ahead was the silhouette of something shelter-shaped.

A new subdivision, still under construction. The spiny shape of it, from our hilltop vista, looked vaguely archaeological. An unearthed skeleton, half-emerged from the red clay. At the center, a clubhouse, an empty pool in the shape of a kidney bean, gleaming green tennis courts. It was surrounded by unfinished houses. Timber frames shuddered. Wind battered the spongy pink insulation. The protective sheeting thrashed, like a rib cage rising and falling. We made our way down the hill, slipping on soaked pine straw.

There was a cul-de-sac of three completed houses at the bottom of the hill. Jae held her finger to her lips, scanning the cars. We bent low and raced around the side of the house on the left. I pressed my ear to the wall, listening for the sounds of a family stumbling awake: running pipes, creaking beds, the click-clack of an expensive goldendoodle on hardwood floors.

Jae knelt in the wet grass. We'd found a small tool kit on the boat. We had stuffed it into a sand-crusted tote bag, along with the nonperishable food and some additional clothes—sweatshirts emblazoned with "Beaches Be Crazy" and "It's Margarita O'Clock."

Jae removed the screwdriver and held it between her teeth. She crept toward the car in the drive: a white Kia Forte. After taking a few steps, she motioned for me to follow. She pried open the door. The soft *snick* of the car unlocking was like a thunder crack.

We froze. Listening. Waiting. The sunrise was a time bomb, a countdown. The rain had slowed to a dull mist. Birdsong trilled around us, rustling leaves, snapping twigs.

Jae opened the driver's side and slipped smoothly inside. I followed suit.

She eased the screwdriver into the ignition. There was something erotic about her careful maneuvering, the tenderness of her attention as she searched for some inner sensitivity, the right friction of pins and wires.

"With a lot of cars, if they're pre-2006," Jae whispered, "you usually don't have to hot-wire. You can just—"

Her jaw went taut as she used deeper force, leveraging the screwdriver at a new angle.

A deep vibration purred beneath us.

I quickly ducked down in the passenger seat, in case the rumble of the car woke any neighbors. The cops would be looking for a pair. Jae eased out of her jacket—a Gators windbreaker she found on the boat—and laid it on top of me as she maneuvered us out of the neighborhood. I waited about ten minutes before I emerged, slouching low, cap pulled over my eyes, knees bent, feet on the dash.

I sat up, stretched my limbs. Fruited plains, bathed in sunlight, passed us by. The country looked less scary today than I thought it would, less unwelcome. It wasn't. Looks are deceiving. But for an hour, at a McDonald's drive-thru, drinking iced coffee and scarfing an Egg McMuffin, watching the sun rise as we drove deeper into Alabama, I felt unafraid.

I filled the tank at an empty gas station outside Montgomery, hat pulled low over my face. I caught a glimpse of my strange new hair in the side mirror. Jae returned with stolen Pop-Tarts and a roll of newspapers. It was Sunday, December 18. We'd now been fugitives for an entire week.

I grimaced at the front page.

"'She Hunted Us Like Animals': Florida Teens Recount Terrifying Encounter with Hollywood Slayer Evie Gordon."

"Here we go," I murmured. Jae had managed to grab three different papers and two tabloids. Jae resumed driving while I flipped through them, reading the most interesting headlines aloud.

"Carlisle Sons Tell All: What We Know About Their Nightmarish Encounter with Evie Gordon."

"Who Is Gordon's Partner-in-Crime? Detectives Speculate."

"The Victors, the Carlisles, and Tate-LaBianca: The Eerie Similarities Between Gordon and Manson."

"'These Boys Are Lucky to Be Alive': Okaloosa County, Florida, Detective Reports."

"Gordon Targets Wealthy Families: FBI Special Agent Shares Theories."

"Female Violence and Rage: A Psychologist Offers Insight."

"'Pure Evil': California Governor Wants 'Severest Sentence Possible' for Evie Gordon."

"Gordon, Wuornos, and the Manson Girls: Why Women Kill."

"Why do they?" Jae murmured dryly.

I read every article aloud to Jae. The longer I read, the funnier it seemed. I could consume the stories objectively, as if I were an anonymous true-crime enthusiast with no skin in the game. A creepy teenager, hungry for the gory details. "Evie Gordon" wasn't me. She was a character. The new Aileen Wuornos, Charles Manson 2.0. A horror-movie villain of operatic, Grand Guignol proportions. Evie Gordon: The Das Kapital Killer. Her motivations borrowed heavily from the Charles Manson school of schizophrenia. Manson believed the Beatles' *White Album* prophesied an apocalyptic race war; the Tate–LaBianca murders were the first shots fired. Evie Gordon was simply picking up where he'd left off. One editorial even went so far as referencing a map, drawing a thick red line between the LaBianca house in Los Feliz and the Victor House, only a mile north in the foothills of Griffith Park. Most seemed fixated on the laziest of iconography: a Hollywood actress, a gory poolside murder, young female killers.

Others let their imaginations run wild. Evie Gordon was a nightmare. A boogeyman. Hide your Rolexes, gents. Ladies, keep your designer purses at home. She can smell the expensive skin care, the unnatural collagen, the veneers, the real silver. At this very moment, she might be reclining on a curved staircase, licking the marrow from a fresh clavicle. At her feet is the scrap heap of a fallen chandelier, the broken limbs of imported furniture, the shards of a silent auction painting. On their knees in the foyer are her followers. You think Unnamed Accomplice is the only one? Oh, no. Her Family is growing. The quiet girl with the key to your house, who watches your children? She could be Evie. The elderly man whose name you can't quite remember, though he comes every week to prune your bushes and mow your lawn? He's an Evie too.

One reporter was fixated on the fact that I'd gone on strike with the teachers' union when I worked briefly as a teaching assistant: evidence that I was Trotsky reincarnate. He quoted Vera Duarte, my former boss, who said that I had a "history of speaking cruelly about clients." Vera Duarte was a Beverly Hills housewife who married a ninety-year-old wheelchair-bound Portuguese aristocrat. Their house cost $22 million. Her tutoring company, West Side Tutoring, was a girl-boss vanity project. I thought we got along. Apparently not. She told *USA Today* that I once called a student's mom "Jersey Shore Marie Antoinette."

Another editorial mocked the pitiful state of my finances, my ninety-nine-thousand-dollar student-loan debt. I was a failure, taking out my resentment on good, hardworking people. To prove it, he listed all the folksy millionaires who'd come before me. Men who'd come from nothing, who lifted themselves up by their bootstraps and made capitalism their bitch. An army of cowboys trudging uphill through the snow, planting their flag on Wall Street. I was the face of the editorial's mockery, but I was only a symptom of a larger malignancy. These gaping wounds walk among us, he warned—the debtors, the renters, the generations at the end of the alphabet, born for the end of the world.

"Do you know where that phrase comes from?" said Jae. "'Bootstrapping.'"

I shook my head and lit a cigarette.

"It was a joke. The whole point of the metaphor is that it's a joke about a narcissist. It comes from some German satirist—I forget his name. We learned about it in an econ seminar. He wrote all these tales about this particular character, a baron, who was this big braggart. The baron would tell these grandiose stories of his adventures and exaggerate how impressive and heroic he was. In one of the stories, the baron escapes a swamp by pulling on his own hair. In an American adaptation, they changed it so the baron pulls himself out by his own bootstraps. But the braggart is a blowhard. He's the butt of the joke. What he's describing literally defies the laws of physics. I told my dad the same anecdote once. He was furious with me, as if I'd made it up just to make him feel like a fool. I kind of get it, though. I was never going to get through to him. What we were—poor, though he'd never admit it, we were *poor*—that was temporary to him. A blip on the road to greener pastures." Jae noticed my expression. "What—what's wrong?"

I shrugged cagily. I was embarrassed to be aligned with her dad's naivete. Still, the bootstrap fantasy calcified, unwilling to be dismissed so easily. I had worked so hard. I had taken on so much debt. I sold my eggs. I went to dinner with old men. I sat in front of dull-eyed kids and tried to muster my compassion. I pulled my bootstraps and I barely moved. How stupid I looked: a Scooby-Doo, sprinting and staying in place; a cloud of electrons, circling a void.

25

"Do you want to learn how to steal a car?" Jae asked as we entered Tennessee. "This one's shit. The service light keeps flickering."

I very much wanted to learn how to steal a car.

We found a sleepy shopping center—a Target, a Home Depot, a Marshalls. She turned in, scanning the edges of the parking lot for a suitable option.

"What are we looking for?"

"Hyundai or Kia, ideally. Ford would be okay too—especially an older one."

"There's an Elantra. The window's half-cracked."

"Where?"

"Three o'clock. Rosebush."

I parked some distance away.

"Get the screwdriver," said Jae.

I pocketed it and slung the tote bag over my shoulder, leaving the old car behind.

It was late afternoon. The streetlamps were wrapped with garland. From the Target, we heard faint Christmas music.

"Yeah, this looks good," said Jae.

She leaned casually against the side while I pried open the door.

"See the plastic under the wheel?" said Jae, climbing into the passenger seat. "That stuff's really flimsy. Just dig your fingers in and rip it down. That's it."

It took some force, but after a few minutes of prying, I was able to tear it off.

"See the ignition lock cylinder? Pull that out. Now stick the screwdriver in—not like that; go easy."

I eased it in the way I'd watched Jae do it before, twisting carefully.

The engine roared to life.

Jae consulted the map, directing me to a side street. I leaned back in the driver's seat, unrolling the window a crack.

Without realizing it, I'd taken the gun from my pocket and was holding it in my lap, tracing my finger over the handle in a way that was slightly too *my precious* for my comfort. I pocketed it and took a soda from Jae's most recent gas station haul. I felt good. Fearless, almost scarily so, because I had no reason to be. An entire country was chasing us—and isn't this what so many women say they want? Men pursuing them, courting them, waiting up late next to the telephone for news of their whereabouts, twirling their hair. A pair of headlights rounding the bend: Could it be Evie?

A funny thing, how the language of courtship mirrors the language of hunting. Chase. Pursue. Stalk. We had become the object of it all. Objects of lust, objects of fear. What was the difference, really? I saw the way they talked about me on the news and in the papers. Scandalized hysteria. I was a nobody. All the journalists had was a handful of images to circulate and puzzle over, to dissect, and devour. A woman's face is never just a thing in itself. It is always slippery with metaphor. A lake of meaning to stare into, a surface to observe your fears, jealousies, and desires. With only the plain fact of my face and the thin biographical details available online, lengthy essays had already been written on my motivations (bad) and moral shortcomings (too long to list). My face was like one of those optical illusions, a Rorschach test. How long does it take to stare at an unexceptional almost-thirtysomething until you see the devil within? Wait for it. Give it time to surface. My blandly smiling face on the college admissions photo: in a certain light, doesn't she portray an undeniable capacity for sexual deviance? Posts were pulled from my Instagram, overanalyzing every detail, searching for evidence of psychopathy, the vague vampiness of a cartoon brunette.

Today was the first day I felt that the power to decide the value of another human's life was not theirs alone. I scanned the road, still stroking the gun in my lap. The man in the nice suit, behind the wheel of that BMW: Did he know my name? Was he afraid? The woman with the severe bun, the dark lipstick, the Porsche SUV—was she scanning the road for Evie Gordon? Did she know I was just two cars away? Did she know I was watching her?

I looked at Jae. The afternoon sun sprayed brightly behind her messy hair, curled around her temples and ears. The tilt of her mouth was sinful. I felt a pulse of giddiness, as if we were embarking on a vacation. A string had been cut. On holiday you could be anyone. Jae could be a stranger at a tiki bar, a ski lodge, a window seat, seduced into a whirlwind romance. I'd said a version of this to Jae before, but she didn't seem as entertained by the fantasy. *This is not a holiday. This is our lives now.* But that was the thing about Jae: She was too cool, too logical. She didn't indulge. Her feet were firmly on the ground.

I wandered. Most of my fantasies were innocent. Wintry cottagecore domesticity in Canada. A vegetable garden. A dog, a cat, a fence to keep out predators. Sharing a bed. Going to sleep with her, waking up with her.

But there were other fantasies. Jae and I storming into a cavernous bank. Marble columns, marble floors. We hoist machine guns over our heads. Magazines of bullets drape our chests like pageant ribbons. We fire warning shots, and everyone drops to their knees. Our steps echo on the marble floor. We're wearing Halloween masks. We're wearing fur coats and salacious three-piece suits, unbuttoned. We take our piles of money to our underground lair.

We are pursued by Batman, who we kill (he's so easy to kill, why do they pretend it's hard?). We trash expensive hotel rooms. We fuck in piles of money. Fantasies of supervillainy, in garish comic book colors, in the seedy low-fi pixelation of bad porn, in the high camp of a music video.

"What are you thinking about?" said Jae, giving my thigh a lazy squeeze.

I cracked open a soda. "Road head."

Memphis smelled like Wonder Bread and Hostess cakes. There was a factory downtown. Behind the smell of sugar and yeast was the fertile, primordial richness of the Mississippi Delta. We got barbecue from a roadside stand and ate it farther north, out of the city, on the side of the river. The water was bloody, a mirror of the sunset. Algae skimmed the surface, sour-candy green. The barbecue was good.

Since Jae had done most of the driving during the day, I let her sleep through the night. We agreed not to stop until we reached Washington. Twenty-four hundred miles. It would take us roughly four days.

I took a coffee break in Kansas City, flipping through *Time* magazine. I was near the end when I saw the headline "Evie Gordon: A Gifted Kid Turned Killer."

The first photo was a seven-year-old me with my parents. It was an interview, the sub-headline read, "Gordon Family Finally Speaks About Their Daughter Turned Murderer."

I stared at the letters until they scrambled, damp and illegible. I couldn't bring myself to read it. What were they saying about me? What eulogies were they writing for the daughter they once knew? *We thought she was someone else. We thought we raised her right.*

I slammed the magazine shut and tossed it in the back seat, ignoring the desire to hold their photograph to my chest, preserving the memory of us as we were, as they were, as I was. Forever withholding the moment of discovering who they believed me to be now.

Night driving was the hardest, especially when Jae was asleep. I distracted myself with the radio. When my mind tilted in dangerous directions, I had to find more creative ways to wheel myself back. I started taking note of funny town names, to tell Jae when she woke up. McCool Junction. Funk. Republican City. Madrid.

The sun was rising in Madrid when I heard my name.

I turned up the volume on the radio.

"—Dinah Victor's sister, Rebecca Fitzgerald, declined to bury her sister in the Victor family plot in Palo Alto, where Peter Victor was buried on Friday. Fitzgerald arranged a separate funeral ceremony for Dinah with family in France and elected for Dinah to be cremated."

I tensed. A separate funeral? In France?

The passenger seat creaked. Jae was waking up.

Why would Peter and Dinah have separate funerals?

I remembered a crumpled receipt. Jae's small, neat handwriting.

"Separate beds," I said slowly.

"Hm?" Jae mumbled groggily.

"At the bayou. You wrote that Peter and Dinah slept in separate beds."

Now Jae looked very awake.

"And Dinah—Dinah wasn't home," I said. "For weeks. It was Peter who was coming to the door. The koi pond was the first time I'd seen Dinah in weeks."

I looked over at Jae. Her expression was hyper-focused.

"The suitcase," I said. "There was a suitcase by the door to the garden. Dinah must've just come back."

Jae frowned. "Right."

"Where was she? France?"

"Maybe she had an acting job."

"No, no, that would've been reported, don't you think? Dinah hadn't acted in years. She retired after Serena—she told me she wasn't interested in that anymore. She just wanted to be a mom."

It didn't make sense.

"Serena never mentioned anything either," I said.

I remember how exhausted Serena seemed. Her vacant stare at the wall. Her jumpiness. Her and Peter, circling each other like strangers.

Serena is smarter than she lets on.

Jae had written this when I questioned her at the bayou. Serena's Lexapro, her spells of sadness, her absence from school. Her behavior had to be related to whatever was going on with her parents. She was the only person who knew what went on inside that house. If only she could tell us.

But first she had to wake up.

"Serena knows," I said. "Whatever was going on in that family— Serena will be able to explain it, when she wakes up. *If* she wakes up."

"She will."

I felt a familiar flare of impatience—of helplessness.

Jae shifted in the passenger seat, rubbing her tired eyes. A distant Starbucks appeared on the horizon.

Jae disappeared inside to buy our coffee, which gave me a few minutes to think. She took over driving. When we returned to the highway, I turned to her, determined.

"There's an alternative, you know," I said, trying to sound mild.

"What's that?"

"You could—you could tell me yourself."

"Tell you what," said Jae, her eyes dull as she stared at the grim Nebraska snow.

"Jae, I found you tied up under their stairs."

"Yeah, I remember that." Jae swerved sharply around some ice on the road.

"So, I mean, you obviously have *some* insight into—"

"Evie . . ."

I pushed forward. "The last thing you told me was that you dropped out. Your dad, he was struggling with alcohol. You're working for DoorDash and Lyft," I summarized. "And then what? Help me get from A to B."

"No."

"No?" I repeated, surprised.

"I don't want to talk about that."

"Is that when you met the Victors?"

"What did I just say?" she snapped.

I opened my mouth, prepared to be bullish, to badger Jae into trauma-spilling. And then I saw her fingers go instinctively to her throat. The still-green bruise, like the stain of cheap jewelry.

After a guilty silence, Jae sighed.

"Yes," she said. "That's when I met the Victors."

"How?"

"I worked for them."

"You were a caterer," I remembered.

Jae nodded.

Of course. There are two ways for someone like Jae to get a glimpse of a house like that, to slip through the membranes between worlds. The first way is violence. The second is service.

"For how long?"

"Long enough. The company let me go."

"Did something happen?"

Jae sighed. "No. They just—it didn't work out."

"Were you still living with your dad?"

"Sometimes."

"Where is he now?"

"Dead." Her voice didn't waver.

I stared at her, stunned. Jae looked at me, daring me to speak.

"Don't," she said. "Don't say it. Don't say anything."

The urge to apologize, to pry, to learn the answers—the how, the when, the why—were almost impossible to resist. But I had to. There was no other choice.

"Where did you live?" I said. "Where did you go?"

Jae gripped the wheel, white-knuckled. She shook her head.

"With your friends?"

"I lived in my car."

We were silent after that. It was almost lunch when Jae spoke again.

"I was desperate," she said. "I got desperate."

Her voice was a hoarse monotone. We had made it to Cheyenne, Wyoming. A roadside tourist attraction greeted us: a giraffe constructed of painted oil drums, eyelashes made of a long-toothed comb. A scrap-metal elephant. Pristine, foamy snow was banked on either side of the highway.

"I went back," she whispered.

"Back to the Victors'?" I was confused.

Jae nodded.

"What happened?"

"I don't remember how I got there." Jae didn't hear the interjection. She plowed ahead, lost in her memory. "I was just at their door. I was so tired. I was hungry, and my dad had *just*—" A muscle worked in her jaw. She fell silent again. After a few minutes, she said, "I was desperate."

I wanted every detail—what was it like, working for the Victors? what happened to your dad?—and yet, contained in that one word was a whole universe. *Desperate.*

"Who opened the door?" I said. "Serena?"

Jae shook her head.

"Dinah?"

Jae shook her head again.

"It was Peter," I said.

Jae's eyes moved. Hatred flickered. Raw, oily, still twitching.

"He didn't recognize me," said Jae. "We never interacted much when I used to come to the house for work. So he thought I was—one of them."

"One of them?" I didn't understand.

"The women," said Jae.

Highest Bidder. Of course.

"I was weak—I was so *tired*—I—"

Jae was quiet for a long time.

"He invited me in," she said. "And then he realized . . . I wasn't there for *that*. He realized I was nobody." Her voice shook. "It was so easy for him."

She cut herself off. We watched the snow blur past. I stared at the faded bruise on her neck. I remembered how raw it looked when I'd found her. Still prickled with blood at the edges, a thunderous purple in the center.

"No one was looking for me," she said quietly. "No one even knew I was missing."

26

I let Jae sleep through the night. We passed a state penitentiary in Montana. It was three in the morning but some of the lights were still illuminated. In another universe, I might be inside there, its California equivalent. If Jae hadn't secured the Nissan and a new ID in the desert. If Jae hadn't come back for me. If Jae hadn't stopped the clerk. If Jae wasn't at my side in Florida, fending off the Carlisle boys.

Jae was the point of divergence. The fork in the path. The difference between my life now, and a life of mystery meat and orange jumpsuits, toilet wine and DIY shivs. I was wanted for murder, not burglary or tax fraud or drug use. There was a very real possibility that my prison sentence would resemble *Silence of the Lambs* more than *Orange Is the New Black*. I'd advise febrile FBI agents about the comings and goings of my comrades in murder. I'd lure the special agent's hand through the dog flap where I'm served food and trap him. I'd carve off his face with a fingernail, thin as a slice of Boar's Head, and slip it over my own like a drugstore sheet mask. I'd escape.

Or I would rot my days away, tens of thousands of days, until I died.

There was also the other possibility: the possibility where I was found innocent. I could argue self-defense. Serena was trying to kill me. The Carlisle boys were trying to kill me. I had a right to defend myself, didn't I? Robert Durst's lawyer successfully argued self-defense, and his client beheaded a man and sawed off his arms and legs. I wasn't a high school sports star or O. J. Simpson, but maybe some hotshot young lawyer would step forward to represent me.

Except where would that leave Jae? She had spent weeks trapped in a prison of another kind. She wouldn't put herself through that again. And I would never ask that of her.

So, Scylla: a life sentence in federal prison or, best-case scenario, an Amanda Knox–like future of unflagging public hatred and scrutiny. But I would have limited access to my family, my friends, the known world.

Or Charybdis: permanent exile and homelessness, a shadow world, a lonely purgatory of home invasions and nonperishables. And Jae.

By morning, we were still in Montana, close to the Canadian border. Jae filled the tank at a gas station. The store was empty, so I risked perusing the magazine racks inside. A stoned twenty-something manned the counter—orange fisherman beanie, neck tattoos, and a heavy beard, a joint tucked carelessly behind his ear.

I scanned the most recent headlines. A US representative from Florida called us "the most monstrous women in America." A popular pseudo-philosopher incel wanted us to be executed live on television. The governor of California called us "pure evil." We were vile, we were vicious, we were barely human. Every description of the murders reminded readers that we were not just any killers; we were *female* killers. Our transgression made us instantly mythological. Signifiers of a mysterious, feminine evil. Black widows, femme fatales, witches. Objects of loathing, objects of revenge fantasy, objects of perverse eroticism. *Bonnie and Bonnie.* No Clyde in sight.

Nestled among the descriptions of my vile viciousness was the *Time* magazine article, the one that taunted me, the one I still couldn't bring myself to read: "Gordon Family Finally Speaks."

I turned away, confronting a rack of maps. *British Columbia: The Essential Guide. Vancouver Island Adventures.* They were small enough to slip into my pocket. I was no Jae when it came to pick-pocketing, but this seemed easy enough.

I glanced again at the stoned cashier. He was already watching me.

I froze.

A slow grin of recognition spread across his face.

I fumbled for the handgun in my pocket.

"There's heat sensors, you know," he said. "On the border."

He jerked his chin at the map I was still holding. *British Columbia Sight-Seeing.*

The wind chimes on the door rang. It was Jae.

She looked at me and the clerk, locked in a stare-off.

"The sensors pick up nonanimal heat signatures," said the clerk, clocking Jae with a wary nod. "I know it seems like it would be easy to cross—but those sensors will fuck you. I mean it. Border patrol will be on you in minutes."

He was sort of good-looking, the cashier, in a shifty, unkempt way. His name tag said "Gabe."

Jae took out her switchblade.

Gabe lifted his hands in surrender.

"Look, you don't have to say anything. No offense, man, but it's pretty clear what you're trying to do. I mean, why else would you be all the way out here?"

Jae took a wary step forward.

"I'm not gonna turn you in," said Gabe.

"Why should I believe you?" I said.

"Why? Because Patrick Bateman ate *shit*." He let out a low

whistle of admiration, hand on his chest. "Who are you gonna hit next? Are you taking requests? I've got some names."

"You don't know anything about us." My voice shook.

I let him glimpse the gun in my pocket. I hoped he couldn't see the quiver in my hand.

"Damn. Okay. Never meet your heroes. Can I give some advice?"

The gun made a soft click as I turned off the safety. No one moved.

"Anacortes," said Gabe quickly. "In Washington. There's a ferry. You don't even have to leave your car. Just drive on. Keep a low profile. Get off at one of the San Juan Islands. Vancouver Island is right across the strait. You could swim."

Jae's eyes narrowed in skepticism.

"That was a joke, Jesse James," said Gabe. "Don't fucking swim. Find a house with a boat in the slip. It's all vacation homes out there—trust me, half of them will be empty. Take their boat and ride as far as you can. I've got a friend who's moved plenty of—"

His eyes cut to the lot. Another car pulled into the gas station. We started moving toward the door.

As we crossed the counter, Gabe offered a funny bow and handed me a greasy Burger King bag. I took it hastily and shoved open the doors, strolling back into the cold with Jae at my heels.

We left the station as fast as we could, Jae at the wheel.

"That was so *stupid*, Evie," she hissed. "What were you thinking?"

I ignored this and opened the bag. Inside was an uneaten burger and fries. I unwrapped the burger hastily and shoved it in my mouth.

"What's that?" said Jae.

"What do you think? It's free breakfast," I said, through a mouthful of pickle. "And it wasn't stupid."

I handed her the sweaty bag of food. Reluctantly, she took a handful of fries.

"Why are you being so blasé about this?" Jae demanded.

"If you thought he was really a problem," I said, "you would have tried harder to stop it. Wouldn't you?"

Jae was quiet.

"Sure," she admitted. "But you can't just blindly trust anybody who tells you they're a fan."

"A *fan?*"

"I'm surprised he didn't ask for your autograph," said Jae dryly. "There's more like him out there, I'm sure."

I couldn't hide my bewilderment. News was so difficult to come by that we'd had to settle for the bare minimum, the lowest common denominator: garden-variety national papers, the snowy broadcasts available in cheap hotels. Cable news anchors proselytizing from their pulpits, senators and sheriffs and FBI agents demanding our heads on spikes. It had never occurred to me that the public's opinion of us might resemble something thornier, more schismatic. Warring factions, defectors, and heretics. It was nice, admittedly, to think there were at least a few people out there—strangers—who didn't want to see us rot in prison for the rest of our lives.

"It makes sense," I said, "what he was proposing. The ferry. The islands, taking a boat. It's not like we haven't done it before."

Jae handed me the rest of the burger. I studied the map while I ate and found the town he mentioned: "Anacortes."

"Where is it?"

"It's north of Seattle. Right on the water."

"So what—we find an empty house with a boat in the slip, take the boat—"

"Turn off the nav system, just like we did in Florida, go totally dark—"

"But how do we get to land in Canada?"

"It's not far," I said, looking at the map. "Look, here's the Haro Strait. And then there's more little towns on the Canada side. We'll ride until we find a place that looks safe to dock."

"And then?"

"We'll find a car and drive."

An exit appeared from the dark highway. Jae took it and drove down a lonely street, parking under a bridge. She consulted the map herself. I left the car to pee, grateful for the head-clearing rush of cold air.

I was shivering when I reentered the car. Jae turned up the heat.

"I like it," she said quietly. "The ferry idea. Anacortes. It makes sense," she admitted, "and it's less dangerous than dealing with the wilderness on land. Better the devil we know."

There were no good options. Either we got chased by bears and died of frostbite, or we risked the open sea.

It was agreed: we'd go to Canada by boat.

27

We traded off driving through Washington. The Cascade Range, if you squinted, was almost the Swiss Alps. The dramatic fantasy ranges of New Zealand. Medieval Austria, where the hills are alive with blond children, sopranos, and fur coats. By nightfall we arrived in a strange Bavarian village, a former railroad stop turned tourist attraction. A Christmas snow globe of a town. A Festival of Lights, a gazebo wreathed in tinsel. It was so charming it felt sinister. From the baroque, candy-colored eaves, I half expected to see Snow White or an elf or a Gilmore Girl.

A lonely motel parking lot allowed us an hour of rest. Since this was by far the most crowded town we'd stopped in, I stayed in the car while Jae secured food. She returned with German beer, soft pretzels, and a fresh stack of tabloids and newspapers.

"There's an interview with Lukas," I read aloud, surprised to see his gaunt face staring back at me from the newspaper. "He was on TV last night."

"Who?" said Jae, distracted.

"Serena's boyfriend."

"Is Serena awake?" said Jae, suddenly alert, taking the paper from me. I read over her shoulder.

"It looks like it was just a pinkie twitch."

"There's an excerpt of the interview," said Jae. "She asks him about Highest Bidder. If he or Serena knew Peter was bringing escorts to the house."

"What does he say?"

I snatched the paper back before she could answer, scanning frantically.

LTH: I didn't know anything about that. Serena might have. They weren't very close. She said all her dad cared about was money. He wanted, like, Epstein money. Like private-island money. Serena said he blamed her mom a lot— since she was this famous actress or whatever, it brought more attention on him, after the investigation.

ABC: Investigation?

LTH: After the housing crash. Serena said a lot of the other VPs at his bank got to stay. But not him. That's why they moved to LA.

ABC: How did Peter treat Serena?

LTH: I don't think Mr. Victor ever, like, did anything to her. But I think she heard some stuff. I don't know—I think she saw him once, with one of the girls—the women. The, um, the sex workers. There was this one night she came to my house, really late. She was freaked-out. She said she didn't feel safe at home. She kept saying, "I saw someone." And then the next day, she told me her mom was filing for divorce.

ABC: When was this?

LTH: Maybe a month ago? Mrs. Victor went to Paris. She couldn't take Serena out of school yet, but the plan was to get everything ready, so they could, ASAP, after she served Mr. Victor the divorce papers.

ABC: How did Peter react to the divorce?

LTH: Well, I don't think Mrs. Victor ever actually got to tell him. She was waiting for the right time. They were both pretty afraid—her and Serena. But

Serena said her mom had a good lawyer. Like, for alimony. I think he repped Mel Gibson's wife. Or the Murdochs. I can't remember.

ABC: That was a billion-dollar alimony settlement.

LTH: Was it? Whoa. Well, I think Mrs. Victor got that guy.

Divorce. My ears rang.

Dinah was filing for divorce.

Of course.

Separate beds.

Separate funerals.

"It was that day, wasn't it?" I said. "Last Sunday. December eleventh. That's when Dinah came home from Paris. To tell Peter she was divorcing him."

I remembered again the suitcase by the door to the garden. The dropped handbag.

Realization passed over Jae's face.

I arrived at three p.m. to tutor Serena. How many hours late was I to the murder? Three? Two? One? The blood was still wet when I showed up.

I closed my eyes. I could see it perfectly.

Peter walks into the kitchen. He's surprised to see his wife standing there. He hasn't seen her in weeks. She hasn't answered any of his texts or calls. He's not an idiot. He knows exactly what she's trying to do. But Dinah's smart: surely, she knows better than to take him to court. She wouldn't dare.

He looks at the papers she hands him. Her expression is determined, but her hand shakes. He looks at the number she's demanding. It was signed by a lawyer whose name he recognizes. A lawyer who has ruined many men's lives. Good men, hardworking men: men who were only trying to protect their wives from their basest selves. Men have urges. Dinah was an alpine spring, pure and cold and clean. Sometimes, men need to drink at more suitable watering holes. Peter has specific tastes. He is the first to admit it. Dinah wouldn't have understood.

No, he says simply, handing them back.

It's already happening.

You're asking too much.

Dinah looks like she wants to slap him.

Peter wants her to slap him. Because if she did, it would open a door he has never dared open. And behind that door is a world where he slaps her back. A world where he puts his hands around her throat—just like he did to the woman he paid, just like he did to the woman he didn't—and says, No, Dinah. You listen to me.

And she would, wouldn't she.

I'm leaving, she says. The lawyers will take care of the rest.

Something passes over Peter's face. Something that reverberates in hers, distorted, like a funhouse mirror. It's fear.

She takes a step back.

He takes a step forward.

The garden. She walks into the ivy and mint, her arms crossed in trembling fury, clutching her phone.

He follows.

She says, Get away from me.

He says, Let me talk.

She says, No.

He says, Just let me—

And then his hand is around her throat. It is soft, from all her creams. Almost too soft. He squeezes.

In the struggle, they land in the koi pond. She is on top of him.

Furious, struggling for breath, soaking wet, he picks up the nearest thing.

A rock.

He hits her with the rock. Furious, screaming, she flies back, then comes forward, blood in her eyes. He has never seen her like this before. How long has his wife dreamed beside him, in her sexless nightgowns, imagining what it would feel like to put her hands around his throat?

He can't breathe. It takes all his strength to hit her again. Her skull cracks. He hits her again and again. His own vision whites out. He's winning. She staggers back. Oh, he's won. He has her. How dare she think she could—that he would just *take it*—

If only he could lift his head. He is sinking. He can't see.

All he has to do is lift up.

If only his brain would just—if he could just—

If—

A scream, swallowed by the trees.

If a tree falls and there's no one around to hear it—

If a murderer murders a murderer murders a murderer murders a—

It was a bad joke. Killer and killed: a closed-loop circuit. No witnesses. No one to exonerate us. Of course, this was why no other suspects had come to light. No one was ever going to emerge from the shadows, twirling the ends of their mustache. Serena would not wake up and reveal her diabolical plan. Lukas would not rip back the curtain and tell us how he did it. No FBI agent or detective was going to divert from the pack and pursue a new theory. Even the cleverest amateur sleuth was not going to jigsaw these pieces together.

"Maybe," said Jae desperately, "maybe that's not it. Maybe . . ."

Maybe. Maybe Peter and Dinah hadn't killed each other. But the thing that was clear now—or rather, the thing that was always clear, I'd just been unwilling to face it—was that it didn't matter either way. It had never mattered.

Because there was Evie Gordon.

28

It was two a.m. when I finally gave in.

Jae slept against the window, mouth open, brow furrowed in a bad dream. I insisted on driving that night, despite her offer to take over. It's not like I would've been able to sleep anyway. Might as well give myself a task to complete. My mind, kept idle—it was unthinkable, the places it might wander. Hope was a dangerous thing to lose. Who was I without it? I was afraid to know.

I pulled into a gas station and filled the tank. I sat in the parked car, contemplating the *Time* magazine in my lap. The article in question, the poison apple I'd resisted for two days: "Gordon Family Finally Speaks."

At the center was a photo of me as a kid. Wild Shirley Temple curls, big eyes, and freckles. It's Halloween. I'm dressed like a shark. My head emerges from its soft, felt teeth. I appear delighted to be eaten—giant grin, both my front teeth missing, a half-chewed red Tootsie Pop thrust in my little fist. I'm holding a pumpkin pail. Clutching my shoulders, ghoulishly tall even while bending over, is my dad. He's dressed as Dracula. My mom is Generic Party City Witch. They wore these exact costumes every Halloween before their divorce. My dad would fill the front yard with headstones he sawed from scrap wood, painted with references that were funny only to him. Dead rock stars, Jimi Hendrix and Jim Morrison. Dead presidents, Nixon and Reagan. He was like a big, mischievous kid. He even built a coffin and would hide in it when kids approached the house. They'd ring the bell, wait for someone to come to the door. When they least expected it, he'd burst out of the coffin and scare them.

There were other photos. Me on the first day of fourth grade, clutching my Lisa Frank notebook. Me in Destin with my mom, at an oceanfront pancake house called the Frisky Dolphin. My mom was obsessed with dolphins: they were all over her house, the prints on her wall, her dangly gift-shop jewelry.

"Do you think Evie is still alive?"

This was the first question the reporter asked my mom.

"Yes," my mom answered confidently. The reporter described her smile as *brave* and *wobbly*. "Of course she is! She's smart. She's always been smart."

"And you maintain there's absolutely zero chance she's guilty?"

"Of course we do," my dad interjected. "We have no doubt that our Evie is innocent."

"Then why hasn't she turned herself in? Isn't it only fair that she submit herself to the judicial process? You could argue that the longer she evades the law, the guiltier she looks."

"Well, you know, the justice system in this country is deeply flawed," said my dad.

"The evidence looks bad though, you have to admit," said the reporter. "And there are no other suspects—"

"That we know of," my dad interrupted. I could picture his expressive Jeff Goldblum hands wagging a finger in admonishment, the troubled V of his wild eyebrows.

"I just want to know Evie is safe," said my mom. "I want people to stop saying the horrible things they're saying on television. And I want them to *stop camping outside my house.*"

Something was wrong.

As I drove, darkness pulsed around me, claustrophobic. Like I'd been zipped inside an animal skin. All my organs corseted together. Every bloodstream and airway winnowed to a seam.

I pulled into a rest stop, threw the car door open, gasping. I stumbled toward the bathroom, leaned my forehead against a cool vending machine, ignoring the numbness of my fingers and toes. I kicked the machine until it burped up an Aquafina and gulped that down. It didn't help. I tried to throw up, but all I managed was stringy bile. I returned to the car, my breath staccato and jerky. I headbutted the steering wheel in frustration, *bang-bang-bang.* Jae's eyelids fluttered open. I kissed her hair. *Go back to sleep.*

I got out of the car again, followed the sounds of a stream behind the rest stop. Fished a cigarette from my pocket and took shivery puffs. The car's headlights drowned out the stars in the night sky. I felt like I was sitting under a world-shaped bowl. A lonely bowl without stars or planets or people. Only a nucleus of darkness, yawning wider and wider. Even the cold failed to reach me. I looked at my fingers. Three had gone numb. I sucked one into the heat of my mouth like a child, to give it sensation. If I stayed out here long enough, I was sure other parts would lose circulation too. Despair was the iceberg. It was always there waiting for our fateful meeting.

Adrenaline was a more powerful drug than any I'd sampled in a college dorm room. It made you fall in love. It inured you to pain. It readied you to march into battle, visions of immortality shimmering on the horizon. The crash was worse than nicotine withdrawal.

And then the clock restarts. The hourglass flips. The last grain of sand falls, and you wake crusted with drool, in a stranger's clothes, in a crashed car, in a foreign country.

29

Jae was awake when I finally returned to the car, sitting on the driver's side. I sank wordlessly into the passenger seat and slept for about thirty minutes. The rest of the time, I was only pretending. My ears refused to pop from the altitude. I was massaging the skin under my jaw, when the sun emerged from behind the white clouds, a dim candle at the end of its wick.

"What's wrong?" said Jae finally.

"Nothing."

This was a lie, of course. Something was very wrong. But the thing that was wrong was my head, and until I organized my thoughts, I couldn't speak even if I tried. I clutched the *Time* magazine article. I had most of my parents' answers memorized by now.

I tried to sleep again. When that failed, I tried to eat. I had no appetite. A list of things I did not have: an appetite, a future, a bed to sleep in, a roof over my head, the possibility of ever seeing my family again, assurance of where my next meal would come from, anything at all to call my own. And I would never have any of those things again. Even Jae felt shadowy today. Impressions of her stumbled briefly into focus, like crystal patterns beneath a magnifying glass—there was her cunning mouth, and here, her clever fingers, the dark, wry curve of her eyebrows—but in totality I couldn't see her. The brush of her lips over my knuckles as I pretended to sleep made a terrifying wave crest in my rib cage. We weren't supposed to feel this much.

I was not an outlaw or a pirate or the next great American serial killer. I was a twenty-nine-year-old SAT tutor from Hendersonville, North Carolina. I wanted to go to Big Sur and stay at the Madonna Inn with my college friends in May, like we did every year. I wanted to save up enough money to go to New Orleans in June with my best friends from high school, who still lived in North Carolina. Two of them had kids now, or would soon enough. Three were married. I wasn't sure if I wanted children or if I even wanted to get married; I suspected not. But I would have liked the opportunity to keep wondering. To apply for a PhD or move to a new part of the country—or back home. I might have a little house. A room and a bed to call my own. A dog in the yard. A girlfriend to love. She'd be a competent professional criminal. She'd have a cunning mouth and clever hands and a string of flowers tattooed across her hip.

Jae stopped to dumpster dive at a Safeway, and I forced myself to eat. Stale bread, an orange, carrot sticks. She attended diligently to my needs. After I ate, I smoked more cigarettes and drank more beer and stroked the gun in my lap absent-mindedly until I fell back asleep. I felt a little better when I woke up, though my head still hurt. Wordlessly, Jae produced some Tylenol. I swallowed them dry. She uncapped a water bottle with the same clinical attentiveness. The gesture made my throat tight.

She will be fine, I thought, watching her cheeks hollow around her cigarette. She never needed me anyway. Cool, cynical Jae, wielder of knives, stealer of cars. If anything, when I tell her, she'll be relieved. Cut loose from her celebrity ball and chain.

"I'm sorry," I said.

"For what?" said Jae.

For not being an outlaw or a pirate or America's Next Top Serial Killer. And for leaving you, I thought, even though I hadn't done it yet.

30

I was in a less sour mood when we arrived in Anacortes. Rain skimmed the windows. A dewy green world, ferns, and thunder. We arrived a little before noon. A thick veil of mist shrouded the harbor, though we could still make out the bridal face of Fidalgo Bay. Islands dense with cedar and balsam fir, sailboats leisurely in the shallows of sea cliffs.

A historic stern-wheeler greeted us as we entered the harbor: the *W. T. Preston*. It looked like a cross between an industrial barge and an old-fashioned Tom Sawyer riverboat, the kind with a big paddle wheel. The marina sprawled. Sailboats and fishing boats, mostly. There were a few houseboats and cruisers too. A cluster of touristy cafés: Dockside Dogs, Zaza Turkish Coffee in a turquoise sea shack, a barbecue stand. Campfire smoke drifted from a nearby RV park. We bought snacks from a convenience store. Sandwiches wrapped in plastic, hummus cups, and bruised bananas. For the journey, Jae took extra food from the store: nuts, crackers, dried fruit, and jerky. Cup Noodles and canned soup.

We arrived at the ferry terminal at noon and waited. There was a six p.m. vessel, the *Samish*, that would take us to Lopez Island. I looked at our map, studying the path to Nanaimo, British Columbia. Jae pored over a sheaf of brochures and real estate listings in the car, in search of a promising target. An empty house, a boat in the slip. We had a fail-safe in case none of the docks paid off: a campground near the Lopez Island ferry terminal. We'd take refuge there until morning. At six a.m., we could board the ferry again and try another island, Orcas or San Juan.

My plan was ripening too, though I hadn't yet articulated this to Jae. My first priority was ensuring that she was set up for success. I'd wait for us to find a suitable empty house with a boat, confirm she knew how to navigate it and that the weather conditions were safe enough for the crossing, watch her disappear on the horizon. Then, and only then, would I take the car and drive to a police station to turn myself in.

I wasn't going to slip away in the night without telling her, nothing so cruel. When the time was right, I would calmly inform her of my decision and that she couldn't change my mind. I would protect her, of course, throughout the entire legal process. I'd never disclose her name or location, only the truth about what Peter Victor had done to her. I would tell them my theory, that Peter and Dinah had killed each other, and if I was successful, Jae might be able to resume a completely ordinary life. Of course, I'd still have to submit myself to the vagaries of the American criminal justice system, but I'd had a long sleepless night to make my peace with that.

There were four lanes of cars at the ferry terminal, each about eight vehicles deep. I sank into the floorboards in the back seat, a blanket draped over me. Once we reached the ticket booth, I'd let it cover me entirely. It's not like anyone was going to search our car, but it was best to operate out of an abundance of caution. We'd come this far. And even if my fugitive chapter was technically nearing an end, I wanted it to be on my own terms—and I wanted Jae to be far, far away when it happened.

Jae inched slowly forward. In the back seat, I settled dreamily into the silence of a decision made. I was and always have been a great compartmentalizer. It's a remarkable pathology. I felt good: I even caught myself whistling.

"Pull the blanket over your head," said Jae sharply.

"Are we at the ticket booth?"

"Just do it."

I obeyed, with a prickle of dread.

Jae started pretending to talk on an imaginary phone. Murmurs and "hms," "yeses" and "nos." She fake laughed. Nearly ten minutes passed before the car moved again. From beneath the thin blanket, I watched Jae pay the ticket attendant in cash and drive onto the ferry.

"What was that about?"

"Stay down."

"Jae, what's going on?"

"Nothing. I think I'm just being paranoid."

"Okay?"

"There were two men in a car. A Ferrari, a red one. I don't know. It felt like they were watching me."

"Where are they?"

"They're right behind us."

"They can probably see your mouth moving right now."

"Shit."

The line of cars filed into place belowdecks.

"I don't like this," Jae murmured, her eyes fixed on her rear-view mirror. "Everyone else is leaving their cars except them."

It was true. Now that the vessel had set sail, most people were headed for the galley.

"You can leave too, you know, if they're creeping you out," I said, tucking the blanket under my chin. "Don't worry. I'll stay here and nap. I could use some sleep anyway."

"I'm not going to leave you alone," Jae muttered.

The words "leave you alone" were a small disturbance in the glass-smooth surface of my mind. I ignored it.

"I'm giving you permission," I said.

I could tell Jae wanted to turn and face me, but she couldn't: not with the men in the Ferrari watching.

"What?" I said.

Jae chewed on the cap of her water bottle. She had a bit of an oral fixation. Cigarettes, her fingernails, stray bits of plastic.

"You can tell me, you know," said Jae, her lips barely moving. "If you're afraid."

"I'm not afraid. Are you?"

Jae didn't answer. She drummed her fingers on the wheel. I sat up as much as I dared, watching her.

"I heard you last night," she said quietly. "You were having a panic attack."

My stomach knotted, remembering. The suffocation. The gasping loneliness.

"You've never had one before last night, have you?"

"I'm fine."

"Evie."

"I don't feel like talking about it."

"I think we have to."

"I didn't make you talk about the things *you* didn't feel like talking about, did I?" I was suddenly furious. My anger came so easily these days.

Jae didn't flinch. "I only talked because I knew you wanted me to."

For a while, neither of us spoke. I listened to Jae eat an apple and tried to sleep.

"They're getting out," Jae warned in a low voice. "Cover yourself with the blanket."

I sank down as deeply as I could, going still. I heard footsteps, deep male voices, a laugh. The sounds receded. I peered out warily.

"They're gone," said Jae. "One of them tipped his head at me when he passed. Maybe it was friendly. I really think I'm just being paranoid."

She scrubbed her hands over her face. It was rare I saw Jae this rattled.

Slowly, the other drivers returned to their cars. I stayed under my blanket until we'd made it to land. I felt the rumble of gravel, the tick-tick-tick of the turn signal.

"Don't move yet," said Jae. "I want to lose this Ferrari."

"Are they following us?"

"They're in the next lane, within eyesight. They think I'm alone. They can't suddenly see another person in the car."

I stayed down until Jae said it was safe. Even then I remained curled in the back seat, ready to dive under the blanket in case they reappeared.

Jae consulted the real estate listings. The first two houses we investigated had empty slips, so we drove on to a third. It was remote, midcentury in style, floating in a lake of cool grass. The moonlit sea was visible behind it. There was a dirt bike in the otherwise empty drive, draped in cobwebs. We tested windows and doors. Everything was locked. The garage looked most promising: it wasn't mechanized, just had two rusted handles that could be lifted, with enough brute strength.

Brute strength was one of my few criminal gifts. Jae wriggled beneath the gap.

"Oh shit—" she hissed. Something clattered to the ground.

"You good?"

"It's dark in here."

I heard the squeal of hinges.

"Door's unlocked."

Before I could celebrate this good fortune, two headlights turned the corner, illuminating the highway. I pressed myself flat against the garage door, which clattered shut with a loud thud.

"Evie?" Jae called out.

I held a hand over my heart, willing it to slow. The headlights were gone.

It was starting to rain.

"I'm fine," I managed.

"Go to the front door," said Jae. "I'll let you in."

A giant spiderweb veiled the entrance, glittering with raindrops. A promising indication of vacancy.

The door swung open, revealing Jae. It was warmer inside, though not by much. The moonlight was bright enough to make out the interior. Every surface was cognac wood, smooth as a cheek. It looked more like a yacht than a home. Hexagonal stone floors, a skylight, walls of windows. The stone fireplace in the living room was as tall as a medieval church. The furniture was all wrong: grandma-ish floral couches, heavy mahogany tables. The yard was a sprawl of manicured greenery, studded with just enough trees for a murderer to slink through with ease. We raided the kitchen first. The fridge was empty except for an expired milk carton. The pantry held only the essentials: a few cartons of chicken stock, boxed pasta, an unopened jar of tomato sauce.

Through the rain-streaked windows, we could make out the reason we'd settled on this house: the sleek white cruiser, rocking beside the dock. We decided to let ourselves rest for a few hours before we embarked for Canada. We'd leave in the middle of the night.

We made pasta in the dark. After we ate, we crept down the hallway to the bedroom. Jae drew a bath. We sank into its heat, facing each other. Jae's bony knees against mine, our ankles intercrossed. I kept the gun on the edge of the basin.

Water lapped against the edge. The drip of the faucet. The drum of rain against the window.

"You're not coming with me, are you?" said Jae.

Her eyes assessed me without judgment. A rivulet of bathwater made a path from her hairline to her chin. I watched it cling to her jaw, suspended, before it dropped into the tub.

"How long have you known?" I said.

She leaned back, her elbows resting on the edge, long fingers skimming the water.

"Since the rest stop last night."

"I wanted to make sure you'd be okay."

"Oh, I'm okay," Jae said, her voice expressionless.

"Okay. Good."

"Are *you* okay?"

"Oh, I'll be okay."

Jae drew her legs away from mine. All the feeling receded from her face. The curve of her mouth was merciless.

Very suddenly, she got out of the bath. I followed her.

"Jae."

She reached for a towel, hastily scrubbing it over herself.

"Jae," I repeated, taking her wrist.

She pulled away, fiercely, but didn't move, her body tilting toward mine. I kissed her. Jae clawed at my hair, knotting her fingers. The rage she was so good at keeping subterranean spit up from the surface, great licks of white heat, scored across my nape and shoulders. I muscled her into the wall, my teeth in her neck. The tension of our bodies vibrating between two opposing states: wanting to fight, wanting to surrender.

Somehow, we made it to the clean moonlit bed, and our dripping hair and still-damp bodies made a mess of it. I kissed her clit. Her face twisted in suffering. I kissed her mouth. She deepened it, roughly. I kissed her again, more tenderly than I'd ever dared.

Afterward we lay there next to each other, watching the rain on the skylight. An unsettled silence brooding, her hands in fists, her shoulders spiky and still.

"I'm going to the police precinct," I said. "Alone."

She said nothing.

"I'm not going to tell them anything about you," I said. "They won't know your name or where you're going. I'll wait until the morning. You'll be long gone by then. You'll be safe."

"No," said Jae, watching the ceiling.

"I'm not going to give you up, Jae. I'm not going to give them anything. Just me."

"If you're going to leave, leave now."

It was then that Jae finally looked at me. Her stoicism succumbed, for the briefest moment, to something damp and lonely. A wet blink, and it was gone.

"I'll leave in the night," I told her. "After you're asleep."

"I won't sleep," said Jae, and I knew that was the closest to a confession either of us would ever get.

Jae never slept, but she did close her eyes and turn away, silently granting me permission to leave.

We had already investigated the boat. It was nicer than any of the others we'd been on. Jae knew how to shut down the transponder, so she couldn't be tracked. We'd done the same on the cruiser in Florida. I didn't pack a bag, and I left her the gun.

It had stopped raining by the time I slipped out the door. I decided to leave the car too, in case something happened, and she needed to alter the plan. The police precinct was a four-mile trek.

The wind was brutal against my cheeks. After about a mile of walking, a pair of headlights swung around a bend. The panic was instant and routine, then quickly followed by relief. I didn't need to be afraid anymore. A cop might find me here and it would be fine: in fact, it would save me the rest of the trip.

Except these headlights didn't belong to a cop car. They belonged to a red Ferrari.

Two men, early forties, expensive-looking, driving at a menacingly slow pace.

They came to a complete stop and rolled down a window.

I tugged the scarf to cover the bottom half of my face.

"Bit late for a walk, isn't it?" said the driver.

He was smiling. It was December, and he looked like he'd just returned from a long summer on an expensive Greek isle. A deep and buttery tan, waxy dark hair, seven-thousand-dollar teeth. On his hands was a pair of pristinely white gloves, as if he'd been golfing. It was almost two in the morning.

"I could say the same to you," I said, as mildly as I could manage.

"What are you doing out?"

"I don't think that's your business."

"We're just being neighborly." He was still smiling. "We've never seen you around."

"I've been sick in bed."

"Your family owns property out here?"

"Yes."

"Oh? Which house?"

I frowned. In the passenger seat, the other rider uncapped a slim bottle of brown liquor and took a swig. He was texting, with a bored expression.

"You see," said the driver, when I'd taken too long to answer, "my family owns *all* the property on this side of the island."

"I didn't say our property was on *this* side, did I?" My voice trembled.

"No," the driver conceded, "but we did see an unfamiliar vehicle riding around here earlier. Strange driver, beat-up car."

Jae.

"So we're doing the rounds—making sure there's no one sketchy around. I'm sure you understand. This time of year, the holidays—lots of burglary, you know. People get ideas. And this island, it means a lot to the people who live here."

I grit my teeth, forcing a smile.

He drove on. Exhaust plumed out, making me cough. I listened to the crush of wheels until the car disappeared. I could hear the ocean, crashing against the rocks. Owls bleating to each other in the high branches. The moon shone between the clouds. Every panicked breath sent another visible puff into the air. In another world, I gun it all the way to the police precinct. An elderly receptionist goes slack-jawed when she sees me, spilling her coffee as she fumbles for the phone. I offer my wrists. I surrender peacefully. In another world, I sleep in a cell tonight. Phones ring across the country. In another world, my mug shot makes the morning news.

31

I ran. The woods were a velvet black, rustling with wind. The low sibilant hiss of animals, the stampeding of my feet and lungs. A bare forest of bones, roots emerging from the dirt like unburied knees and elbows. A branch slashed against my cheek, a seam of blood. I couldn't breathe and I couldn't stop.

The red Ferrari was already parked in the driveway when I reached the house. I watched the man from the passenger seat peer inside the stolen car. Then the window of the house. He pressed right against it, his hands cupped over his eyes. I wasn't sure why since the front door was wide open. The driver, I'm sure, was already inside.

"Oh, it's you," said the man, when I approached from behind, red-faced and gasping.

"It's me," I said, grabbing a fistful of his shirt and slamming his face into the stone.

Jae and the driver were in the bedroom. Jae was against the wall. The driver was holding her there. He was pressing a handgun into her throat. All the veins in her arms went taut. Her jaw was lifted in challenge: she looked ferocious. But that didn't matter, did it, when there was a gun to your head.

"I knew it," he said, his eyes finding me in the open doorway. His voice shook with the pleasure of being right, years of unfounded fears of home invasion finally confirmed. "I knew it."

"You knew what?" I said.

"*I knew it!*" he exploded. "*I knew it!*"

"Congratulations," I said.

"This is my property. Do you know what they would do to you if this was—say, Alabama? If you trespass on a man's property, he can legally kill you."

"We haven't hurt anybody." It was a house. It didn't feel injury. It was indifferent to us.

I froze as the man turned the gun away from Jae to me. His hand shook. Gone was the menacing smile from the road. His fears had come to fruition. Until this moment of confronting whether he would actually kill someone over this, he had been happy just to be right.

"You think you can—" he gasped out. "You think you can just—you think you can—"

"We did," I said.

He was wrong to let Jae out of his sight. While he was focused on me, she swiped the Glock from the bedside table. She pressed the gun against the back of his skull, while he pointed his gun at me. The three of us were like a perverse solar eclipse.

"SEBASTIAN!" screamed a garbled voice downstairs, crashing through the kitchen. "SEBASTIAN!"

It was the man from the passenger seat. I'd smashed his phone and left him crumpled on the concrete outside. I guess he wasn't as unconscious as I'd thought.

The driver—Sebastian—took a step closer to me.

"Don't," Jae warned. "I'll shoot."

The other man stormed blindly into the bedroom, brandishing a kitchen knife. His face was a ruin of blood.

Jae shot him as he ran toward me. He fell to the ground like a fish hitting a wet deck.

I dodged out of the way of his falling body, which was the only reason Sebastian's bullet didn't hit me. Jae shot at him, too, but missed. The bullet hit his shoulder. Blood spurted from the wound. He touched it in shock. His white glove came away red with gore. His hand trembled so badly he almost dropped his gun, and he ran. We followed him onto the dewy lawn. Jae's gun was out of bullets. I'd picked up the fallen kitchen knife, the one his friend had intended to kill me with. Sebastian's aim was bad, and he wasn't hard to catch. Jae held him down, wrestling his gun away. Besides that, I don't remember much. There was only the doing, the execution. When you do something so unnatural, there is an emergency hot-wiring of your synapses, clever electrical maneuvering that steps in to save the broken fuse. The deed happens, and you are there and not there at once. It's only after it's done that the lights turn back on, and your memory returns, but because you've broken something so fundamental, the memories come only in pieces. Some today, some tomorrow, some ten years from now when you are in a grocery store and you are picking up a bottle of hot sauce and you drop the hot sauce because you're clumsy and it spills all over your hands and an aproned teenager rushes over to clean you up and says ma'am don't cry it happens all the time and you remember how long it takes to kill someone with a knife, the sound it makes, the crunch and the squelch of tissue opening.

Jae knelt in the grass, panting hard. I could feel her hands on my face, clutching me, pressing her forehead against mine. There was so much blood on us. My fingers made fists of Jae's shirt, trying to stay upright. My head slipped through her hands.

I don't remember walking back to the house. If it weren't for Jae taking the lead, I might still be in the grass, with the dew and the body and the lonely red-and-white glove, abandoned some feet away. Jae guided us, packed a bag with stolen winter clothes. We didn't have time to clean ourselves off properly—just a quick wash in the sink, to get rid of as much blood as we could. The keys were on a hook by the front door.

The boat winked in the moonlight, accepting our weight. The key turned smoothly in the ignition. The sea was choppy, but I could see land. It was everywhere, scattered in little islands. If we went south, we could claim one of those wild islands and live there like marooned bandits. There was a little cabin on the boat, with sleeping quarters, a toilet, a kitchenette. Jae emerged from below with a steaming Cup Noodles. She wrapped it in a thick sock, to protect my hands. She blew on it, then handed it to me.

"How do you feel?" said Jae, pressed against me in the captain's seat.

I shook my head, unable to speak.

Sebastian was going to kill Jae, so I killed him. His friend was going to kill me, so Jae killed him. It shouldn't have been so easy as that. But it was. I felt like I could have killed Sebastian and his friend a hundred times, a hundred ways. If I had no weapon at all, I might've squeezed Sebastian's neck until his head popped like a balloon. His eyes, angry grapes beneath my thumbs. I might've hooked my fingers in his mouth, snapped his jaw like plywood. If time allowed, I might've done it slowly. I might've gotten creative.

That had once felt like an uncrossable Rubicon: the idea of murdering someone in cold blood. I'd always clung to the idea that good and evil were stable identities, matters of intrinsic moral fiber, doled out patiently at birth by an omniscient god—not decisions you make every minute of every day of your life, subject to sweeping highs and lows as volatile as a heart monitor.

But taking a life was not hypothetical. You either do it or you don't. And until you're there and the knife is in your hand and it's Sebastian's life or hers, you don't know. You don't know.

I know. Not knowing was no longer a sanctuary I could take refuge in.

"What are you thinking?" murmured Jae. "Talk to me."

I tried to speak and couldn't. Words felt elastic and strange; they traveled shapeless to my throat and back again, darting like small fish. The moment I came close to producing a word, it lost all meaning. I remembered what Jae told me in the car, when she explained why it took her so long to speak: it was just a matter of finding the lever. There were so many things to say and scream that I felt impotent in the face of them. But I could kiss her. Kissing Jae struck a bell inside me that rang and rang, that somehow contained more understanding than speech.

32

I was shivering so hard I felt like my jaw would break. We'd made it over the Canadian marine border, but we were too miserable to feel relief. First there was the icy wind, like fists prickled with needles, battering our faces. Then we went numb. Then the numbness became a kind of tender, face-shaped bruise. I couldn't speak. Jae was only slightly better off. We were under each other's clothes, using the other's body heat. The wind and waves refused to relent. All there was to do was suffer it. Outrun the clock. People have survived worse. Trenches. Rats and snow and bayonets. I don't know why these were the images I kept returning to: men blue with cold in no-man's-land, unrelenting hails of bullets, snuggling up beside a corpse. An icy breath or grenade away from becoming one yourself.

The sun rose, and the wind settled. We took turns ducking down into the cabin, making cup after cup of boiling water to hold in our gloved hands, letting the steam thaw our frozen organs. It was beautiful out here: we could see that now. There were still no marinas though. We'd passed one, in the middle of the night, but the wheel was stiff with frost, too difficult to turn, and we couldn't see well in the cold, thrashing dark.

"I have an idea," said Jae, blowing steam from her cup, "but you won't like it."

"Anything to get off this fucking boat."

"We drop anchor and swim," said Jae.

We were so close to shore. There was a beach, a proper beach. Most of the coastline was too rugged, all rocks and trees. I closed my eyes. I opened them. The sandy beach was still there.

"We'll freeze."

"It's daylight now," said Jae. "If we keep going, if we find a marina, we can't approach in broad daylight. You know we can't. What if the police have found Sebastian and the other Ferrari guy by now? They'll be looking for this boat. We don't have much time. And we can't do last night again." Another torturous, arctic night on the Pacific. We would not survive that.

"There's a flotation device in the cabin," Jae continued. "We can use it to keep the bag dry. We'll have dry clothes and shoes when we reach land. And look, the beach is empty. It's completely empty. We might never get a shot like this again. We can bring the boat as close as possible to shore. I'll jump in first. You can toss the flotation device and we'll lower the bag. Then you jump in."

She looked so resolute, so sure of herself. It was funny, how contagious someone else's bravery could be. If you trust someone enough, they can make you do just about anything.

I don't remember a single thing about the swim to shore. A black curtain dropped in my mind, and reality played out just beyond it. I caught flashes of what my body was experiencing: the shriveling of my lungs, water so cold it seemed to transmute into a solid right as I penetrated its surface. Once ashore, we flung off our sopping clothes and changed trembling into dry ones.

We treaded through the damp woods. It was chilly, though not nearly as cold as it had been at night, on the water. Mist rolled sleepily over the evergreens. After hours of walking, even beauty becomes monotonous. Our minds were empty, willing our bodies through the basic mechanics of drawing the next breath, taking the next step. When the red barn appeared on the horizon, I was sure it was a mirage.

It was a sheep farm. Their faces turned indifferently toward us, then away. Inside the barn, we went slack in the bales of hay, peering through the window. About fifty meters farther was a small house. There were two cars in the driveway. An old lady washed dishes at the sink. Occasionally, she looked up, said something to someone unseen over her shoulder, and resumed washing. Suddenly, through a side door, an old man emerged from the house. He wore a heavy beanie, like a Brooklyn hipster. He was very tall and Nordic-looking. When he removed his beanie to scratch his head, great tufts of snowy hair spilled out. He was wearing a windbreaker that looked too light for the cold, and he was heading right for the barn.

"Shit," Jae murmured, grabbing me by the wrist and dragging me outside.

The barn door made a sound like a thunderclap when it clattered shut.

"Who's there?" the old man barked, and Jae bullied me into a small woodshed behind the barn. We sardined ourselves like corpses in a coffin, narrowly avoiding being stabbed by a garden hoe.

The shed was pitch-black and windowless. We held our breath, listening to the old man grumble to himself inside the barn.

Finally, the barn door clattered shut again. Jae's head went so still in the crook of my neck I was afraid she might actually be dead, until I felt her fingers knot in the back of my jacket.

We listened to his footsteps disappear.

"Wait," Jae whispered into my neck, "wait."

It was thirty minutes before we let ourselves escape the woodshed and tiptoe back into the barn. The hay helped to keep us warm, and so did the sheep. Jae rested her head on my shoulder, our eyes fixed on the house.

"What's the plan, chief?" I said quietly.

"Wait until dark," said Jae, "and then we take one of the cars."

"I feel bad taking from them," I admitted.

"I was thinking we could leave the watch."

"The watch?"

"I took it from Sebastian's," Jae admitted. "A Cartier, just sitting in one of the drawers."

It wasn't perfect but it would have to do. We wouldn't be able to survive without a car.

And so, we waited. For an hour or so, the sun blazed, and it was almost warm. As soon as dusk fell, the temperature plummeted again. We shivered together in the hay, listening to the slow, even snoring of sheep. The light was on in the kitchen and living room. The elderly couple moved around the house, following their domestic routine. Hockey played on the television. The old man watched it standing up, pacing, taking swigs from a bottle. Occasionally, he entered the kitchen to help his wife with some culinary task and then returned to the TV again. Jae and I murmured to each other in low voices, her legs in my lap. We shared a crumbly Hershey's bar to commemorate our successful border crossing.

Jae's eyes traveled over my face.

"What?"

"Nothing." Jae was trying very hard to seem aloof, which only made her look more shy. I liked that I could make her feel that way.

"What do you want?" I said, desperate to peer inside her brain, eager for a distraction. "If you could have anything, right now, what would it be?"

Jae took a bite of chocolate, mulling it over. "A house."

"A house," I repeated, nodding. "What do you want it to look like?"

"Small. Not too small, just—you know, cozy. Good kitchen."

"You know what I've always wanted? A breakfast nook. Like with a booth. And a Tiffany light fixture hanging down. Black-and-white checkered floors, like really classic."

"You've already thought about this."

"That's the exact kitchen of this house my dad and I used to visit all the time. We told the agent we were 'in the market.' I think she knew we were lying. We always said though—if we could Frankenstein a dream house together, we'd take the kitchen from that house and stick it in the exterior of the house next door."

"What did the house next door look like?"

"It was an English Tudor. It was old, built in the 1920s, I think, and it wasn't very big—maybe two bedrooms. But it was so beautiful. All that sunlight. It had a greenhouse. And a fountain."

"Did it have a garden?"

"I think so."

"That's what my house will have," said Jae. Her throat moved. "A garden. With lots of flowers."

We were down to the end of our chocolate bar. I gave Jae the last piece.

"What kind of flowers?"

"Hang on. I think the lights have gone out."

"Hm?"

"Look. The farmhouse."

"Oh, yeah," I said, standing, brushing off the hay. "The windows are dark."

Jae left the Cartier watch on the hood of their truck. We took their second car, a Toyota Corolla. In the rearview mirror, I saw an upstairs light turn on inside the house. A few seconds later, it turned off again. Woolly trees staggered from every direction of the road, spruces and firs and evergreens. Occasionally I'd catch a glimpse of the sea, and the glacier-tipped mountains of the British Columbia coastline beyond.

The drive had the shagginess of a dream. It felt like being underwater, or on the moon. An uninhabited world of flora and water and mountains. We were astronauts. Astronauts must prepare themselves for loneliness. They train for isolation the way Olympians train for marathons.

We drove inland. At the mouth of an inlet, we found a lumber town that had seen better days. Next to a McDonald's was a strip mall: a Dollar Tree, a mattress store, a clothing store advertising a 70 percent clearance sale, an electronics store that had gone out of business, and a shuttered furniture store called the Brick. All the windows were covered in cardboard.

Jae parked at the back of the mall. There was a staff entrance to the Brick, but the door was chained shut.

"I need bolt cutters," said Jae.

"Are we going to stay here?"

"Why not? It's gone out of business. There's cardboard all over the windows. I doubt anyone's going in or out. We can hide out for a couple days, don't you think?"

I shrugged. "I guess so. I thought we might find another house."

"Not yet," said Jae. "Not for a couple of weeks, at least. If they've found Sebastian by now—houses are the first place they'll look. After them and the Carlisles, it's too obvious a pattern. Not to mention we left both crime scenes on boats."

It was a fair point. There was a Home Hardware store next to the strip mall. Jae left for bolt cutters. I picked up McDonald's for us and waited in the car. She returned a few minutes later with a tool kit. We slipped inside through the back.

There were piles of water-stained, flattened cardboard boxes by the staff restroom. In the break room, a moth-eaten couch, a sticky microwave, bags of trash. An empty doughnut box sitting on a table, a deflated birthday balloon tied to a plastic chair. A Ping-Pong table. A small television that looked like it was purchased in the nineties.

The storeroom wasn't much better. Cracks of light splintered through the cardboard taped to the windows. Most of the furniture was gone. But there was a king-sized sleigh bed and a living room set. An ugly dining table and chairs. Stray furniture littered the dusty showroom: a buffet table, still tagged with a "Going Out of Business: 90% Off!" sticker. A recliner. A pile of bohemian rugs.

"I'm gonna dump the old folks' car," said Jae through a mouthful of Big Mac. "I'll find us a new one."

I didn't want to be left alone, though I didn't admit this out loud.

"I won't blame you," said Jae, "if you don't want this. You can still go home."

No. I couldn't. It was a childish whim, a last-ditch tantrum before I accepted my lot. Home was Before. Now there was only After. Maybe, in some other world, we're good people who meet wholesomely at a farmers' market, or a bookstore, or on a dating app, and we make only the right decisions, and we're rewarded with long lives, home ownership, and several beloved pets. In that world, we never know what the other looks like after they've just killed someone. In that world, we never clean a stranger's blood off each other's hands.

33

Time passed strangely in the furniture store.

Some days it dripped luxuriously slow. Other days seemed to accumulate behind me with no memory of how I'd spent them.

The Brick was nowhere close to the Tudor dream house with the garden and the breakfast nook, but it was shelter. Once it became apparent that the store was abandoned, we decided to stay for a couple weeks. Jae, ever the doomsday planner, engineered an escape route through the staff bathroom window, in the event we needed a getaway. Every three days, she snuck out unnoticed in our new, stolen pickup truck for a McDonald's or Save-On-Foods grocery run.

Christmas was quiet: it came a few days after we arrived. A stolen bottle of Sangiovese, a clandestine trip to a drive-in. We shared fries with gravy and a chocolate shake. New Year's was quieter: prosecco and Ping-Pong in the break room, sex on the rug pile, a McDonald's apple pie. We were able to fix the snowy TV in the break room, so we could keep up with the news. The murders of Sebastian Onasis and Evan Barclay—the man whose face I'd slammed into the wall, the man Jae shot—had made the rounds, of course, but so far no one had linked them to us. Some pundits posed the theory, drawing parallels between the attempted Carlisle murders and the successful ones on Lopez Island. Nashville Hair did a segment on it, lambasting the "idiotic" FBI for not making the connection. We were grateful the holidays seemed to temporarily slacken the urgency around our crime spree, but it seemed only a matter of time before they compared DNA samples and traced it back to us.

I still held out hope that Serena would wake up and tell the world about her parents' volatile divorce, the escort she'd witnessed in her own home, the alimony her mother was demanding. But she remained unconscious. Her aunt Rebecca gave a teary interview in which she insisted she would "never, under any circumstances, pull the plug." Not while Serena's pinkie still occasionally twitched, or her eyelashes fluttered. Any day now, Rebecca assured us, her beautiful niece would open her eyes.

We settled into a routine. Jae was an early bird. I was not. When I finally stumbled out of the sleigh bed in the afternoon, Jae had usually eaten some sort of breakfast—coffee and dry cereal, unless she'd made a McDonald's run, in which case we might have a McMuffin. There was a very old, stained coffee pot in the break room that we spent a few hours sanitizing in the bathroom until it felt safe to use. At night, we played house: a TV dinner, flipping through stolen Dollar Tree paperbacks beside a cardboard fireplace, sex in our sleigh bed. If it weren't for the way we flinched every time the wind rattled the doors, our fingers twitching for the gun we kept with us at all times, the scene would have felt almost ordinary. Lovers going to bed together, suburban routine, domestic bliss. But playing house was no different from playing pirates or playing outlaws. The fantasy was no less impossible.

During this time, I often felt as though I didn't know how to take care of Jae. She was strange about tenderness, received it like a blow. Still, I looked for ways to smuggle it to her, but more and more it seemed kindness wasn't what she desired from me. There was only one kind of affection she permitted: sex, the kind that danced along the edge of brutality. She wasn't the first partner I'd been with who liked a bit of cruelty, but Jae took it better than any of her predecessors. She smiled at pain. Her ability to withstand it scared me. She was tough—I already knew she was: Why did she need to keep proving it? It almost felt like she was atoning, seeking punishment, only I didn't understand for what, and why I needed to be the one who delivered it. But I loved to give Jae what she wanted. She was beautiful when she got what she wanted.

It was funny, how mysterious her mind still was to me. I could dedicate my life to studying her, filling notebook after notebook with my observations. But would I know her any better? Do we know the famous musician after we read their five-hundred-page biography? Does the therapist know the patient after they've uncovered their psychic wound? Does the wife know the spouse they sleep with every night, the person they share a life with? I've thought about that often: "sharing a life." *I want to share my life with you.* Maybe it's possible. You can share a life, not a body. You might spend all your time with another person, but you are not inside their skin, wandering the landscape of their mind. You can feel you know them to their very bones, but it is only that. A feeling you have. A feeling that might be more like a fiction, or a projection. Your certainty of your partner, who they are, and what they can be—the thing you call knowledge—might be another way of shrinking them down to a size you can comprehend. This was the kind of partner I was used to, the kind who wanted to name what I was in relation to them, to compensate for some lack of their own, yin and yang. But people are not funhouse mirrors: we can't stand in front of them and search only for ourselves or our absence. "Opposites attract" felt like an antique holdover, medieval and inert, destined for obsolescence. A self-fulfilling prophecy for straight people who lacked imagination.

Jae never named me as This, in order to name herself as That. In her infinite, mysterious possibility, she preserved my own. Knowability is not what makes you worthy of love. Shouldn't we keep some curtains closed, some doors locked? When did absolute transparency become a precondition for romance?

Maybe this was too utopian. Or maybe these were simply the terms I was being asked to accept, at the exclusion of all others. Either way, I accepted Jae's terms. She accepted mine.

34

It was January 7 when the murders of Sebastian Onasis and Evan Barclay were finally traced back to us. DNA at the crime scene was
matched with our DNA from the Carlisle house. From there, it
didn't take a genius to infer the obvious: we'd escaped to Canada.

We prepared ourselves for the inevitability that the police
would come knocking. Jae continued to develop our escape plan.
The pickup was parked in a nearby junkyard, hidden from plain
sight. An emergency bag was hidden in the truck bed. We hun-
kered down at the furniture store for three days, surviving on our
current rations.

On January 11 Jae finally dared to leave the bunker for a food
run. I brewed coffee and turned on the television.

It took me a minute to recognize the girl's face on-screen. Lank
blond hair curtained a wan, sour-milk face. A tongue darted out to
wet chapped lips. A hospital bed. An IV drip.

The girl lifted her eyes to the camera. They were Serena Victor's
blue eyes.

Lukas was beside her. Serena's limp hand was in his lap, and he
was stroking it as dutifully as a cat. Serena gazed out the window.

"Tell me what the last forty-eight hours have been like," said
the interviewer gently. She was young and blond and pretty: Serena, in ten years.

"I don't know where to start." Serena's voice was hoarse.

"I can't even imagine what it must be like for you. To wake from
a coma, after almost four weeks, and discover your parents are dead."

"Not dead," Serena corrected, "murdered."

This was it. I was standing in the moment I'd been daydreaming about for weeks, the moment that might finally exonerate me. It didn't feel real.

A sympathetic head shake from the interviewer, a hand on her chest. Lukas appeared dumbfounded, out of his depth. The coffeepot beeped, announcing it was ready. I didn't dare move.

Serena took a deep breath, gathering her words. "My mom— she'd been in Paris for a few weeks. With her sister. We were going to move there, together. Me and her."

"What about your father?"

"Um. No. My mom . . . well, my parents were about to get divorced. My mom, she'd been wanting to for a while. Mostly because of me, I think. She didn't think it was a good home environment."

"What was home like?"

Serena looked down. "I don't really know how to talk about it."

Lukas stroked her knuckles.

"There have been reports," the interviewer said carefully, "about your father's use of an escort service called Highest Bidder. Can you tell us about that?"

Serena's head lifted. She looked confused. "What?"

The interviewer glanced at Lukas nervously.

"It's—it's come out, since, um. Since he passed," said Lukas, "that your dad—"

"My dad? *My* dad?"

The interviewer looked shocked. "You didn't know?"

Serena seemed torn between laughter and disgust. "My father is dead. He was *murdered* and you're—you're trying to—"

"I thought you knew," said Lukas.

"Lukas, are you serious? You know my dad. He's—he's not like that—"

"Did your mother know?" the interviewer interrupted.

"How am I supposed to know?" Serena snapped. "She's dead."

The tenor of the interview had changed. Gone was the quiet, sickly girl. Serena looked like she wanted to rip the IVs from her arm and storm off camera.

"When your mother told you she planned to divorce your father," the interviewer tried gently, "did she explain why?"

Serena's anger slowly faded; her fragile expression returned.

"She just said she wasn't happy. I know—I know they slept in separate beds." Serena swallowed. "But she never gave me details. She didn't want to burden me. I was pretty unhappy as it was. I hated it there."

"Hated it where?"

"That house," Serena whispered.

Now it was Lukas who interjected. "Wait. I'm still confused. You said—there was that night, you came over, you kept saying you 'saw someone.'"

"I did. I did see someone."

"Who?" said Lukas.

Serena shook her head. "You'll think I'm crazy."

"We won't think you're crazy, Serena," said the interviewer.

Serena drew a deep breath. "It started in the fall. Maybe a couple weeks after school started. I can't remember."

"What did?"

"The sounds."

"Sounds? What kind of sounds? Like . . . sounds in your head?"

"No," said Serena impatiently. "*No*. Not in my head. I'm not crazy. I know it was real. My parents refused to believe it—but it *was* real."

"Can you describe the sounds?"

"They were—" Serena stared out the window for a long moment. "They were in the walls."

"You heard sounds in the walls?" the interviewer repeated slowly. "Like an animal?"

"That's what I thought at first. Squirrels, maybe. Or a raccoon. I kept asking my parents if they could hear it too. They said no. I tried to ignore it, but I kept hearing it—little scurries and footsteps. We have a pretty old house. The acoustics can be kind of weird; sometimes a sound down the hall can seem like it's right next to your ear. A couple times, it was like that. Like an animal breathing right into my skull."

"So what did you think it was?"

Serena looked embarrassed. "I don't know. A ghost. There's all kinds of weird stories about my house. People who've died, like famous actors and stuff. Hallways that don't exist—that's a real myth, by the way, that there's, like, secret hallways in the house. Apparently, the architect wanted to build them, like for servants, I guess. But obviously he didn't follow through—it's just, you know, folklore. But at that point, I was hearing so much stuff that even though it's not like I really believed in any of that—I don't know. I wasn't counting anything out."

"What did your parents do?"

"They brought an animal control person in. He didn't find anything. But I kept hearing things. I told my parents it was still happening."

"Did they believe you?"

Serena gave a grim, humorless little smile. "They took me to see a psychologist."

"What did the psychologist say?"

"That it wasn't psychological."

"But we know you take medication," said the interviewer delicately, "for depression, no?"

"Yeah. But that's different from imagining things in the walls, isn't it? That's why I stopped talking to my parents about it. They thought I was crazy too. But the sounds didn't stop. The steps, the—the breathing. That's when I started to think maybe they were right. Maybe I *was* going crazy. It was bad enough that I could barely get out of bed. I didn't want to leave my room. I was scared of the rest of the house. My mom even took me out of school for a while."

Serena drew her gaze from the window and looked down at her lap.

"But then"—she licked her lips—"I found out I wasn't crazy at all. There was something in the walls. A person."

"A . . . a person?"

Serena nodded. "I was up late, studying for midterms. I came down to the kitchen in the middle of the night to make coffee, and"—an unfocused look came over Serena's face—"the fridge was already open. I couldn't see anyone, so I thought maybe one of my parents had left it open earlier by accident, but usually if someone forgets to close the door it makes this annoying little jingle until you shut it. I wasn't scared or anything, at first. But then I saw this . . . creature."

Serena breathed raggedly. Lukas stroked her hand.

"At first," she said, "I thought it was some kind of big animal, because it was on the ground, on all fours, crouching like . . . I don't know. A jungle cat. A wolf. There's coyotes, you know, and even mountain lions, lots of them, actually, in Griffith Park. But then the creature moved, really fast, like it meant to run. It was trying to move like an animal, but there was something wrong about it. Our fridge has this blue light that's pretty bright, so I could see it clearly. It was human. Not an animal. There was a person in my kitchen."

"An intruder," said the interviewer.

Serena nodded. "They fled. I didn't chase them or anything. I was too scared. They went out through the back garden. I woke up my parents immediately. But they didn't believe me. I mean, they *said* they did, but I know they didn't. They didn't take me seriously at all. They did change the locks, but it was—I don't know, probably three days later? I heard the sounds in the walls again. And this time . . ." Serena picked a bit of skin around her thumbnail, shaking her head in a pained way. "I just couldn't stop thinking it was a *person*. There was a person, living in our walls. Taking food in the middle of the night. Watching me sleep."

"What did you do?"

"I searched the house. I thought we might have, like, hidden doors or something. I know it sounds crazy."

"Did you find anything?"

"Nothing." Serena shook her head. "I searched inside all the closets, the attic. There was nothing. That freaked me out even more. I was going insane. My mom was insisting we had to move. My dad refused. She called me every day in Paris, updating me about her plan. The school she was enrolling me in, all that. I felt bad, about leaving you"—Serena glanced apologetically at Lukas—"but I had to leave. I felt so crazy. And then I—I saw her again."

"'Her'?" said the interviewer, alarmed. "You mean, the person you saw in your kitchen?"

Behind me the creak of a door. It was Jae, holding a bag of McDonald's in a limp fist. I stood to greet her, urgently waving her over. Jae didn't move. Her eyes were focused on the television, her body frozen in the doorway.

Serena nodded. "I saw her on the back patio. She went right over the gate. This time I recognized her immediately. I knew her—she was my SAT tutor."

"Evie Gordon," the interviewer prompted.

"No." Serena shook her head. "Not Evie. Her name was Jae. Jae Park. We fired her. Evie Gordon was her replacement."

The coffee machine beeped again.

"I don't think Jae ever left our house. I think—I think she stayed."
Serena's breath trembled. "And then she murdered my parents."

The Victors' front door was open when I arrived.

It was so strange. The dining room was empty: stranger. The
whole house, in fact, was empty. I don't count Dinah and Peter:
they were only meat, by that point. An empty house.

But it wasn't empty. There was a person in a closet. She was
tied up with electrical cord. The cord was frayed with bite marks.
I broke down the door to free her. Whoever killed the Victors,
maybe they tied her up, I thought. Worse, maybe the *Victors* tied
her up. She gave me no answers: she was traumatized and speech-
less. And I was patient.

Jae put the McDonald's bag on the floor, slowly. She stayed in
the doorway, watching me. A car insurance commercial chirped
from the television, oblivious. The coffee machine beeped again. I
felt like smashing it with my bare hands.

"Jae," I said, finally breaking the silence.

Jae was very still. Her chest heaved. She stayed rooted in place.

"She's lying," I said slowly, prompting her. "It's okay. We
thought—we thought she'd help. But you were always more skeptical, and you were right."

Jae didn't move.

I didn't understand.

"She's *lying*," I repeated.

Jae still wasn't saying anything.

And I still wasn't understanding.

"What's going on?" I said.

Jae didn't move.

"No. No. I'm not doing this again," I said. "You can't pull that
card again. *Talk to me.*"

Jae's lips parted; no sound emerged.

"Serena is lying," I tried again, as patiently as I could. "Jae, you didn't *live in the walls.*" I felt insane even saying it out loud. "That's not—you're not—Jae, she's making it up, she's painting you like—like someone from a horror movie, for fuck's sake."

My voice rang terribly, echoing in the break room.

"Say something," I said.

Jae shook her head. Carefully, she took the switchblade from her sock. Her eyes were steady as they followed me around the room.

I was starting to understand.

Jae took a step back.

"No." I crossed the room and lurched for the back of her shirt, but she threw me off with a strength that shouldn't have surprised me as much as it did.

She pinned me against the wall and brought the blade to my throat.

Her breath was a panicked rattle. So was mine.

I wanted to scream. I wanted to gather all the rage in my body into a material shape and release it into the world to wreak havoc. I was so angry it paralyzed me. I was so angry it didn't feel like anger at all. It was more like grief. Or horror. Something I'd never felt, something I didn't have a name for yet. My body was resisting it, all my bones and muscles knitting together to push it out.

"What did you do?" I whispered, but I knew.

I knew.

It was always Jae.

It was Jae in the garden. It was Jae in the koi pond. It was Jae by the pool with the rock. It was Jae in the closet, with the cord she knotted herself.

It was Jae, waiting for me.

Jae's eyes stared helplessly into mine. My body felt porous, enterable, and transparent.

Her grip went slack around the knife. She stared at me with big, wounded eyes. She looked hurt. I was hurting her. Poor Jae. Poor Jae, who killed them all. Poor Jae, who told me so many lies—was any of it true? Poor Jae, who let me think she was their victim.

I remembered the cry from the dark closet.

Help.

I had almost made it to my car.

I was going to drive away. I was going to call the police, from a safe distance. I was going to go home and call my parents. I was going to get high with my roommate and watch *RuPaul*. I was going to crawl into bed, my own bed, not a motel bed, not the driver's seat of a stolen car, not the master bed of an antebellum Florida mansion, not a sleigh bed in a closed-down furniture store. The next morning, I would wake up in that bed again. And the morning after that too.

My life. My whole life was right there.

And then I heard "please."

I could take the knife. It wouldn't be hard at all. It was amazing, I thought, watching her back away, watching her process the violence on my face. The violence I might've done if I'd been quicker.

But it was Jae who was quicker, of course. She ran before I had the chance. This didn't surprise me much, in hindsight. I was sly; she was slyer. My talents and gifts were no match for Jae Park.

Part III

Dream House

35

Speaking has always been difficult for me. Writing is easier, or at least I thought it was. I used to be a very dedicated diarist.

I am out of practice. I have had to erase so many beginnings and start again. I want to get it right for you.

I will start here: I am a good listener. I am not good at most things, but that one I know is true. Teachers used to write that on my behavioral reports when I was a kid. "Listens well. Takes direction well. Quiet." That was before I turned bad.

When I was little, I thought being told I was good at listening was a stupid thing to be good at, like being good at eating or breathing. But there is an art to it. Voices contain all the subterranean life in us that wants to get out. Voices are powerful instruments, even if they are not as legible as faces, with all those muscles and control gauges. Think about the uncanniness you feel when you hear your voice in a video recording or a voicemail. That is not what it sounds like in your head. But the immediacy of the voice—the wanton vibrato, all those sensitive micro-frequencies—contains information. Sometimes I think the voice is even more intelligible than words. It comes before words, which most of us are hopeless at using anyway, no matter how big our vocabulary or how many books we have read. Whoever says the right thing? But the voice. That is the raw material. The antecedent. A quaver, a whisper, a break. If you know how to listen, it says enough. And I am a good listener.

As a child, being good at listening was code for being good at doing what I was told. Being a good listener as an adult is a finer-tuned skill. It took patience and practice. I had a lot of practice at the Victor House.

Peter Victor had the calm voice of a hostage negotiator, living among land mines. Dinah's had a shallowness, airy-fairy and affected, like it dipped only as far as her throat. Serena's was self-consciously deep, moody, straining for the maturity she desired. New voices came and went. Clamors of them during Friday-night book clubs. Pairs of them, masculine, stiff, uncomfortable, when the plumbing needed fixing, or the garden needed maintenance. I was grateful for new voices when they arrived. I liked the guessing game. Imagining the person behind the voice. Filling in the lines.

Your voice was a new voice. Though I heard it only once a week, on Sundays, it soon became my favorite. Your voice was like the lowest string on a guitar, resonating with authority and gravitas. It brought to mind glasses of red wine and cigars and sloe-eyed femmes fatales in black-and-white movies. It was rough-edged and husky. What kind of face went with a voice like that? I wanted to know.

Listen, Evie. I know what you are thinking about me. I am a nightmare. I hide in walls. I lie to nice girls. I make them think I am like them. I am guilty of those things, but one thing I am not is naive. I knew this was never going to end well for me. Serena would wake up eventually and tell the world what she knew. I could not be Pencil Sketch or Anonymous Partner-in-Crime forever. I was never Partner to begin with. I might not be much of a mastermind, but I was definitely no henchman. No, I was always Public Enemy Number One. You had to have known there was another story unspooling, unseen, alongside your own.

It sounds bad. It is bad. I hand myself over for judgment, hatred, kicking, whatever you want. Whatever makes you feel good. Empathy and understanding, those are horizons I will never meet. But I will sail my ship as close as I can. I do not care if they never understand me. I do not even care if you never understand me. I just want to tell you. There are so many things I never got to tell you.

36

First: vomiting, and more vomiting.

Second: finally smashing that beeping coffeepot.

Third: scarfing down the McDonald's abandoned on the floor.

Fourth: promptly vomiting again.

Weak-kneed, I sat on the bathroom floor with my head in my hands. I thought about marching to the Dollar Tree, borrowing a cashier's phone to dial 911.

Then I remembered I was in fucking Canada.

I made the trek to the pickup that Jae had left in the junkyard. Though she may be a cunning, two-faced, murderous bitch, she at least had the decency not to take it for herself. She could easily steal another, I was sure. Jae could pick a pocket and replenish our entire inventory within a day if she wanted. The truck was probably a gesture of pity, and one I was in no position to refuse, no matter how badly it bruised what little pride I had left. Sure, Jae had imparted her carjacking wisdom to me, but I'd never tried to steal one on my own and in such a hysterical state.

I asked her once, how did you get so good at stealing? Not just stealing. Surviving. She explained it like this: When you don't have money, it doesn't just transform the way you think, the way you're perceived, the way you navigate the world. It transforms space itself. You live under a completely different sky. Your sunshine is different. Your moonlight. What's light to them is dark to you—and the opposite might be true too. The difference is sensory. Your sight, your hearing, your taste: they all conform to your circumstances. What's edible, audible, and visible to you might not be to them. Architectural blind spots and vulnerabilities prickle into existence as if seen beneath an infrared light. All things are enterable. All things are livable, with enough imagination. When you don't have money, your imagination is forced to expand beyond the limits of what's tolerable to rich people, who don't need imagination at all. When you are rich, the opposite happens: the world shrinks to particularities and patterns. I can drink water only at this temperature. I can sleep on beds only with this thread count, this mattress height. I can't live in a house without a dishwasher, an in-unit washer/dryer, a view of the ocean. The imagination folds in on itself. Space crystallizes and becomes intractable, opaque. When you are poor, space does the inverse: it hollows out. Anything can be a door. Anything can be a place to rest.

I nodded along, as if I understood, because I hated not understanding. I liked to imagine myself as equally streetwise, as if I could somehow catch wisdom from her like a contagion. But I couldn't. Growing up, I had always imagined myself as the one with the least, indulged my little self-pities, hoarding them with stubborn pride: my scholarship-kid insecurities, my side hustles and quick-cash schemes. In college, I was the one on gift aid, the one who had to take out student loans, the one who couldn't jet to Paris on a whim for winter break, instead stockpiling my tutoring money for an economy flight on a budget airline to Asheville. How myopic I was to think this was what it meant to live *without*.

I'd gone to private school, for fuck's sake. I went to one of the best and most expensive colleges in the country. I always had a warm bed to go home to, three square home-cooked meals, parents who were still alive. Who loved me.

I drove. Jae had also left me all of our money, and we'd saved a decent amount, roughly nine hundred dollars. I drove without destination. I drove without regard to traffic laws. I drove like I had a death wish, which I didn't, genuinely, but I can't say that in the hours after Jae's departure I had much regard for life either. I wasn't driving anywhere in particular, but if pressed, if forced at gunpoint to say where I was going, I would probably have admitted that I was trying to go home. Not Los Angeles. Hendersonville, North Carolina. How I would get to North Carolina from Vancouver Island was a mystery to me—forgive me, I wasn't all there. I was thinking more about how I would be welcomed when I arrived. Would my parents greet me with open arms, after my face was screened on every television in the country, grinning above the "MURDERER" marquee? They'd believed I was innocent, before I killed Sebastian—would they still believe it now?

And yet I couldn't help nursing some hope that if I crept meekly to my mom's door, she'd open it. I was good, once. Or at least I was good at pretending to be. Would she listen, if I explained it exactly as it happened, improbable as the story might sound? What other options did I have, now that Jae had confessed that it was *her* who was Evie Gordon, Hollywood Robin Hood, all along? Jae had tricked me. She'd lied to me. She'd possibly—probably—even set me up to take the fall. Jae knew I came every Sunday. She knew the time. What other conclusion was I meant to draw?

While I drove nowhere in an unfamiliar country, I rehearsed a speech I would never give. *Mom, I was duped.* I was outwitted by a criminal mastermind. I can hardly believe it myself, but that's the truth. I'll start at the beginning. I was the one who discovered the Victors' bloody crime scene. The blood was still wet, that's how fresh it was, which probably should've been my first clue that the true murderer was lying in wait. I would've called the cops, but then I heard someone cry out for help: there was a woman tied up under the stairs—I won't jump ahead, for the sake of dramatic storytelling, but keep an eye on her, Mom, that's all I'll say—and then the kid I tutor came home, assumed me and the woman were trying to burgle her, and attacked me. I knocked her out in self-defense. An accident, I swear. Problem is, then her boyfriend showed up and saw me standing over her "dead" body. Naturally, we ran. I'd just seen dead bodies for the first time. I'd just rescued a person who I thought was the victim of sex trafficking or kidnapping or, honestly, I had no idea—she never actually said, she let me fill in the blanks myself—and kudos to Jae—that's her name, Jae—because I took the bait completely. Not all the blame lies with Jae: I was the idiot who asked her all the wrong questions. Who stopped asking her questions altogether. An important thing to know about Jae—please, I cannot overstate how important this is—is that Jae is really hot, okay, especially once she got cleaned up. Plot twist. Okay, here's the thing, there's really no getting around this part: I may or may not have had carnal relations with her. Mom, don't make that face. I was lonely, and like I said, the sketch doesn't do Jae any justice. Anyway, things got wild out there. You can't imagine what it's like. The panic, the adrenaline. The fear. We stole a boat. I held a gun to a teenager's head. I killed a guy. It's funny to think about now: How many times have I been called a murderer on television? How long does it take to become the thing you're branded? For me, it took ten days. I was never going to be proven innocent, was I? How pathetic that this was a lifeboat I once clung to. Maybe it was never a wrongful accusation: maybe it was a clarion call. The true nucleus I'd been orbiting all along. A prophecy in the wings, waiting to accept the truth of who I was always going to be.

A killer. I was a killer.

At least now, when I go to prison, it'll be for a crime I've actually committed. I'm trying to follow your advice, Mom. You always say, no matter how bad it gets, you've got to find the silver lining.

I swerved off the highway into a ditch. Not on purpose. Just regular idiocy. Heartbreak, rage, despair, et cetera, it's embarrassing, you get it—they probably played a part too. It happened fast. One minute I was fantasizing about my childhood bedroom; the next, I was dreaming about putting my hands around Jae's throat. Then I was in a ditch, and the hood was smoking.

"Shit," I muttered, "shit, shit, shit—"

I slammed the accelerator. The truck made a pitiful sound.

I was on a major highway. There was nothing around me except woods and mountains.

I climbed out of the driver's seat and threw open the hood, staring down the machinery beneath, willing it to make sense.

Red-and-blue lights danced behind me.

Sirens.

I started to laugh.

The cop pulled up behind me. I heard his door open and shut.

"Ma'am?" the officer called out. "Do you need help?"

I turned around, pushing my sunglasses on top of my head. I gave a dazzling smile.

"Hello, Officer," I said, "as you see, I've driven into this ditch."

His expression fell at the sight of my famous face.

"Oh no . . ." He fumbled for his walkie-talkie. "Oh no . . ."

"I would appreciate some help."

"Backup," he stammered. "I need backup. I—"

I lifted my hands slowly in surrender.

"Get on the ground," he barked, "get on the ground."

I did as he said. There was no point delaying the inevitable. The fleet arrived soon after, with pomp and circumstance, helicopters and dogs and cars that slowed down on the highway to watch the show. I understand. I would've slowed down too. It's not every day you get the chance to watch the capture of a serial killer.

"Where is Jae Park?" an officer barked in my face. "Where is she? Where is Jae Park? Where is Jae?"

Where is Jae? I wondered placidly, gazing out the police car window. She could be anywhere. I thought about lying—just to fuck with them, the way Jae had fucked with me. What trail of bullshit breadcrumbs might I scatter?

The trouble was this: How do you lie about a liar? Where do you even begin?

37

The first thing I need you to know is that most of the things I told you were truthful, Evie. Of course, that will mean little to you, coming from me. I never lied to you about my childhood or my parents or the Carmel House. I never lied about our eviction or my mom's cancer. My lies were lies of omission, namely the SAT tutoring. In other instances, especially regarding the Victors, I lied by following the script you wrote for me. You were particularly credulous when it came to the Victors, prepared to see the worst in them and the best in me.

I did briefly work as a caterer in college, but that was not how I met the Victors. I was Serena's SAT tutor. That was my third job after I dropped out, alongside DoorDash and Lyft. Serena liked me a lot. In fact, she liked me too much. She blushed whenever I spoke. She could barely hold eye contact. Serena always asked me to tutor her in her bedroom. When I complimented her album collection, she started showing up to our sessions in T-shirts printed with bands I had mentioned in passing. Her taste in music was dreamy and gothic, fuzzy eighties and nineties shoegaze and post-punk. She said things designed to impress me or make me laugh. I was being paid, so I always acted impressed or laughed. It was flattering at first, the moony-eyed attention she gave me. That soon passed. The change happened invisibly, a subtle rotation in my tolerance levels. Serena was jumpy and eager to please, and putting her at ease was its own difficult labor. Every session was a tightrope act: Be nice but not indulgent. Be cool but not frosty. The problem was that I had become reliant on these tutoring sessions. We met twice a week, for two hours each session. That was almost half my weekly income.

Finally, it happened: Serena gathered her courage and invited me to see the Breeders with her. She had bought two tickets. I made a lousy excuse about having plans that night. I was apologetic. I tried to seem genuine.

The next day, I received a text from Mrs. Victor. She was firing me for "inappropriate behavior." My tutoring supervisor quickly followed up via email: he was letting me go. When I applied for other tutoring agencies, no one got back to me. I had been blacklisted.

It was only a few weeks later that I got a phone call from jail. It was my father.

The police station looked like a suburban high school campus, with neat geometric hedges and coffee-colored brick. I told the receptionist I was picking up Jordan Park. She said there was no Jordan Park in their system. But he called me from here, I insisted.

A woman in the waiting area interrupted and said he was probably taken to Santa Ana.

"That's what they do in Irvine," she said loudly, more to the receptionist than me. "They dump their problems elsewhere."

I had heard rumors of this in Orange County. People plucked from benches, stranded from their belongings and carts and tents, and driven to nearby cities.

It was eight p.m. when I found him. He was asleep on the public library steps. His head was tilted at an unnatural angle, and his eyes were half–squinted open, a sleeping habit of his that disturbed me as a kid. I shook him awake. He stared at me in an unfocused way, and then vomited on my shoes. When he was finished, he began to shake.

The ambulance took an hour to arrive. The ride to the hospital another twenty minutes. He was brought to an emergency room, where he was treated as an inconvenience. I lost my temper. It is not too much to ask, I insisted, for my father to be granted some grace. Some dignity.

Six hours later, the nurse declared him dead.

It was a seizure. Alcohol poisoning had led to irreparable brain damage.

I could not pay the bill. I gave the hospital the address to my dad's studio apartment, which I later learned he had not been renting for the past six days. I had been crashing with my friend Minho for weeks in Northridge. Whenever his girlfriend complained about how often I stayed over, I slept in my car.

For an entire week, my dad had been sleeping elsewhere. Where, I had no idea.

After his body was cleaned in the mortuary, they referred me to a local funeral service, though I knew I couldn't afford it. There were other options, they informed me. The hospital could keep the body for up to two weeks. The deceased could be donated to a research society, or the county could arrange for a burial or cremation, at no cost to me. I did not know what research society to donate him to, so I picked the latter.

The hours that followed I do not remember. I drove. Sunshine flooded the car, bright and mocking. I did not eat or drink. I did not bathe myself and I did not cry. If someone crossed my path to ask me my name, I was not sure I would be able to tell them.

I accepted a Lyft ride in Silver Lake. I accepted a ride in Eagle Rock. I accepted rides in Pasadena, in Alhambra, in Burbank. I remember sitting in my car, my mind spinning the same dead-end circuits, arriving at no particular destination. I ended up in front of the Victors' house.

It was Peter who answered the door. I did not lie about that either.

He was confused to see me. It took him a few minutes to recognize that I was Serena's tutor. He did not know that Dinah had fired me. He told me it was a school day, so Serena was not home. He said they were leaving next weekend to tour universities in Europe, for Serena's fall break. I pretended I knew this and had forgotten.

I went to Starbucks to charge my phone. I had no new messages. I asked Minho if I could come over. He said no. His girlfriend was upset with him. I begged, but he did not change his mind. I typed the words "my father is dead," my thumb hovering over the send button. I stared at the arrangement of letters. F-a-t-h-e-r. D-e-a-d. The longer I stared, the funnier and more unreal they looked. I tried Kevin Ahn, but he had blocked my number. I texted a girl I used to sleep with at UCLA, who I had not spoken to in five years. She did not answer.

When I returned to the street, my car was gone. In my dumbstruck state, I had parked in a red zone, and it was towed. The release fee, plus the towing charge, would cost me $560. I could not pay this, so I returned to Starbucks. I slept outside under a table of stacked chairs. I met an older woman, Sylvia, who took pity on me. She showed me how to break into different cars: most times, she broke in only for a warm place to sleep, then abandoned the car by morning. I did this for seven days.

Then I remembered something Peter had told me. They were going on vacation.

You know how ideas start. Bad ones, good ones, they all start the same way. Nasty little germs. This germ had a host, an inky, vegetal place to grow teeth and tentacles. Los Angeles is never dark, but its dimmest hour is around three a.m. I went on foot and arrived before sunrise. I hopped the fence in the back garden, snuck past the koi pond and the bridge, the pool, the ivy, the mint. I started to jimmy the back door handle, but it swung open of its own accord, inviting me into its cool, dark interior. I remembered something Serena had told me a long time ago, about the house's original architect, who wanted to build secret passageways for servants behind the walls. The hallways are a myth, she said.

They are not a myth. I found them. Unlike the Victors, I knew how to look.

38

Here's the funny thing about being wanted in several states: no one knows exactly where to send you. California wanted me for the Victors. Florida wanted me for the attack on the Carlisles. Washington wanted me for Sebastian Onasis and Evan Barclay. Canada didn't want me at all. The FBI was involved, which was flattering. My crime spree crossed both state and international lines. I was dangerous on a global level.

At a Victoria jail, an FBI special agent interrogated me in a bright room. I was handcuffed with a loose chain and given hot coffee and food. He introduced himself as Special Agent Cruz. He was small and stocky like a wrestler and had beautiful hair and teeth. He smiled a lot. I was scared, and he knew this. The interview was mostly an exchange of shallow biographical detail, to get me nice and comfortable so that when the knife came, I'd offer my throat easily. Yes, I am from North Carolina. Yes, I went to a very expensive college. Yes, I lived in New York. Yes, I moved to Los Angeles. Yes, I tutored the SAT.

"What was that like?" he asked me.

"I don't know. It was a job. It paid my bills."

"Did you like being an SAT tutor?"

"It was fine."

"I hated the SAT," he said, with a conspiratorial smile designed to put me at ease. I was not at ease. "I did terribly."

He seemed to have done pretty well for himself. I didn't say this out loud. I was going to be keeping all my smart-ass comments to myself, from this day forward. I was a new woman. Well-mannered, sympathetic, and innocent. There were no mirrors in this interrogation room, but I arranged my expression into one I hope looked pious.

"How many students did you have?" Cruz was feeling comfortable now. He had done interviews like this so many times that perhaps he genuinely believed I was comfortable too. The coffee, the French fries, the bright room with the windows—not a dark interrogation room with a wobbly chair and a sweating thermostat. We're just two people, talking. The handcuffs are a funny accessory. Ignore them. We're just two pals chatting.

"Usually about five a week."

"Did you want to be a tutor?"

"I was good at it," I said.

"But that's not the same as wanting to do it, is it? I see you have a lot of degrees here. Bachelor degree in liberal arts, a master's in art history. You were a salutatorian in high school. A straight-A student your whole life. What did you want to do? What did you want to be?"

What was all that hard work for? That's what he was asking me. The truth was I didn't know. I never knew. I just liked being in school. It was the closest thing I had to a safety net. Or maybe it was something like Stockholm syndrome. It was what I understood. The clear design of it, the easily navigable benchmarks. Every week, there were dozens of opportunities for me to succeed. I did it for the A. The gold star. It separated me from others. Achievement was its own high. The As were not cumulative. I was not stockpiling credit to cash them in for some greater raison d'être. I wanted to be successful—a vague term that remained one-dimensional—but I had no model for what that looked like outside of school. School was my dominion, and I was its emperor. Outside of those walls, I was no one.

"I guess I was just good at school."

"Did you want to teach?" said Cruz.

"I like teaching."

"Did you like teaching Serena Victor?"

I held Cruz's stare. It was the first time he had mentioned the Victors, and despite the casualness he tried to affect, he couldn't swerve around its significance. Something new had entered the room.

"Yes," I said mildly. "She was very easy to work with."

He smiled at me. I smiled at him. He rested his cheek on his fist. I rested my cheek on my fist. We gazed at each other, like lovers in a standoff. When this didn't go anywhere, a new FBI agent came in. Her name was Special Agent Afuye.

"Here's what's going on," said Afuye, standing over me. Cruz remained in the room, still observing me like I was the most interesting painting in the museum. "California has already begun the extradition process. Canada is cooperating. They do not want you here, and I'm sure you're not very interested in my advice, but trust me—you do not want to be here either."

"I'd like a lawyer."

Afuye looked bored. She sat down in the chair opposite me.

"This is going to be a very long process. Are you prepared for that? Because it can go much easier than this. We can help you, but in order to do that, we need you to cooperate. For example, you can tell us where Jae Park is."

I laughed. They still didn't get it.

"You're never going to find her."

"We have a lot of resources."

"It doesn't matter. You won't find her. She could be anywhere," I said. "She hid in a family's house for weeks without getting caught."

"Jae can't evade capture forever."

Fools. I was like them, once. I almost felt bad for them, but they'd have to learn their lesson the way I had, the hard way. Never underestimate Jae Park.

39

A rotten smell grew in the house. It would be easy to conclude that rotten smell was me. I did not think so. It could have been the Whole Foods rotisserie chicken the Victors left spoiling in the trash, or the plastic tin of cantaloupe Serena forgot to throw away before her European college tour, souring on her nightstand. A housekeeper came, about three days into my stay, and threw all this away. She did not climb into the walls when she was finished. She entered and left through the front door. When she was gone, the smell lingered. Maybe it was me after all.

I still believe it was the house itself, finally free to release its natural stench. Without the Victors, it sagged like a woman released from her corset. She had no one to perform for anymore. Water stains, leaks, drywall crumbling. Stairs that groaned, though no one climbed them. Floors that creaked, untreaded. This was a very old house, and I think it wanted to die.

There was, of course, the alternative: I was not its only ghost. There were others. Servants, maybe, or children. An old Hollywood actress, a drunk. A lunatic brother returned from war, rambling from a locked bedroom. I saw figures like this sometimes, but my vision was not its most reliable in those days. Even though the Victors were gone, I still spent most of my time in the walls, in darkness, in the event of an early return.

Even within the walls, there was a lot of traveling to do. The house had its own maze of hallways, like a structural counter-narrative, a matrix of space without any rhyming counterparts.

Sometimes, hallways appeared out of nowhere. Once, I found an elevator chute that went from the attic to Peter Victor's study. When I looked for it again, it was gone. There was no presiding logic to the architecture, other than nihilism. Illogic was its own rule. The hallways were wide enough for a broad-shouldered man to slink around without touching the walls, and they were as tall as any room. They were everywhere, creating space for themselves like organs, insisting on their anatomic importance.

Soon, I knew every inch of their house as though it were my own. I knew the ideal radial degree of the faucet for a perfectly hot bath. I knew that they never used the third guest room bathroom on the first floor, so this was safe for me to use in the middle of the night, or in the daytime, when the house was empty. I got very good at controlling my bodily functions. I knew the expiration dates on their expensive truffle mustards and fig jams, their soy cheese and tempeh strips, Serena's vegan exotica. I had developed tastes of my own: which oil paintings I liked, which candles, which gourmet crackers and bars of soap. I was careful, of course. I never took enough to be suspicious. I knew they would come back, eventually, and they did. The initial plan was to stay a few nights, to buy myself some time until I figured out how to return to my old life. But that road seemed impossibly long, and I couldn't find the entrance. I had been living paycheck to paycheck. I was in debt. Where would I begin? Who would give me a loan, how would I start? Who would employ me, where would I sleep at night? Now that I was inside the Victors' house, I saw how much room there was for me, and how easy it would be to stay. I did not even have to live underground. I was intestinal, nested inside them like a Matryoshka doll.

After the Victors came back, the house sat up straight again. It sucked in its stomach and behaved itself. I could not hear it breathing anymore. There were too many other sounds. It was still easy enough to feed myself on their scraps, gulp water from taps, and return once more to my secret hallways. The Victors were creatures of routine. Before she fled to Paris, Dinah charted the same path every day: from bed to shower, from shower to kitchen, from teapot to patio. She went to yoga. She meditated by the koi pond. She made an elaborate salad she never finished. All of this I gathered aurally. The only family member I regularly watched was Peter.

There was a small hole I discovered in a hallway. Using my pinkie finger, I was able to make the hole bigger. It looked directly into Peter's office, between the shelves of a bookcase. His office was not very interesting. He worked in there at night, after dinner, on his computer. Sometimes he worked there in the morning, usually on the telephone. I wanted to learn more about how he made money, but no matter how many of these calls I listened to, I could not make sense of it. My unfinished bachelor's degree in economics had not helped me understand our eviction, and it did not help me here either. Anything meaningful was disappeared into jargon, an untranslatable language: CDO, subprime, tranche, triple-B. I eventually concluded that this untranslatability was by design. The jargon of the finance world was merely a way to obscure the red strings of causality. To gamify the relation between banker and borrower, the conspiracy of interdependence. I remember the furrow of my father's brow as he pored over those bank statements after our eviction. He passed them to me, hoping I might better understand them. Why shouldn't I be able to? I had all the resources of my education. But I did not understand, and I felt stupid for it. Now I believe that no one understands it. Not Peter, not any of them. It's a performance. Bad actors can learn lines, too. They walk onstage and speak with confidence, like a child in a foreign language class: memorization without comprehension. Words, numbers, people: none of it was real to them.

There was a painting on the wall of his office that interested me. It was a David Hockney print, famous enough that even I recognized it. There was a pool. One figure swims in the pool, in what appears to be tighty-whities. He is deep underwater and looks like he might hit the wall. The other figure stands over him, on the lip of the pool. He has smooth golden-blond hair, like a high school villain in an eighties movie. He wears crisp white chinos and a salmon-pink blazer, and his hands hang casually at his sides as he watches the swimmer. What was interesting was not the painting itself but that Peter Victor habitually re-created this scene with absolute literalism.

Every Monday, Dinah went somewhere and was gone for the rest of the day. On these days, Peter "worked from home." He would begin in his office, which I could observe from my hole. As soon as Dinah's car left, he'd place a call. Sometimes he jerked off while he waited. Eventually, he'd get up from his chair and go somewhere else in the house. At this point, I'd take the hallway to the master bedroom, which had a view of the garden and pool. It was safe to watch from there. Dinah was gone and Serena was at school. I could hear quite clearly what was going on outside, since Peter and Dinah usually kept the window open.

First, Peter would admit a guest through the back gate. A sex worker of some kind, always female. The appearance of femaleness seemed to be his only requirement. Other than that, the women were all different. Black women, white women, Korean women, Mexican women. Young women, old women, middle-aged women. Skinny women, fat women, short women, tall women, and everything in between. I noticed there were a few women who came several times. Most I saw only once.

Peter Victor did not fuck these women, but he did ask them to strip naked. Once they were naked, he asked them to get in the pool. One time, a middle-aged woman protested that she could not swim. Peter told her this did not matter, and she could remain in the shallow end. He asked the women to hold their breath underwater. He would stand over them and time them. He did not jerk off. He did not push them. In fact, he did not touch them at all. They stayed below the surface all by themselves. When the women rose, sputtering and gasping, he asked them if they were all right. They always said they were. He asked them to do this over and over, timing them. Once, a woman held her breath for almost four minutes. She was young and tan, with dark sleek hair and a flat chest. After about an hour, the women would climb out of the pool, and Peter would give them a towel. The women were never admitted inside the house, not even to use the bathroom. Once they were gone, he came back inside, and I'd return to the hallway. Usually this was when Peter pleasured himself in his office. After I realized this was the conclusion to the routine, I stopped watching and wandered elsewhere.

Peter's poolside ritual made me wonder how long I would last, if I were one of Peter's women. One Saturday, after Dinah had left for Paris and Peter and Serena were spending a long weekend in Monterey, I went to the backyard pool. I hadn't been outside in weeks. I let myself enjoy the sun on my face for almost an hour before I slipped out of my clothes and entered the water. I held my nose, sank quietly and peacefully to the bottom. The lack of oxygen stretched at the fibers of my brain like taffy, and I looked up. I was in the ocean. I thought how easy it would be to stay here, with the coral and fish. I knew what awaited me if I returned to the surface. For every minute that passed, the horizon would be another ocean farther, the current stronger, the sharks hungrier. The salt would spray, and the sea would open its throat and the swim to land would be too treacherous. There was no land to swim to. We tread water, working and working and working but the mouth kept expanding, always asking for more. It would take something ugly and violent and beautiful to tilt the world on its axis. Robin Hood, reversing the terms of the debt, taking payment in pounds of flesh. Fire flickering on red faces, mobs, and dark mansions. Blood and cake. Could I be saved? I was already at the very bottom. Or was there another level beneath this one, a trapdoor? I felt suddenly afraid, and in my panic, I shot up for air. I scrabbled at the limestone edge of the pool and staggered back into the house.

The Victors returned the next day. I heard Serena's slow, shuffling footsteps in her bedroom, which was the room I usually slept closest to. She seemed like the least dangerous family member if I ever got caught.

And I did get caught, once. By Serena, ironically. She was up late studying. I thought she had gone to sleep by the time I crept to the kitchen for food. I escaped through the back garden, and after several hours of crouching in the bushes, I was able to return through the kitchen. A small fuss was made, and the locks were changed, but I don't think Peter and Dinah sincerely believed Serena had seen a person creeping around their house. After this, I'd often hear her looking for me. She came close, several times. The only other family member who seemed to sense me was Pickle the dog, but he was old and senile and easy to gaslight. He barked at me, trying desperately to alert his family to the trespasser. They did not listen. They patted his raggedy white head and talked to him in baby voices. Sometimes I let him lick the sauce from empty cans before I disposed of them.

I dreamed about leaving often. The first time I gave my exit strategy any real, serious thought was when my replacement came. You. On Sunday afternoons, I'd wait patiently in the hall between the kitchen and dining room, listening for your arrival. You almost never tutored Serena in her bedroom, as I had. You usually worked in the dining room. You were tougher than I was, skillfully navigating all of Serena's attempts to divert your attention away from the SAT. You carried yourself with authority. You walked the halls so naturally, as if you owned a house just like this. Even hearing you ask the same solve-for-x questions I had asked a hundred times was somehow exhilarating. As a teacher, I had affected a cool remoteness, which tended to produce good results. I was not mean, but I was sparing with praise. Students worked hard to impress the teacher who was difficult to read.

Your approach was different. You were more controlling, supportive, and far less patient. More than anything, I could tell you were eager to just do the problems yourself and do them correctly. Listening to you teach, I was surprised how much I missed it.

Once you were introduced to the house, I became bolder. Several times, I made small alterations to Peter's office. I moved books. I hid pens and files. Once, I even made a pencil scratch to his beloved painting. I do not know what emboldened me. Maybe I wanted to scare him. Maybe I wanted to confirm I still existed. I had lived in the walls for at least two months. Sometimes, in paranoid moments, I imagined that I'd already crossed over, another ghost in the house. When I stole things as a child, and no one noticed, I believed I had developed the power of invisibility. Now, the suspicion returned. If I stood in front of Peter, would he see me? If I closed my hands around his neck, as I often fantasized, would I leave a bruise? If I held his head underwater, would he sink? It would take physical force: I knew that much. I did not have Peter's power. If I wanted to hurt someone, to really hurt them, I had to resort to old-fashioned violence. I had to put my hands on them. But to do that, I first had to know that I was still real. That I had ever been real, a person with history and flesh. A person born to a mother and father, whose names were Mila and Jordan, and who once lived in a modest but beautiful house on Carmel Avenue, and who had a daughter named Jae. Named after the blue jay, my mother's favorite bird to draw. According to my father, my name meant both "talent" and "good fortune." I was intended to be the natural conduit between the two.

Look how far I had come. How far I would go.

The boldest thing I ever did was confront Peter himself. It was not much of a confrontation, though, considering how drunk he was. He did not seem at all surprised. He was sitting beside his desk. There was an empty highball glass in his hand, which he was staring at in a distracted way. When I entered through the door, like an ordinary person, he smiled at me. Serena was spending the weekend with Lukas, so Peter was alone. Earlier that day, for the first time, he hired two women to go underwater at the same time. I think he had wanted to do something like that for a while. There was a middle-aged woman, Chinese, maybe. The other woman was Black and looked much younger. They went into the pool together and disappeared beneath the surface while Peter stood over them, drinking vodka at eleven a.m. Suddenly, the older woman shot to the surface, choking, and heaved herself onto the lip of the pool. Her face was a dark, swollen red, and she massaged her throat while the other woman, clearly a stranger to her, tentatively rubbed her back. Peter brought her water and apologized. He was nice to her. Then he asked her to do it again.

It went on like this for over an hour. Maybe that's why I visited him in his office that night, long after the women were gone and my own nausea subsided, once Peter had drunk himself into a stupor so thick, I knew I could say all the things I wanted, and he would think I was no more meaningful than a dream.

I sat in the chair opposite his desk. He watched me through cloudy, hooded eyes. Behind his glasses, his eyes were the same gray color that streaked his dark blond hair. He was not bad-looking, if you went for that sort of thing.

"My wife's home," Peter slurred.

"No, she isn't," I said. "She's in Paris."

"Oh," he said, "good."

"Does she know?"

"Does she know about what?"

"Why do you do it?"

He had a sly little smile. "Do what?"

I lifted my chin at his David Hockney print. "That."

He craned his neck to stare at it.

"My wife gave me that as a birthday present," he said, and burped, "two months ago. Gave it to me right in front of my daughter. Acted all innocent about it—Dinah. A silly power play from a silly woman."

"So Serena doesn't know, but your wife does."

That awful, sly expression was back. "Knows what?"

I stood up from the chair and walked around the room. I felt drunk, as if I had caught his stupor like a contagion. I picked up a heavy crystal paperweight and imagined bringing it down on Peter's head. When I turned back to face him, he was asleep. I dropped the weight, and it shattered. It cut my hand when it broke, and I felt relieved to see the blood. I wiped my bloody hand on his face and the front of his shirt. His eyes fluttered briefly, but he was too far gone. What could I do? This was not an interrogation room. I was not a detective, coaxing a confession. I already knew what Peter had done. He was clever: he was the architect of so much suffering, but he never dealt any blows himself. When the police come to kick you out of your house, allowing you thirty minutes to pile everything you own into the front yard while your neighbors watch, Peter and his kind are nowhere to be seen. His invisibility worked so much differently than mine.

I have caused a lot of harm. Most of it I regret.

But I do not regret what I did to Peter Victor.

40

Hey, Jae, here's an SAT question for you: How many scapegoats does it take to kill a family and get away with it?

Once the FBI gave up on trying to strike a deal in exchange for Jae's whereabouts—they sincerely believed I was covering for the woman who'd ruined my life—I was extradited to California. The district attorney of Los Angeles charged me with the first-degree murder of Peter and Dinah Victor, and I was shipped to LA with a US Marshal. They went back and forth on whether I would be flown on a commercial airline, but decided that given my celebrity, I'd bring too much unwanted attention. I was ferried to Anacortes in an FBI van. From there, I was taken all the way to California. Once I arrived in LA, I was booked at a federal facility downtown. There was a giant crowd of people outside holding uncreative signs ("Burn in Hell," "Bring Back the Death Penalty," etc.), waiting to watch me get escorted inside. A small troop of supporters shouted that they loved my work.

The intake process was exactly as humiliating as you might expect. I was stripped and photographed from all angles. Swabs were taken on the inside of my mouth. I was fingerprinted, tested for tuberculosis. I was given a beige shirt and beige pants to match the beige walls and floors and ceiling. My room—they called them "rooms," not cells, and "housing units," not cell blocks—was 105, right under the stairs. There were no bars on the doors, and the windows were made of plate glass. The bunk beds jutted from the wall like bookshelves, and the thick, polyethylene foam mattress reminded me of gym mats in high school. There was a space-age aluminum toilet and sink, and everything was beige except for the mattress, which was a deep forest green.

My parents came to California. When I saw them, I cried the way I've never cried before, not since I was a child. They were kind to me, kinder than I deserved, just as I knew they would be. Their kindness only made it worse. I could barely look them in the eye. The guards wouldn't let them touch me. During their first visit, my mom moved automatically to hug me—which was allowed; I was almost positive it was allowed—but they wouldn't permit her to come within five feet of me. The guards were cruel about it. My mom was scared. My dad too. They pretended that they weren't, like everything was fine, but I knew.

At night, in my cell, I tried to convince myself it was only the guards they were scared of—their guns, their barking orders—though I knew some small part of them was afraid of me. Evie Gordon. The serial killer who'd stalked their newspapers and TV screens for weeks. The murderer responsible for the SWAT team who'd invaded their living rooms and kitchens, who answered all their calls and watched their every move.

My dad took out a second mortgage on his house to help me find a lawyer. His name was Patrick Heath. I met him for the first time in the detention center visiting room. He was younger than me by exactly eleven months, and had a very Irish complexion and ears that stuck out. He had thick, dark hair and a trustworthy face, and though he was broad-shouldered and tall—six feet at least—his hunched posture and meek smile made him appear much smaller than he was. Heath studied theater at UCLA, and when that hadn't panned out, he went to UC Berkeley for law school. He grew up a few miles from downtown LA, in Manhattan Beach. I learned that he was half-Jewish and had a fiancée who was also a lawyer ("corporate," he admitted sheepishly, "to pay our bills"). Heath accompanied me to my arraignment, where we pleaded not guilty. Once my trial date was set, we spent a lot of time together in the detention center visiting room. Heath believed I was completely innocent of killing the Victors, and that I'd assaulted the Carlisle boys and killed Sebastian Onasis and Evan Barclay only out of self-defense. Maybe he was just very good at pretending he believed these things. He was an actor after all.

Heath placed an inordinate amount of trust in me. He was impressed by the many degrees, I think, and by the fact that I understood all his cultural references. He thought I would be "powerful" on the stand.

The first time we met, he asked me to tell him what happened at the Victor House in as much detail as I could recall. I told him about finding the bodies. I told him about my panic and confusion. I told him about running and hearing the "help" from behind the door. The "please." I told him about discovering a filthy, terrified woman tied up beneath the stairs. I described the hallway. I described untying her. I described Serena coming home and trying to call the police. I described when she hit me with the lamp. I parted my short hair for him and showed him the scar on my scalp.

Here's the thing about being named a criminal. You no longer know when you're acting or not. There was a little tremble in my voice as I told Heath this story, and if you asked me whether it was the product of genuine fear or something I'd affected as a survival mechanism, I don't think I'd be able to give you a straight answer. "Evie" was not a stable identity anymore. The unthinking animal that lived in my skin, she was one thing. But then there's the way I appeared behind interrogation windows, immortalized in newspaper ink and television pixels and buffering web pages— the little bits of me scavenged from a crime scene and Frankensteined into a three-dimensional figure that also went by "Evie."

When I laughed, when I cried, when I ate the mystery meat they brought to my "room," when I sat, when I stood, when my face twitched unconsciously, when I coughed, when my nose itched, when I crossed my arms, when I uncrossed them, I was forced to watch myself not from inside my own skull but as Them. I was nothing but surfaces to read and judge. Everything I did felt like a performance. The difference no longer mattered. Now, even when I cried, I had no idea if it was something I'd taught myself to do to curry favor, sway an opinion, survive.

"Where was I?"

"You thought Serena was going to kill you," Heath reminded me gently.

"Yes," I said, "so I grabbed the first thing I could to protect myself. It was the vase. When Serena came at me with the lamp, I threw it. I didn't even think."

Heath didn't take notes as I talked. He watched me the way I imagine a theater director watches an actor during a scene.

"She fell down. Her eyes sort of rolled back in her head. I was pretty confident she was unconscious. But of course, I was scared for the worst. I wanted to call the police. But Jae—I didn't know her name yet—she begged me not to. In the end though, the choice was taken from us completely. Lukas came. Serena's boyfriend."

"So you ran."

I searched Heath's face for judgment. I didn't find any, though that didn't mean much. I don't think I have any talent for reading people. I thought I had accurately read Jae and look how that turned out.

"We ran."

"You and Jae."

"Yes."

"You were together the whole time?"

"Yes," I admitted. "We were together."

In the biblical sense!
I didn't say that.

Most of the hours I spent confined to my "room," I daydreamed. Jae and I in a stolen Maserati, the Monopoly man hog-tied and gagged in the trunk. We drive along the beach in the Hamptons, wind in our hair, swigging bourbon from a flask. We pull up to a beautiful house: plantation-style columns, Range Rovers and Teslas and Porsches parked along the circular drive. There's a party inside. We walk arm in arm up to the front door. A woman in a sleek designer dress answers. She looks scared when she sees us on her stoop. There is already so much blood on us, in delicate constellations. We cross the threshold into the marble foyer. She backs away. We take another step. She falls. The fall catches the attention of her guests. The music stops. A hush falls. Jae withdraws a knife. I smile.

I wondered what Jae would think, if she knew about my fantasies. Would she like them? Would she play along?

Then I remembered that I hated her fucking guts.

41

I loved your Sunday visits. They quickly became the center of my world.

Believe it or not, in your own oblivious way, it was you who encouraged me to leave the Victors. Not directly, of course. You had no idea I existed, and I hoped it would stay that way. But I could not help thinking of you constantly. There was little else to occupy my attention. Your throaty voice, the forthright way you strode through the house, the unkind things you murmured under your breath when Serena left the room. You have a habit of doing that, did you know? Your inner monologue, so urgent it fizzed over. There was so much life in you. Could there be as much life in me?

The morning after my confrontation with Peter, I decided to leave for good. The house was quiet. I slunk through every hallway, listening carefully to each room. I did not know the day of the week. I couldn't even tell the time of day from the walls of Serena's room, since the hallway entrance was in her closet. The best space for that was the closet beneath the entryway stairs, which could be accessed from the interior hallway network through a hidden door. In this closet you could tell, at least, whether it was day or night.

I knew the best way to leave would be through the back. I crept from the hall into the house. It was either late morning or early afternoon, by the look of the sunlight. I entered the kitchen. It was empty. I thought about taking food for the road, but I wanted to be as light on my feet as possible, and besides, I had no idea when Peter and Serena would return. My courage was so fleeting I was not sure I'd ever feel brave enough to leave again. I tiptoed outside, shielding my eyes against the sunlight. The garden was even lusher than I remembered. Someone had been busy planting flowers.

If it were not for those black-eyed Susans, I wonder how differently things might have gone. Could I measure it in serotonin levels, in cortisol and adrenaline, the flood of tenderness, anguish, outrage that swept through me when I entered the garden? It brought me to my knees. I had not seen those flowers since I was a child, then there they were, fruiting with wild abandon. They were my mother's favorite flower. Justice. That is what they symbolize. I had a string of them tattooed on my rib cage. In the garden beside them, impossibly, was a flower with a virgin-white bulb, framed in red petals. I knew these were sweet Williams, because we always had a bouquet of them on the kitchen table in the Carmel House. They were my father's favorite.

Memories, like houses, are vulnerable to time—they weather, fade, and fall apart. I had let mine fall into disrepair. They mostly lived in the Carmel House, a forbidden place. The walls my mom painted with such gentle affection to hang her watercolor flowers. The Yamaha keyboard where my dad knelt beside me to teach me the popular English songs he loved, "Hey Jude" and "Your Song," songs I still cannot listen to with any sort of stoicism. The lake of morning sunlight we waded through in the kitchen, where my mom cooked the braised cabbage that her mother once cooked for her in Kyiv, the cabbage that she failed to make taste like the kimchi my father claimed not to miss, the table where I read and did my math homework, where my mom bent to kiss my cheek at random moments simply because I was there, and she felt like it. Because I was hers. Because she loved me.

"Mom," I whispered.

It had been weeks since I'd spoken a word out loud.

"Stand up," said a voice behind me.

For a single, wonderful, terrifying moment, I was sure I'd see my mother standing behind me. Her dark bob, the strands that hung in her face, the ones I tugged on when she held me in her lap. The long, elegant fingers she combed through my hair. Maybe Dad would be beside her.

Slowly, I got to my feet and turned.

"Who the fuck are you?" croaked Peter Victor.

I ran. I leaped over the bank of flowers toward the gate, speeding past the pool, where I nearly slipped and fell. Fingers closed around the back of my shirt and jerked, hard. I tried to crawl away, dragging myself over the low bridge, but Peter pinned me beneath his knees. He looked savage and strange, his breath sour with vodka. He had been drinking again this morning. His eyes stared into mine, unseeing.

He thought I was one of his women.

The ones who went under the water.

I heaved myself up, knocking Peter onto his back. In the struggle, he ended up in the koi pond. His hand was around my throat, trying to pull me under with him. He was too drunk: his grip on me was savage, if unstable. He took big, gurgling breaths, heaving himself up, submerging again when I pushed him. His inhalations became more ragged the longer we fought. He was losing. Eventually, his head came up for only a single, gasping breath, bubbles streaming from his nose. His face was turning purple. We could have been struggling like this for five minutes or an hour, I had no idea. All I know is that the bubbles stopped, and then the gasping. He was dying. He was dead.

Dinah was stealthier behind me. She had her phone. She made a sound, not quite a scream, when she was close enough to see who we were. Her dead husband, and a murderous woman. I caught my reflection in the dark water. A stranger stared back at me.

I remember this moment of recognition. Dinah's shock. My shock. The fact of Peter's death. I remember standing. What I do not remember is killing Dinah, but there is no question that I did. Little flashes return to me sometimes, the images unrelated and impressionistic. A granite rock kicked off a cliff side. A watermelon bashed with a hammer. A black-eyed Susan, pristine, untouched.

42

Like everyone, Heath was desperate to know why Jae had done it. He had seen Serena's interview. I imagine nearly everyone in the country had seen that interview. The scope of our fame was still hard for me to completely fathom. In jail, I was shielded from the media circus. It was Jae everyone was fascinated by, according to Heath.

The public wondered how we met. Two SAT tutors: Had we known each other beforehand? When did we start planning the murders? Ever since Serena put a name to the famous pencil sketch, journalists and internet sleuths had dug up what little dirt they could find. Jae had a mother who died of ovarian cancer in Kyiv. She had a father who died of brain damage in a Santa Ana hospital. She went to Irvine High School. Jae's math teacher reported that she was formidably bright, almost unnervingly so. Her English teacher reported that she expressed interest in creative writing, though she could be shy and uncommunicative in class. Her art teacher reported that she was the best in the year, as did her music instructor. Journalists unearthed that she'd received a perfect SAT score.

It didn't take long for more scandalous stories to emerge. A childhood friend, Cho Minho, told the press that he and Jae had once played in a punk band together called Blood Boys ("not my idea," I recalled Jae telling me dryly). He said his mother used to pack him an extra lunch to bring for Jae, after they learned that Jae's father wouldn't allow her to bring Korean food to school, afraid that she would be bullied for it—never mind that most of her classmates in Irvine were also from Asian families. A former UCLA classmate, Divya Choudhary, told a journalist she used to date Jae— they weren't "girlfriends" but they were "seeing each other." She described Jae as "quiet" and "mysterious." Divya broke things off when she found out Jae had also slept with her roommate.

Troubled Lesbian Heartbreaker was a much better story than Sympathetic Genius Orphan. The press got plenty of mileage out of these new anecdotes. But the biggest revelation was about Jae's father. He was a drunk. In 2009, the Parks were evicted from the three-bedroom home they purchased on Carmel Avenue. Jordan, likely due to his struggles with alcoholism, had difficulty holding a job at the end of his life. In the weeks before his death, he was squatting in an apartment complex, and he was arrested twice for drunk and disorderly behavior. Apples and trees: that was the implication.

I told Heath that Jae was virtually mute. We barely spoke. He begged me to tell him otherwise. To trust him.

"We didn't talk," I insisted. "She was traumatized, like I said."

"You were with her for *four weeks.*"

"And?"

"It's very hard to believe that you spent a month together saying nothing."

"I don't know what to tell you. It's the truth."

Heath didn't believe me, and that was fair. He had a good bullshit detector, and this was some of my worst bullshitting. But I couldn't admit the truth. Dignity had little use to me in jail, yet it was the only thing I had. To the meager handful of people who actually believed I was innocent—my parents, my friends, some internet weirdos, two prison guards, and of course Heath—Jae was an irredeemable villain. To admit that I had slept with her? That I *loved* her? I couldn't face the humiliation. I was on self-harm watch, so I had nothing to off myself with, but I would happily asphyxiate on my own vomit before I let anyone pity me for being some cunt-struck chump.

"It's okay," said Heath gently, "if you have complicated feelings toward her. You can tell me. You can trust me."

"Complicated feelings?" I said. "Like Stockholm syndrome? That's what you think?"

"I don't think that."

"Then what are you trying to say?"

Heath chose his words carefully. "I think that you're trying to protect her."

"You're allowed to think wrong things," I said. "That's your right as an American."

He laughed unkindly. "If you're not protecting her, then you're protecting yourself. Because you're ashamed of something."

"Are you a therapist now? You're right. I'm ashamed of a lot of things."

"Help me help you. That's all I'm asking."

"Okay."

"Tell me about Jae as you knew her."

I observed Heath across the table. He made a steeple of his fingers and rested his chin, observing me back. I could do this for a long time. Jail had made me patient.

"Why?"

"Because the more I know, the better I can help your case," said Heath. "It's Jae they want. But until they find her—and if what you've told me about her is right, it's possible they never will—then you're the only one they can prosecute. But you're a stand-in, Evie. They don't really want to put you away. You didn't commit any crime."

"Yes, I did," I corrected Heath quickly. "I killed Sebastian."

Heath put his face in his hands. He was exasperated with me. "He was trying to kill *you*."

"I staged several successful home invasions. I put a gun to a kid's head."

"Evie."

"I stole a boat. Two boats. Oh my God—*three boats.*"

"Evie, you were just trying to *survive*—"

"I stole a lot of cars."

"That was Jae. She was the experienced criminal."

"Aren't I at least an accomplice?"

"I don't know," said Heath, tired. "Are you?"

Jae asked me once, "What's the worst thing you've ever done?"

"Bullying," I told her. And I was a bully. That was true. There was this smart-ass in my seventh-grade math class who competed with me for the best scores. To fuck with him, I used to take his things from his locker and throw them in the girls' bathroom, then dare him to fetch them. There was a girl with a mouthful of braces who used to eat awkward food at lunch, the sort of things that get stuck in your teeth—apple peels, popcorn kernels—and I'd take unflatteringly zoomed-in photos of her with my friends and laugh at them. This was in middle school. In high school, I cyberbullied a girl who was on student council with me freshman year. Sometimes my friends participated. Mostly, I did it alone. That was all me. I laughed. I enjoyed their humiliation.

Jae never did anything like that. I called her a saint. I was worried she wasn't cruel enough to tolerate someone as unsaintly as me.

43

After I killed the Victors, I had to make some quick decisions.

I couldn't run out into the street. I'd cleaned off the blood splatters in the bathroom, but I still felt exposed. I didn't know where to go. There were a lot of police that monitored these hills. The street was purely residential: mansions and security systems, expensive 24/7 cameras monitoring the area from every gate. A feral-eyed woman sprinting from a fresh crime scene in the Los Feliz hills would be arrested on the spot.

So I came up with another plan. I tied myself up so when the police came, they'd think I was an almost-casualty of whoever had killed the Victors. I could play traumatized. Once I got to the hospital, I'd slip away. This plan was obviously risky, but I did not see any other option. Fleeing was impossible, and besides turning myself in, staging my own attack was the only thing that might explain the fact of my DNA everywhere. I chose the hall under the stairwell for several reasons. One, I thought if my plan went awry, I could free myself quickly and escape into another hallway. Two, I knew there was a coil of electric cord inside, which was once connected to the landline. Three, if struck by bravery, I could attempt to leave through the main door after all. It was not a foolproof plan by any means, but it would have to do.

I retreated to the stairwell. First, I tied my wrists to the rafter. It was more difficult than I anticipated, requiring a lot of teeth and tricky finger work, and then frantic, painful rope burn, to make it look as though I had been there for a long time.

Once I was tied up, two new problems presented themselves. The first was Pickle the dog, who was howling and sprinting around the house as fast as his arthritis could take him. The second was that my ears were ringing. I do not know if it happened in the fight with Peter or with Dinah. Something must have struck the side of my head. I could barely hear. Being inside the stairwell was like being inside the belly of a sea creature. Sounds were drowned out by the house's cavernous inhalations. I wondered if the house knew its Victors were dead.

I could make out faint footsteps. I took my chance and cried out for help. The door shuddered, then went still. It shuddered again. I composed myself. Any minute now, the police would find me, and I would be ushered onstage. A new performance would begin.

The door burst open. Light flooded in. It was not the police.

It was you.

Driving made me sentimental. Hours and hours passed with my head against the window. I had never left California before. I stared at the mountains, great, big blue ones that throbbed like fresh bruises against the sky. California is beautiful, I would think. Arizona is beautiful. New Mexico is beautiful. The earth turned over, hot, tender red dirt like the inside of a mouth. The horizon thinned as flat as a ruler's edge. In Texas, you could see storms approaching from miles away. It was thrilling to watch them come, to know that the chemistry that governed those storm clouds was not so different from the chemistry that governed me. No one can be expected to carry all that weight. Eventually, it must come down.

44

Days limped along and slurred together. In jail there were two breakfasts: one was a little disk of egg, with perfect gelatin edges like it came from a can, with a side of toast and plain yogurt. The other was microwave pancakes, the small, silver-dollar kind, with a pat of butter and syrup, and two Jimmy Dean sausages. There were three lunches: bologna and American on white, ham and American on white, or American and tomato on white. Bag of off-brand potato chips, and Granny Smith apple. Dinner had the most variety. Plasticky baked ziti, chicken and dumplings, beef stew. Taco night was my favorite. I was not allowed to interact with the other prisoners—I was a violent security risk!—but the guards told me this was the other prisoners' favorite too. It's nice to have things in common.

I read a lot during the day. We were allowed ten books at a time, though legal books didn't count, and Heath had lent me plenty of those. We were allowed one cubic foot of storage for legal materials underneath our beds. When I wasn't reading, I exercised. I wasn't allowed to use the gym facilities or the rec room, but three times a week, they let me run in the small courtyard, early in the morning before the others were awake. My cell was big enough for me to do some exercises on the floor: push-ups, sit-ups, yoga. I kept my cell clean. I slept terribly, in twenty-minute intervals at most. We were woken early every day, and they often shone a painfully bright light into my room late in the night. I was convinced they did this on purpose.

My parents continued to visit me. The guards still forbade them from touching me. My mother did not hold me to her chest and assure me she understood all my decisions. Honestly, we didn't even really speak, not about my case or anything serious. I asked them what TV shows they were watching, and about the weather in North Carolina, and if there was any interesting gossip. They indulged this shallowness for as long as they could, but inevitably, what they really wanted to talk about was me. What I'd done. What I'd *not* done: that's what they wanted to hear. But I couldn't speak. I kept wetting my lips, clearing my throat. I didn't know where to begin. When I reached back to find the start, time bent in unnatural ways. No matter how many different configurations Heath presented, how many different ways he made it Jae's fault, I couldn't shake the feeling that it was me. I'd done everything they said I did. I was every bad thing they called me.

Several uneventful weeks passed. My first trial, the one in California, was still months away. The most eventful thing that happened was that the governor of California went on the news and said he believed I was guilty and that I deserved a life sentence for my crimes. The governor of Florida responded to him the next day: "Don't worry, friend. Since your state can't kill her, ours will." I hadn't even killed anyone in Florida.

A few days later, I woke early for my run and did something funny to my ankle. This was exciting only in the sense that I got to visit the infirmary. In jail, going to new rooms was always exciting. After the infirmary, I was given a bologna and cheese sandwich, even though I'd had bologna and cheese sandwiches the last six days in a row. I read John Steinbeck's *Of Mice and Men*, which I'd already read four times before. The detention center library had a lot of John Steinbeck.

At three p.m., a guard told me I had a visitor. This was strange.

We weren't allowed visitors after three on weekends, except for legal personnel, and Heath wasn't supposed to come until Tuesday. I was taken to the North Wing, on the fifth floor. Heath was waiting for me in the visiting room.

"What is it?" I said.

"I wanted to tell you in person," said Heath nervously, still standing. "I thought about calling, but I think this is better."

"You're being weird and ominous. Sit down."

"I'm sorry."

"Sit down."

"Evie."

"What's going on?"

Heath sat down. "They found Jae."

They didn't find Jae. She turned herself in. That's a very important difference.

The details of her deception were described in a viral *New York Magazine* article. Heath brought me a copy. It's called "The Girl in the Walls." Subtitle: "How Jae Park Survived in Liminal Space."

Jesus fucking Christ.

Jae wore a gray beanie and a hospital mask, to avoid recognition. Her modus operandi was always the same. She attacked fast-food joints—Subway was her usual target—to steal from cash registers. Despite the fact she was wielding a knife and robbing the store, she was described as polite. One employee reported that Jae once brought ice to a teenage sandwich artist who was so startled by Jae's entrance that she burned her hand in the Subway toaster oven. At a Subway near the World's Largest Dinosaur in Alberta, an employee said that Jae brought them all bags of bread to tide them over after she locked them in a bathroom.

Of course, none of these employees knew that the thief known as the Canadian Subway Burglar was Jae Park, top billed on America's Most Wanted list. It wasn't just her disguise: she was too efficient and professional to ever get caught.

There was a close call near Golden, British Columbia. A manager spilled olive oil on the ground, and Jae slipped. The employees described the scene as if it were a Looney Tunes cartoon. A police officer arrived on the scene, but Jae was able to stun him with his own Taser gun and flee the scene. It would be two months before she would be in police custody again.

After burgling Subways became too dangerous, Jae moved into a Home Depot near Edmonton. She slept mostly behind a soil display wall in the nursery, where she constructed an elaborate mini studio apartment for herself. The Garden Center was adjacent to the Home Depot storage facility, and between these walls Jae slept on carpet taken from the flooring department. She was even able to take security cameras to observe employees' comings and goings. She regularly stole food from the break room and, at night, from the cash register displays. Like Subway, the corporate sequence at Home Depot was routinized and predictable. The employees never discovered Jae's hideaway: it was found only because she disclosed its location after turning herself in to the police.

—EXCERPT FROM "THE GIRL IN THE WALLS: HOW
JAE PARK SURVIVED IN LIMINAL SPACE"

45

I was so used to solitude that it took days to adjust to the fugitive existence I now shared with you. The simple fact of another human addressing me was overwhelming. I was being addressed: that meant I was alive. Until I found a way to explain everything—a task that became harder, not easier, as time passed—it was best to say nothing at all. Remaining private and mysterious was easy, so easy that I wondered why most people chose to opt out of it in daily life.

I let you make up your own conclusions about me, and you did, most of them undeservedly sympathetic. This was the first of my many mistakes.

Maybe if you had been different, I might have spoken more readily. If you were gentler, tractable and naive. But of course, you are none of those things. Your mind is sharp and suspicious, and of all the obstacles that faced me, that was the most difficult to overcome. My impression of you as a tutor was that you liked doing things a certain way and expected them to be done exactly as you intended. You were respectful to the Victors but too proud for deference, even the fake professional kind. I have never met anyone quite like you. It was like courting a power line. Energy crackled off you, violent and unpredictable. Even in repose, there was something merciless and unforgiving about your face. I could picture you in school: a loudmouth arguing with teachers, a straight-A busybody. Bulldozing through obstacles, scaring them out of your way through sheer, terrifying moxie. Bossing other students around, leading clubs, captaining teams. The opposite of the sort of student I had been—sullen and troubled, scaring others only so they could not scare me. A dark stare and the bad-kid stink of cigarettes and coin laundromats and free school lunches.

I liked to watch you drive. How easy you were behind the wheel, how confident and ruthless. You muttered under your breath a lot, usually savage things about passing drivers. I still do not know if you realized you were doing this or not. You are restless, in general. Your knee was always bouncing, your hands twitching on the wheel, your eyes scanning the horizon for predators. The sheer forward momentum of you was exhausting. You are bad-tempered, but in a way I did not mind, because unlike most bad-tempered people I have known (men, usually), you did not make your anger my responsibility. You could often be stubborn, and I think you were used to being able to bend others to your force. You had no idea how patient I could be. Once you caught on, we cohabited smoothly.

You are surprisingly thoughtful, a quality of yours that I thought might embarrass you, if I ever called attention to it. You are not nice, exactly, but you are observant. When I was hungry or tired or thirsty, you took care of it. I felt looked after. I liked looking after you, too, in this silent, uncredited way. We never asked each other if we were okay, because you are like me. Your needs embarrass you. Emotional spells, wounds interior and exterior, fears, anxieties, weaknesses of any kind, are private and shameful matters, to be dealt with alone. You never asked me for reassurance, and generally, you required little to no coddling. Your presence did not draw energy from me. Your emotional weather was not contagious. You were self-contained and capable, your own planet, your own orbit, content to cross mine only sometimes.

You are smart, but not as smart as you think you are. Your intelligence is important to you, so I always played along. Besides
stealing for you, or servicing the car, I did not know how else to
curry your favor. I did not immediately understand why I wanted
to so badly. Maybe I just felt indebted. You saved me. You could
have abandoned me dozens of times, but you never did. Despite
how badly I frustrated you, you did not demand my history or
claim ownership over my privacy. I kept waiting for questions that
never came. There was a close call, once, in Texas. One of my car-
dinal rules was to never lose control, and I did. It was dusk, and
the opening notes of "Hey Jude" played on the radio. There we
were. Me, a child. My dad, thick-haired, handsome, and gentle,
kneeling beside me on the carpet, directing my fingers across the
keyboard. I slammed my hand on the radio, leaving you and me in
the kind of fraught, meaningful silence that demands explanation.
Your eyes flicked to me, curious, but you didn't say a word. It was
the kindest luxury you could have afforded me. Silence its own kind
of intimacy.

Despite all you shared with me, you remained unreadable.
Maybe that explained the grip you had on me. You were slippery
and elusive, giving just enough to placate me before showing a
new face, proving how much I still had to learn. Like me, you
were tricky and performative, skilled at avoiding vulnerability. Of
course we were different in so many crucial ways, but there were
also times where you felt close enough to taste the food I ate,
to suffer my injuries as your own. Not since Minho, who used
to bring me his mother's kimbap for school lunch, had I met
someone who shared so readily. Not feelings—those you rarely
shared—but water, food, cigarettes. Within hours of knowing
each other, you were looking after me, passing me water bottles
to drink from, the lip still wet. I would have taken anything you
offered me.

It was not long after, in Florida, that you dyed and cut my hair. I was so taut I could barely breathe. I gave myself miniature tasks to focus on, to distract myself from your proximity. You defeated me easily. You held my jaw with tender authority, mocking every effort I made to ignore you. When you were finished, you told me I looked good. A cruelty. Within days, every nerve ending was a filament under your magnet. All the chambers of my heart hollowed around your shape.

Of course, things would fall apart. As soon as I had Tom Craddock under my knife in Louisiana, it was only a matter of time before you learned the truth about me. We cannot change our fundamental chemistry. When the time came, I put a knife to your throat to make sure you understood. Look, Evie, look into my eyes and face it. The lights are on, but no one is there. No one ever was.

Peter Victor was first. Then Dinah. Then Evan Barclay. And you. It sounds cold, since you are my only victim who's not actually dead, but it is you I feel most guilty about. If I had not killed the Victors and dragged you with me to the road, you'd still be in Los Angeles. You would have tutored Serena as if it were any other Sunday, and I would have listened through the wall. You'd have returned to your car without me, driven home, or to another student's house, or to dinner. Maybe you would meet up with your friends, or a girlfriend. I had no idea what kind of life you sacrificed for mine. I was too selfish to imagine any life of yours that did not include me. I daydreamed often about encountering you in traffic, at a red light or a gas station. You'd meet my eyes, as cool and indifferent as if I were part of the scenery, and glance away. I would give you anything you asked for, but I could not give you that better, more beautiful world. You did not choose the life I dragged you into. You did not choose me.

I knew what I needed to do.

46

Jae confessed to everything. She confessed to murdering the Victors. She confessed to murdering Sebastian Onasis and Evan Barclay single-handedly. She said she drowned Peter in the koi pond. She said she bludgeoned Dinah with a rock. She told them she did it because she wanted to. Though the confession transcript was not published in its entirety, journalists were able to get ahold of key excerpts, which were widely reproduced and analyzed by internet true-crime aficionados, podcast hosts, and Nashville Hair, who called it "horseshit."

"But why did you want to kill them?" Special Agent Afuye asked her. "Did the Victors do something to you?"

"No," said Jae. "Not to me."

"To someone else?"

"Yes, they did things to someone else. Everything you do happens to someone else."

Jae also confessed to living in the Victors' house. She described the internal network of hallways, which made it very easy to navigate in secret. The Victors' house was now being managed by Abigail Victor, Peter's older sister. Though Peter and Dinah's will clearly stated everything would be left to Serena, Abigail had still taken the matter to court. The rumor was that the house was sealed up like a crime scene. Journalists who wanted to investigate Jae's claims about the architecture were denied admission from the LAPD, who installed a gate. The house was routinely patrolled by officers, who often caught ballsy teenagers attempting to break in.

There were also the crimes that did not happen that Jae confessed to, like coercing me into going on the run with her. She described the scene like a kidnapping. I was bullied into the car at gunpoint. I was ordered, on pain of violent retaliation, where to drive, where to stop, when to eat, when to sleep. Other than bargaining for my life, screaming at her, and cursing her name, I refused to speak to her. Jae honored my wish.

Statement of Ms. Jae Park {March 21, 9:45 a.m., interviewed by Special Agent Aisha Afuye}

SPECIAL AGENT AFUYE: Why did you keep Ms. Gordon alive?

PARK: I don't know.

SPECIAL AGENT AFUYE: It seems like it would have been easier to just get rid of her.

PARK: I guess.

SPECIAL AGENT AFUYE: But you didn't.

PARK: No.

SPECIAL AGENT AFUYE: Did Ms. Gordon fight back?

PARK: Yes. She was smart.

SPECIAL AGENT AFUYE: How did she escape?

PARK: We were at a motel in Canada. I was able to sneak us into a vacant room through the window. Normally at night I would lock her in a bathroom so I could get a little sleep.

SPECIAL AGENT AFUYE: You did this every night?

PARK: Yes. I don't sleep that much anyway so I didn't usually keep her in there the entire night. Only a few hours at a time. But that night I was really tired, which she must've realized. I was swerving a lot on the road. I think she figured I'd actually passed out.

SPECIAL AGENT AFUYE: So what did she do?

PARK: She flooded the bathroom. We were on the second floor. She ran the taps in the shower and sink until they flooded, and the room below us must've noticed the leak. It had come into our room too, but I was asleep. The night manager came to investigate. I had to let her out, and as soon as I did, she took the car keys and ran for it. I thought about attacking the night manager but it seemed too risky.

SPECIAL AGENT AFUYE: So Ms. Gordon took the car?

PARK: Yes. Like I said, she was smart.

SPECIAL AGENT AFUYE: And what did you do, now that you didn't have a car?

PARK: I stole another one.

47

Even though we rarely told each other how we felt, my body made it clear. I wanted you. But you were never cruel with your power. I think, miraculously, I might have had some too. Maybe that was the lesson. Power is a part of every romance. It is essential to the transaction. Can you court someone without paying for it? Can you be courted without surrendering something? Is there any kind of romance that exists without bargaining, without negotiation, without debt? I had no money to give you. You had no money to give me. Value did not factor into our attraction. We had none. Power was something else in our case, pouring freely between us, from your mouth to mine and back and back. Was that power, or was it something I do not have words for? I used to have so many answers. Now there are only a few things I know.

48

Heath filed for my case to be dismissed in California, which was easier to do than I expected. As he explained it, the prosecution had a weak argument anyway. They had no physical evidence against me. They didn't have a confession. The most damning witness was Tom Craddock, but he was hurting his own credibility by evangelizing to anyone who listened about how he'd been "saved by God's grace." The Carlisle boys had become controversial figures once reports of their drunken wrongdoings became widespread: DUIs, a totaled Mustang, a speedboat crash that put a teenage girl in a coma. The only other eyewitness was the security guard from the Walmart in Indio, who went on every news program and described how he'd interrogated me—alone, no Jae in sight—and nearly got me to break.

Washington had a very strong case—I was going to be facing those charges after I stood trial for the Victors—but then the state dropped those charges too. Jae Park was the one they wanted, and now they had her. She gave herself willingly. She pled guilty.

The public still believed this was all nonsense, of course. The preachers remained in their pulpits, undeterred by public fact. Nashville Hair still led almost daily cries for my execution. Nevertheless, after three months, I was freed from jail. I went home to North Carolina to live with my mom.

For the first three weeks, the street was bombarded with protesters. Once you've created a mob, it is very hard to kill. Hating me was a religion: it gave people purpose, community, camaraderie, even friendship—maybe romance. I'm sure I could take credit for at least a couple flings. One #EvieDidIt truther, a little depressed, a little lonely, tired of his chafing right hand, catches the eye of another outside my house. News vans were parked there 24/7, documenting the hostility. I thought about speaking to each member of the mob one by one, maybe making them a nice cake, showing them what a nice girl I was. But then I remembered that I didn't know how to make a cake, and that I had never been a very nice girl, even before I was a serial killer.

The numbers dwindled, week by week. A month afterward, there were only five protesters camped outside. I felt sort of bad for them. It must be hard, to have a moral cause, to have something you believe in so vehemently, and then to have that taken away from you. The ones who stayed were evangelical. They did not spit at me or anything like that. Three of them were college students, and the other two middle-aged. One day, while driving my mom to work, I asked their names. One of them opened their mouth to answer; another slapped them on the arm to shut them up before they could. Two days later, they were gone. The vitriol was mostly online. #EvieGordonIsGuilty still trended on social media, at steady numbers. Florida was the only state that never dropped their charges against me. The Carlisles were preparing a new assault case to present to the district attorney. The governor, apparently, encouraged them personally. Jae Park was not enough: they wanted the full set. Heath kept me updated on those developments, in case we needed to prepare for trial again.

Mostly, I stayed home at my mom's and watched Animal Planet. No one in my hometown would hire me. I tried the bookstore and the library and the public school where my dad used to work. I tried the local restaurants and the mall and the movie theater. The teenager who greeted me at the door was eating popcorn clandestinely from a fanny pack: it spilled right out of his mouth when he saw me walk through the automatic doors.

So I stayed home. I smoked cigarettes. I did crossword puzzles. I did not read books. I did not watch the news. An entire election passed without my noticing, as well as a beloved TV news anchor's rape scandal, an oil spill, a Category 5 hurricane in Texas, the rise of a white nationalist group in the Florida Panhandle, and a global scuffle with Russia. I did not watch anything that could be considered mentally stimulating or emotionally vexing. I stuck to reality TV, broad comedy sitcoms, and sports. I became fat, and then, once I realized I was fat, I became very skinny. Photos of me, both the fat and skinny versions, appeared in tabloids and did the mockery rounds online. "Grotesque Female Murderer Exposes Cellulite on Evening Stroll." "Evie Gordon Drops the Weight: Is it Lipo or a Guilty Conscience?"

I ran at least five miles every day, sometimes both in the morning and at night. I listened to podcasts when I ran, the happy chat-radio kind about pop culture and other inanities, to drown out the noise of my own mind. I couldn't stand any sort of silence whatsoever, even when I slept. I fell asleep to *Friends* or *The Office* or *Parks and Recreation.* My depression wasn't really the crying kind. It was more the oh-the-futility-of-man, sleep-perchance-to-dream, cry-for-this-stage-of-fucking-fools Existential Dread kind. It repulsed me. I spoke about it to no one, though of course my mom noticed it because I couldn't leave the house. When I did, even to do something as small as visit the grocery store, all I could think about was how much every person I encountered must hate their lives. That was the weirdest character of my depression. It projected outward, imagining the miseries of everyone I saw, presumptuous and arrogant. I missed when my greatest desire was immortality. Now the thought of living forever made me physically ill. Some Sisyphean shit I wouldn't wish on my worst enemy.

I had a few offers from literary agents to write a memoir. It was basically easy cash. My agent was a very sweet and well-intentioned lesbian boomer who lived in Seattle—"Not too far at all from where Sebastian and Evan were murdered!" her offer email chirped, as if that were an appealing calling card. We wrote a proposal and landed a publishing deal. The cash I made from the contract signing helped me pay off the rest of Heath's legal fees and about a quarter of the student loans I still owed. Most days I was too depressed to actually write the book, but that was a problem for future me.

My serotonin levels had movements and overtures like an opera. They shivered through me in such powerful waves it left me sleepy. Visitors made my mood plummet. A garbage man smiled at me once and I burst into tears. How can he smile? What does he have to smile about? Existential dread was so boring. There were days I did not talk to anyone. The thought of speech was impossible. My cheeks were stiff. If I asked my mouth to smile, it couldn't. I was so scared of my own mind. I wanted everything to return to normal. For all my hormones to return to sea level.

They did, sort of. After about thirteen months, I began to emerge from the fog. Boredom meant I was discontent. If I was discontent, I might have the drive to become content. I had a direction. My mind was craving stimulation again. I could watch television dramas with my mom, the serious kind that were nominated for Emmys. I read novels. I watched the news and felt moved by its tragedies. I felt pretty certain that I would not be able to get a job, but like so many other unemployed members of my generation, I could still claim that faithful refuge: graduate school.

After months of research, I decided to apply for a PhD in sociology. A PhD would accomplish a few things: (1) it was fully funded and I would have a stipend to live on; and (2) it would defer the rest of my student loans. Though most of the highest-ranking programs were in California, I refused to apply to any of them or any program in a big city. I wanted to stay close to my parents.

I was admitted to three different programs. I chose UNC–Chapel Hill and began the following fall. I went by my middle name, Theodora, Theo for short. Theo Gordon, hello. Theo, that's me. I repeated the name to myself in the mirror, *Theo, Theo, Theo*, to convince myself I was her. I let my mom cut my hair short and dye it brown. The good thing was that Theo could be whoever she wanted to be. I decided Theo would be nice. As Theo Gordon, first-year sociology student, very nice, I was assigned a studio apartment in graduate housing. Though I had applied for a studio, I hadn't expected to get one as a first year. Perhaps they were afraid to give me a roommate. I was once a famous murderess.

The first semester was quiet enough. I had no nerves. I had the disturbed confidence of someone with nothing to lose and no one to impress. No one thought I was very nice. Instead, I got a reputation for being rude or spacey, depending on how generously I was interpreted, because I often did not reply when addressed as "Theo." I wasn't as good at being Theo as I wanted. Because I was going by a different name, it took people a beat to figure out who I was. At the welcome orientation, a girl in my cohort stared at me for thirty minutes across a canapé table before finally following me into the hallway and demanding to know if I was related to Evie Gordon. Another boy in my cohort, Vivek, was smoking a cigarette in the hall; he overheard and started laughing.

"Gabby," said Vivek, blowing a plume of smoke. "That *is* Evie Gordon."

Afterward, in our seminars, Gabby and her little clique of friends avoided me and exchanged glances whenever I spoke up in class. Vivek was nice to me: we often smoked cigarettes after seminar. No one in my cohort really wanted to talk to me, which was fine. They were all much younger. I was beginning to feel like going back to school had been a laughably bad idea. But I couldn't afford not to keep deferring my student loans.

It was second semester when everything went to shit. I had started teaching: I'd missed teaching a lot. The first week went well, or at least I thought it had. I was teaching mostly freshmen. Only one of my students recognized me, a gothy true-crime fanatic named Mei. She was late to every class, but her writing was phenomenal, and she always stayed after class to probe me about the Victors. She had a loud, funny, nasally voice. Another student must have overheard us talking about it one day and googled me. She mentioned me to her parents offhand.

Within twenty-four hours, two hundred complaints were sent to the school. Within forty-eight hours, a petition to "GET THE SERIAL KILLER OFF CAMPUS" had 6,745 signatures. By the end of the week, the complaints had ballooned to seven hundred. The petition had 14,000 signatures and counting. Nashville Hair did a segment about it. I watched it on my phone at the campus diner, shit-faced at two in the afternoon, as I was on the days I didn't have to teach. I'd been showing up drunk to seminar for months.

I dropped out. I moved home again, became depressed again. I went to AA and dedicated myself to the Twelve Steps like it was school. I sobered up quickly and threw myself back into physical fitness. I finished the book. My editor hated it. She said it didn't make any sense. I started drinking again.

A movie came out, about Jae. A horror movie. It was called *The Girl in the Walls*. Serena Victor was the protagonist. They made Jae look like the Japanese girl in *The Grudge*, which many reviewers called out as racist. It got bad reviews, generally. Jae was a Wes Craven character, a girl under the stairs, a boogeyman. I was a pretty minor character in the film. The actress that played me was really hot, which I appreciated. The actress who played Jae looked nothing like her. She was too small and feminine, with big round eyes and a Freddy Krueger grin. Our characters never kissed. We did not have sex. I was basically little more than a prop, bullied from hotel room to vacation home under threat of death, whimpering in passenger seats in a brief montage sequence.

A month after the film was released, my mom woke me in the middle of the night. Groggily, I let her drag me into the living room. The TV was on. Jae's face was on-screen: it was a still image of her from her arraignment, in her orange jumpsuit.

"Jae Park Escapes Federal Prison."

I laughed.

I had to hand it to her. That bitch was nothing if not consistent.

The prison guard who helped Jae escape would stand trial next year in California. Her name was Rosa. Her face was all over television. She was twenty-five years old, with a heart-shaped face and long brown hair. She was very pretty. She claimed she was "seduced" and "duped."

Listen, girl. I get it.

I slept poorly for almost an entire year after Jae's escape. I watched the cracks under doors for footsteps, the shadows that moved across the lawn. I started going on long walks at night, my eyes drawing haunting shapes from the silhouettes of mailboxes, from the dark woods behind houses. I peered into car windows and listened to the sounds of owls hooting. I followed the trails of rustling animals. I stepped through the woods and stared up into the trees. Sometimes, I imagined I saw her perched elegantly on a branch. Not inviting me closer, not scaring me away either. Her cool Mona Lisa eyes, her beautiful mouth, half-amused.

I walked home. Once inside, I pressed my ear against the walls and listened for the sounds of breathing.

"Jae?" I whispered into the vent in our bathroom, running my fingers along the wallpaper. "Jae?"

Sleeplessness does wild things to the mind. Sometimes I heard voices speak back to me, but whether that was terror or wishful thinking, I couldn't say.

About a year after Jae's escape—they had not caught her, of course—I received a package in the mail with no return address. Inside was a composition notebook.

I opened the first page. It was a drawing of a house. The line work was simple and clean, beautiful. It was an English Tudor, like something from a storybook. There was a fountain and a greenhouse.

There were more drawings. A kitchen, with a breakfast booth and a little Tiffany light fixture hanging down. The floors were checkered classic black-and-white: I could see the pen strokes, every tile carefully colored in. Sunshine poured in through a skylight.

There was a garden. In the garden were rows and rows of sweet Williams and black-eyed Susans, labeled with their English and Latin names. In the gazebo was us.

There was writing, after the pictures. Pages and pages of it.

Speaking has always been difficult for me. Writing is easier, or at least I thought it was. I used to be a very dedicated diarist.

I am out of practice. I have had to erase so many beginnings and start again. I want to get it right for you.

I will start here: I am a good listener. I am not good at most things, but that one I know is true.

This was how it began.

49

I loved you, Evie. I love you. Those are the things I know.

50

Evie Gordon, Hollywood Robin Hood, is retired. The people think she doesn't exist. The people, in fact, think she never existed: Evie Gordon is just some psycho serial killer who did it for shits and giggles.

Most of the country still thinks I killed them all, by the way.

The truth is, Evie Gordon *did* retire. She doesn't stalk the hills of Bel-Air anymore, though she does think about it sometimes. Mainly, these days, she drives. She goes to expensive neighborhoods, and she looks for a Tesla. A Porsche. A vintage Mustang. (Teslas, mostly.) She follows them. She follows them all the way home.

I am in Los Angeles visiting Patrick Heath, my old lawyer. The Carlisles are suing me for two million dollars in emotional damages. We're preparing for a trial. In a fit of boredom, ennui, nostalgic menace, whatever you want to call it, I decide to follow some cars. It's been nearly five years since I've been back in Los Angeles, so at first, when I follow the Tesla into the Los Feliz hills, lined with English Tudors and Spanish Colonials and Swiss chalets, I don't immediately recognize the street I used to visit every Sunday.

The neighborhood is mostly the same. Muscle memory takes over and brings me right to the most famous house in the neighborhood.

I walk up the drive, over the moat (yes, a real moat), through the lush front garden of succulents and lemon trees, to the huge oak front door, which, the last time I'd been here, was flung wide open.

Today it is closed, so I ring the bell.

A man answers. He can't be an inch taller than five feet six. He has dark skin and the pearliest, most beautiful teeth I've ever seen.

"Hello?" says the man. "Can I help you?"

"You don't recognize me?" I say.

His big smile begins to fade. "I'm so sorry." He has a gentle British accent. "I don't think we've met, and I'm afraid I was not expecting visitors. What's your name?"

"Evie Gordon."

"Evie," he repeats, incredulous. "Evie Gordon?"

"Yes. I'm sorry for not calling ahead. I didn't know who lived here. I didn't even plan to come."

"Evie Gordon," he repeats, stepping back. Not in fear, but to invite me inside. "Evie Gordon, please come inside."

I step into the foyer and he begins to talk in excitement. He introduces himself as Ajani Effiong. He is an English film director. Maybe I have seen his film, *Animators*? It's a zombie film. I apologize for not having seen it. He says do not apologize. He explains that he has just moved to Los Angeles to work on a comic book movie. He says he is still very new to the city. Before, he and his wife lived in Dublin. He says as a horror filmmaker, he could not resist the Victor House. He calls it the Victor House. He maintains a constant stream of chatter. I like this coffeeshop, I don't like this neighbor's dog, I want to get a dog myself but I don't have time, my wife is an artist and she hates the house, she says it is full of bad spirits, I don't feel the bad spirits, actually the house is a little disappointing to tell you the truth, all that talk of hallways and mysteries but it's really a very ordinary house, we haven't found any passageways, and we have looked, we have really looked, my wife wants to paint every room, if we get pregnant here she thinks the baby will be strange, I tell her nonsense, it is not quite the house we thought it would be but it's beautiful, she is finally warming up to it, I think, she says Los Angeles is full of ghosts, I say nonsense it is so young there is no history here, there is no culture here, she says no there are old things here there are things besides America these things do not just leave, this land is broken, I say of course it's broken all land is broken, oh, but there is a Mexican place we like just down the street, there's no good Mexican food in Dublin.

"My wife isn't home," he explains. "She has an exhibit coming up. She's an artist. Hopefully she'll make it home for dinner. We would like to make dinner for you. I'm sure she would love to meet you. I'm glad to meet you. We have read a lot about you. I even have your book. I'm sorry—I haven't read it yet, but I will. I've heard such interesting things."

He stares at me with unapologetic directness, smiling.

"Can I bring you something? Tea? Water? Would you like to look around?"

I wander to the main staircase.

"Are you all right?" he asks. His smile falls.

"I think I want to look around alone," I say. "Is that okay?"

"Yes, it's okay. Are you sure you're all right? You don't look well."

I don't feel well. I feel insane. The house has walls, they stand around me, they have material weight, I could feel them if I touched them. I rest my hand on a banister. It is real. I wonder if the house knows I'm here. There are new paintings on the walls: big, bold colors, abstract shapes, mouths that smear bloodily across geometric faces. They are new eyes. Do they recognize me? The cottage door beneath the stairs is still there, round and sinister, beckoning me closer. How could I have once found this place so beautiful? What was beautiful about it?

"I'm sorry," says Ajani. "I'm so sorry."

"What?" I say, turning to him.

"I was so excited," he says, with an embarrassed smile. A look of deep shame crosses his face. "When I saw you. I didn't think. It is not exciting for you. It is very different for you. A terrible thing happened here. It happened to you. You saw such awful things."

"I came here," I say.

"I'm afraid to leave you alone."

"I won't do anything."

"Oh, no, no, you misunderstand me—I'm not afraid for the house. It's just a house. And besides. I'm a renter." Ajani smiles. "But I am worried for you."

"I'm okay," I say. "But I would like to be alone, if that's okay."

After Ajani leaves me, I go to the door beneath the stairs. It opens for me easily. I use the light on my phone to illuminate the space. I see you, in a trick of light, as I once had all those years ago. Haunted eyes in the dark.

The hallway is low, at first, to account for the stairs. It should have ended there. I encounter a wall. I bend down.

Anything can be a door.

You told me that once.

I feel along the wall. I stare into the darkness and wait for my vision to adjust. I push.

The hall reveals itself. It grows, just like a house, and it fattens, just like a body. It has a strange, intestinal curve to it, which I follow for some time, deep into the belly of the house. A staircase, curving and rickety, takes me upstairs to another dark hallway, narrow but tall. I open a door, which takes me to a closet, which opens to a beautiful bedroom with a domed ceiling, painted a deep blue-green. The room is empty, except for an easel. This was Serena's room, once. Through the maze of hallways, I return downstairs, through the dining room, into the kitchen. I can hear Ajani on the other side of the wall, the whistle of a teakettle. He is murmuring to someone on the phone.

"I'm leaving her alone," he says. "I think she has gone through a very serious ordeal."

I drop to a crouch and press my ear to the wall. It is warm, like a cheek, like something with blood. I shine my light on the floorboards. There is something scratched into the wall, very faintly.

E-V-I-E.

It's me.

It's you.

I trace my fingers over the letters, imagining you in my place, carving them so many years ago. Every organ in my body lifts and churns like a house in a tornado. A structure, brick and mortar, furniture and appliances, plucked easily from the ground like a toy in a child's fingers.

You were here.

There was no return address, on your letter. That makes sense. After all, I might still be harboring spiteful feelings. I could turn the pages over to the police and direct them right to you. It would be fruitless: you'd escape again. You'd find a way. You always find a way. I never would have turned you in, though. I meant what I said in Washington. You could have told me everything when I still had the chance to look into your eyes and tell you that I don't care what you did. I don't care about them. I never did. I was angry that you lied to me. But my anger was never for them. It was grief for myself, my future, my hopes for a life. I think I always knew it was you. Deep down, in some hidden corner of my mind, I already knew and had made my peace with it. You controlled the aperture on my field of vision, but I saw you, Jae. I saw more of you than you know.

You wrote in your letter: "You did not choose me." As if what conspired between us were as impersonal as an arranged marriage. As if I were no more culpable than luggage wheeled onto a train car. But you were not something I suffered. You were not something that happened to me. Yes, a conspiracy of time and space and circumstance put us in the same room together, but accidents of longitude and latitude are only that. I was in a place at a time. We appeared to each other as sphinxes in a crossroads. We told each other riddles. I'm not cleverer than anyone else. I only stayed for longer. You allowed me further than the rest. Don't mistake fate for beauty. There are always choices: hundreds, thousands, millions of them. Soft walls to press up against, to see how much they bend. I did choose you, Jae. Has no one ever chosen you before? I chose you so many times.

I don't know how long I lie there, staring into the dark space, listening. Long enough to hear Ajani call my name in confusion.

The house makes a sound, like a sharp, human inhale.

I turn.

"Jae?"

An exhale. I try to remember what your breathing sounded like, but it's been so long. I watch the darkness. There are no more sounds. I hold my breath, listening. Waiting.

A floorboard creaks.

I shouldn't hope for it, but I do. Of course I do. Why else would I come here? Why else, but for you?

"Where are you?"

Silence.

My skull aches with the effort of listening. Of looking.

"Evie?"

I hear a door open.

It's Ajani, from the foyer.

I look one more time. Nothing.

I make my way back through the hallways, to the room under the stairs, through the door, into the light of the foyer. The sun is setting outside. Ajani keeps more windows open than the Victors ever had.

"Where did you go?" he says. "You were gone for such a long time. I looked for you."

Where did I go?

I was with you.

Acknowledgments

I can't begin this list of gratitude with anyone but my literary agent Stephanie Delman—the woman, the myth, the legend—who has changed my life in ways I still can't believe. Your tireless advocacy moves me every day. Thank you for helping me navigate the first-time publishing insanity with so much patience and joy and laughter, and for reminding me to celebrate whenever I convinced myself I was the unwitting butt of an elaborate *Truman Show*–style prank (low-key still waiting for that rug pull . . .). Thank you to Khalid McCalla, who plucked me from obscurity: without you, I'm not kidding, I might still be SAT tutoring. To Emma Finn, my UK agent: waking up to your contagiously cheerful UK dispatches has made me rethink my distrust of mornings. And to Alison Malecha, international rights seller extraordinaire: thank you for bringing this novel to countries I never believed possible. I'm grateful to Elizabeth Pratt and everyone else at Team Trellis for your enthusiasm and care. As a lifelong film and television fanatic, I must thank Jasmine Lake, Mirabel Michelson, and Addison Duffy at UTA for the mind-boggling work you've done to make those dreams reality. Thank you to Zakiya Dalila Harris, Alison Wisdom, and Danya Kukafka: this process would have felt so much more overwhelming without your kindness.

To my editor Jessica Williams, "thank you" feels hilariously inadequate. Your brilliant vision and profound understanding of this book and these characters has never faltered. I never in my wildest dreams thought I would find an editor I could trust this deeply. Thanks for always getting my references and liking my weirdest jokes. To my UK editor, Lettice Franklin: it is such an extraordinary privilege to be edited by you. Thank you for gifting your dazzlingly beautiful brain to this book. Peter Kispert, thank you for championing this novel and for always being just a quick email away. I'm so grateful for the thoughtful care and generosity of Victoria Cho's early feedback. Thank you to copy editor Stephanie Evans and the team at HarperCollins for the incredible work you've done for this book.

This novel probably would not exist without the brilliant teachers and friends I was fortunate enough to encounter during the four years I spent in UC Irvine's PhD department in English. Thank you to my former UCI students for your intelligence and enthusiasm: I learned so much from so many of you.

I'm nothing without my people. Zoë, always my first and favorite reader: thank you for believing in me and this book and all the other hundreds of thousands of words I've made you read. No one's feedback means more than yours. Margaret: there are so many inside jokes I want to make but I'm forcing myself to be sincere, as a gift to you, because you deserve it for putting up with my bullshit for almost two decades. My life and my writing are so much better for knowing you. Jess: you read this novel when it was just a ten-thousand-word baby, and encouraged me to continue when my belief in myself and my work was at its all-time lowest. Your kindness and fierce support have meant so much to me. Rae, my dearest best soul friend, research assistant, and brave champion of villains (congratulations): thank you for being the Thelma to my Louise 'til the day I die. Ryan: I'm so lucky that one of the preeminent ear-readers of our time is also one of my best friends. You're the best cheerleader and support system I could ever ask for. Alexandra: thank you for literal decades of friendship and brotherhood, and for making all of our many road trips far less terrifying than Evie and Jae's (with the exception of Slidell).

And finally, and most importantly, my family. There are simply none better. There are so many pieces that had to fall into place in order for me to build a life around this thing I love, and every single one of those pieces can be traced back to you. Thank you for giving me so much trust and freedom and love. Mom, Dad, Jake, and my baby Ozzy: without you, this is all meaningless.

About the Author

HANNAH DEITCH is a former SAT tutor with an MA in English from UC Irvine, where she studied Marxist theory and contemporary pop culture. She previously worked as an arts magazine editor and holds an MA in journalism from USC. Her work has appeared in the *Los Angeles Times, LA Weekly,* and the *Los Angeles Review of Books.* She currently lives in Los Angeles. *Killer Potential* is her first novel.